VIRGINIA RISING

This is a work of fiction. Names, characters, organizations, places, events, and incidents are either the products of the author's imagination or are used fictitiously.

To Al and Hondo, with love

CONTENTS

CAST OF CHARACTERS

Forest Service:
Woody Brooks
Brian Calvin
Violet Carter
Greg Foster
Emmylynne and Scott Fox
Rick Givens
Richard Golden
Bill Harris
Wesley Lexington
Walt Newman
Gray Wallace
Darryl White
Jimmy Wilson
Contractor: Harley Fremont and Gemma

Sheriff's Office:
Dexter Dreyfus
Blaze Edwards
Sami Foster
Rolland French
Elliott Green
Jacey Jenner
Sara Levitt
Chris Reynolds
Carla Wiley

State Police:

Carver Grayson
Jeff Langley
Stone Stevens
Christopher Wray

Ku Klux Klan:
Gerald and Fran Brown
Toby, Carl, and Jay Burden
Billy Dean
Junior, Rose, Russell (Shrimp), and Louise (Big Lou) Kendall
Ray, Ella, Ray Jr., Buford, Elaine, Sarah, Jimmy, Dan, and Belle
Parker
Hank, Melba, Samuel (Red), and Buster Ross
Ben and Beth Rover
Herb Smith
Ma, Pa, Orville, and Wilbur Wright

National Alliance:
Ethan, Clark, and Adam Davies
Earl and Leland Graves
Duke Kent
Joe Miller
Nathan Poke
Gene and Dave Speller
Bedford and Gus Springer
Edgar and Erasmus West
Evan, Wendell, and Steve Wilton

Campers:
Armstrong Family
Athey Family
Beck Family
Butler Family
Carpenter Family
Duvall Family
Ledlow Family
Magee Family

Mann Family
Maxwell Family
Payne Family
Vickers Family

Other:
Cliff Bronson
Clay Freeman
George Fry
Jack Fremont
Hal Quinones
John Whitman
Diner: Vera, Dwight, Rachel
Protest: Anthony Stanhope and Sergio Hernandez

A nation that destroys its soils destroys itself. Forests are the lungs of our land, purifying the air and giving fresh strength to our people.

FRANKLIN D. ROOSEVELT

CHAPTER ONE

Russell Kendall and his sister, Big Lou, were the youngest members of the local Klavern, known as the Ku Klos Knights of the Ku Klux Klan. Both kids were still in high school. Russell, known to all as Shrimp, was a junior, and Big Lou a senior. Shrimp was not a school team sports fan. He'd joined no teams, though he'd been invited. Big Lou was the tallest girl in school, and said she had no interest in joining any "pansy-ass sports team." Her preferred sport was tormenting everyone shorter than her, which meant most everyone at the school.

The two had arrived home from school when Big Lou pounded Shrimp's left shoulder. The first hit landed, followed by another, harder punch.

"Shrimp Kendall! You were so rude today! You should have said hello at lunch time, and not just walked by me. Make sure you never ignore me again!"

"Fuck! That hurts!"

"Don't. Do. It. Again. I will hit you if you do."

Shrimp was almost as tall as Big Lou, but being two inches shorter meant he was the shrimp of the family. He was often a target of his sister's behavior, but they were of one mind when it came to the KKK, as they were taught by their parents, Junior and Rose. Both parents worked outside the home so they rarely saw just how mean Big Lou was, and how often she hit Shrimp. Shrimp had learned it was better to take the beating, and get it over quickly. He also learned not to tell on Big Lou. She generally hit him where his bruises wouldn't show. He really didn't want people to know a girl hit him.

Shrimp had not even told his best friend about being bullied by Big Lou. He again considered if he ought to say something. He decided against it. Shrimp was concerned that his standing with his friend would change if he knew.

Shrimp's best friend was Red Ross. Red's given name was Samuel, but his face turned bright red when he was angry, even as a baby. Red was the youngest son of Hank and Melba Ross. Both families lived in the same neighborhood in Pembroke, Virginia.

Shrimp was happy he was leaving for Red's house soon. It had not been soon enough. His shoulder was going to ache. He decided to head over to Red's house earlier than planned. They were going to a meeting that qualified for extra credit at school. Maybe Shrimp would get a "D" in the civics course. It'd be better than flunking.

Red's dad was on the porch as Shrimp walked up.

"Good afternoon, Shrimp! Red told me you were coming by. I hear you're having some trouble with that civics class."

"Yeah. I'm not enjoying it. But I intend to pass it somehow, and the extra credit will help."

"How're your mom and dad?"

"They're fine. Both are still at work right now. I couldn't catch a ride with them so Red offered to drive."

"Red said he was happy to go with you. He's inside, if you want to go on in."

Shrimp tried not to let the screen door slam as he walked in. The house had the same layout as his own and he made his way toward Red's room. It was in the same location of this house as his room was in his.

Being in the Ross home always brought back memories of good times to Shrimp. Shrimp looked at a few photos on the hallway wall. Right now he was gazing at photos from past Klavern events. One photo had Hank in full KKK regalia. Hank Ross was the Klavern leader, and Shrimp admired him for that.

Shrimp looked next at the Ross wedding photo. It reminded

him of something Red's dad frequently said about how Hank and Melba had belonged to the Klavern for more than 30 years, joining right after their marriage in 1988. Shrimp thought people dressed funny back in those days.

Shrimp looked at a few photos of the Ross family. In the passing years Hank and Melba had five children, who were now in their late teens and early twenties. Shrimp looked at more photos. He could easily recognize Ross family members by their tall and lean physiques.

Shrimp smiled at some photos of group gatherings. He saw himself in a few. He thought about the many great times they'd had. Ross family gatherings, regardless of reason for them, often turned to conversations about the Klan, and all that the Klan had done for them. Shrimp had seen them get teary-eyed when talking about how Klavern members had helped Melba back to good health ten years ago by feeding the family, visiting, and helping with housework, while she battled breast cancer. Shrimp knew that no one in the Ross family would turn their backs on Klansman in need. They had said so many times.

Shrimp briefly thought back to the days when Melba was ill. Red had been really scared his mom would die. He and Red became friends about that time, as the families had gathered often. Shrimp and Red became inseparable in the years to come, though they were a couple of years apart in age.

Like today, the friends often dressed alike in Wrangler jeans, a tight white t-shirt, and huge belt buckle. Both wore high-top PF Flyers, black with white trim. Red was the first to get tattoos on both arms, and Shrimp quickly followed suit. At school Shrimp wore a denim jacket to cover the tattoos. He and Red talked about getting full sleeves after Shrimp was out of high school.

Lost in thought, Shrimp jumped as he heard the screen door slam as Hank entered the house.

"I didn't mean to scare you. I thought you'd be in Red's room already."

"I'm early, so I was just looking at the pictures. I'm trying to give Red a little more time to get ready."

"There are a lot of good memories in those photos. Plus, we have more good memories to make. Are you coming to our cancer-free anniversary party in a couple of weeks?"

"Oh, yes, my whole family will be there. Mom has started planning her cake already. Yes, it'll be chocolate on chocolate."

Once a year the Ross family had the party. For years, Shrimp and Red sat at the "kids tables" and grumbled about being treated as kids. But Red had not moved to the "adult tables" when he turned eighteen last year. Instead he continued to sit with Shrimp. Shrimp could always count on Red.

In Shrimp's mind the anniversary party was always the same. He found comfort in the familiarity. The party was held at the Ross place, on the weed and old car strewn front lawn. Most people brought their own chairs for seating. Hank provided lots of tables, but always seemed to be short of chairs. Many kids used the old cars for seating, for playing, and for mischief making.

As always, the entire Klavern was invited to the party. Like everyone else, the Kendall family would attend. As usual the party would start at noon and last into the evening. It always ended in a bonfire. In between the start and the end, lots of food was cooked and eaten, and lots of drinks were consumed. The adults had kegs of beer to last them through the day. The kids drank pop or water, though sometimes there was also lemonade.

Shrimp's mouth started to water as he thought about the cake his mom would make. Rose was always in charge of the cake and ice cream. The cake she baked at home the morning of the event. Rose had always made a sheet-sized chocolate cake with chocolate frosting. Though she said she considered shaking things up a bit, she never did. The vanilla ice cream was made right after dinner. Shrimp loved to have a few spins on the handle so he could brag about what delicious ice cream he made. It was always the event of the year for Shrimp and most everyone else in the Klavern.

"I'm looking forward to coming. It's always the best party of the year."

"We're looking forward to it too. I'm glad you'll be there. I'll enjoy having a slice or two of your mom's cake."

Shrimp left the hallway and entered Red's room. "Hey, Red. I came early. I hope you don't mind."

"I was playing Fortnite. I'm almost done here, and then I need to get a shower. I'm hungry. I'll see if mom will fix dinner for you too."

"That'd be great. I didn't eat before I headed over. I'm starved."

A couple of hours later Red drove them about twenty-five miles away to Christiansburg, Virginia. Shrimp eyed the town hall. It was on the square, at the corner. It was a not a large building, but even so rarely filled up with people at events like this one. This time was as Shrimp expected; there was plenty of seating available with only about fifty people in attendance.

On the way there Shrimp and Red had commented that they knew how the meeting would go. It was going to be silly and trivial, but at least Shrimp would earn extra credit points.

"I know there will be the usual complaints about street vendors."

Red had replied, "I think the major topic will be about keeping shooting outside the town limits. How many times have we heard about people shooting up signs in town?"

Instead they listened to a local resident make a case against the KKK. Both Shrimp and Red decided they would go straight home, and talk with their parents about all they had heard.

Junior and Rose were sitting at their places next to each other at the kitchen table. The house, built in the 1970s, was a starter home with plain finishes. Nothing had been updated in the years they had lived there. It had the usual wear and tear from family life.

Shrimp had his own room, so he felt their home was a castle. His mom often said she'd like a larger home someday, but the had years passed, and soon the kids would be moving out, so Junior said they were fine right where they were. He said he loved the neighborhood.

When Shrimp came into the kitchen his mom was saying the old refrain about getting a dishwasher. He heard his dad's usual response, "Maybe next year, Rose." But Shrimp knew next year would never come, as the space was too small to add a dishwasher. He wondered why they kept talking about the same things. Shrimp was about to shake up the kitchen table banter.

Shrimp told his family about the town hall meeting. He told them that it had started with a KKK history lesson about the different waves of the KKK, ending with the modern wave.

Shrimp commented, "Red and I almost left because it was kind of boring, but the speaker, George Fry, went on to talk about how he had grown up in this area in a conservative family. He'd said they flew the heritage flag like many of their neighbors. He said that he grew up thinking that Confederate flag flying was merely a matter of preserving history, but after the current president was elected, and after the killing in Charlottesville, he had a change of heart. Fry asked everyone who had a heritage flag to remove it.

"Dad," he asked Junior, "Are we really supposed to take down our flag?"

"No, Shrimp, we'll never do that. Who does he think he is?"

Shrimp told his parents that several people clapped when he said to remove the flags, but there were also some gasps. They decided to stay and hear what the speaker had to say. About that time Big Lou joined them in the kitchen.

Shrimp continued, "We were at Charlottesville, and I didn't see it how Fry did. He said the president was wrong to say both sides had good in them. He said he did not think any KKK had good left in them. Mom, he made it seem like all KKK were bad people, making bad decisions, and we were responsible for crime and violence in the county. I know that can't be right. Right?"

His mom responded, "Son, you know us, you know our friends, we are good people. You know everyone in the Klavern. We look out for one another. We're not just members of some club, we're a family. We don't believe that America's a place that should welcome just anyone who wants to come here. We believe in separatism of races. We believe the Aryan race is superior in all ways. These beliefs have served us well."

Shrimp added that he and Red saw nothing wrong with racial separatism, but Fry's tone had made it seem ugly. Big Lou remarked, "Shrimp, you're the only ugly thing around here."

"Fuck off, Louise!"

"Kids! Stop it! Russell Gene, watch your language!"

"Well, I got angry when Fry said that KKK members were responsible for crime and violence in the county."

Shrimp said he was even more upset that Fry wanted people to say they were against the KKK. Shrimp mentioned he could see Red getting angry too, by the redness in his face and his crossed arms.

"Red and I talked about staying behind and beating him up, but several people went up to talk to him, so we came home instead.

"There's more. Fry asked people to step up and help turn things around. He said they needed to shine a light on KKK activities."

According to Shrimp, Fry had told the crowd, "I think it's time to name people belonging to the KKK. And I think it's time to stop frequenting their places of business. I hope you all have had enough and will join me!"

"What does it mean, dad? Will people find out we're members? Will we be attacked?"

"No, Shrimp, I don't think so. No one in the Klavern is going to tell other people who they are or that they're KKK members. I don't know how other people would know who was Klan, and who wasn't. How was the crowd responding? Who else from the Klavern was there?"

"There was applause for Fry a few times as he spoke, but also a few boos. Mostly it sounded like people liked him, and what he said. Orville and Wilbur Wright were there. They were the ones booing."

"Well, then, there's nothing to worry about. Orville and Wilbur will help us decide what to do about this Fry guy. Thanks, son, for bringing this to me. I'll talk to Hank, and we'll be sure to bring this up at the meeting later this week."

Shrimp was glad he had brought this to his dad's attention. He knew Junior would know just what to do.

Shrimp decided he'd write a short essay on the meeting for his extra credit, and forget about it. Tomorrow at school he'd remember to tell Big Lou "hello" every time he saw her. Shrimp was happy school was almost over, and he'd be a senior. Unless Big Lou flunked he would have long days away from her.

CHAPTER TWO

Junior asked, "Shrimp, are you going to the meeting to-night?"

Shrimp didn't always attend Klavern meetings, but since he had heard George Fry speak a few days ago, he decided this meeting would be interesting.

"Yeah, I'll come. When are we leaving?"

"You have about five minutes to get ready."

Now Shrimp was on his way to the gathering in the family car with his dad, mom, and sister. He expected there would be discussion about Mr. Fry. He hoped his own name would get mentioned as someone who had heard Fry speak. Maybe he'd even get called on to speak.

"Dad, do you think they'll want to hear from me or Red?"

"Maybe, or maybe we should let the adults speak."

Shrimp's shoulders drooped a bit as Big Lou smirked at him. He thought it was a good thing it was a short drive.

Klavern meetings were held in the basement of a local church. When renting the space several years ago they called their group a "closed bible study group." Several members of the Klavern were also members of the church, including Shrimp and his family, so no questions had been asked.

Shrimp was quick to exit the car and enter the church. He headed straight to the basement steps. The stairs to the basement were well lit, but the windows in the basement offered in little natural light. Overhead fluorescent bulbs provided lighting.

Shrimp thought it often felt damp in the room, and tonight was no exception. He was glad he'd brought his denim jacket along. It was too humid outside for Shrimp to wear it, but too damp inside not to put it on.

In the basement there was room for about seventy-five people. Chairs for the group were stacked along one wall. After a nod from Junior, Shrimp went to help set up chairs for the meeting. Since he'd done this many times, Shrimp knew to set up about forty chairs. As Shrimp was setting up chairs, Junior set up some tables for refreshments. These would be available during and after the meeting.

Another wall in the basement was covered with storage cabinets. Three of those cupboards had locks only the Klavern leader had keys to open. Shrimp had seen inside the cupboards many times, but had never dared to touch things unless asked to do so.

Shrimp's dad was with Hank Ross at the first cupboard. They were getting the coffee maker, and coffee supplies, including Styrofoam cups, sugar, creamer, and stir sticks. They also pulled out paper plates, napkins, and plastic forks.

"Shrimp, if you're done there, come help with this."

"Okay. I'm almost done." He didn't mind assisting since they always were some of the first people to arrive. It gave him something to do. He glanced at Big Lou. She was on her phone playing a game. She almost never helped with set-up.

As he walked over to the coffee supplies cupboard Shrimp saw the second set of cupboards was still locked. He knew they held robes for those who wanted to don them. Wearing them was required for some ceremonies, but generally the members would wear their street clothes to meetings. Tonight was a street clothes meeting. Shrimp liked the ceremonies, and had his own set of items to wear. It made him feel important when he had them on. It made him feel a part of something bigger than himself.

Another cabinet held flashlights, candles, boxes of crackers, beef jerky, and cookies stocked alongside multiple weapons and bullets. The Klan planned to never be unarmed should anything occur while they were in the basement. There was also an emergency exit. Shrimp had never been to a meeting where the weapons were needed. He thought it'd be exciting if they were ever needed.

As Shrimp had been busy helping with set-up, several Klan members had come into the basement. It was starting to get noisy from all the greetings and small talk going on. Shrimp waved at people as they waved at him. Red had flashed him a quick smile and wave as he arrived. Red's family always brought two cars as Hank liked to arrive very early to meetings.

It was almost time for the meeting to begin and people started heading to their chairs. Shrimp had noticed people usually sat in the same seats at every meeting, even though none had been assigned.

This meeting was previously scheduled, but members were encouraged to attend this important session after Orville and Wilbur Wright reported about the town hall and what George Fry had to say. Junior and Hank had heard about it from their sons, and had made several calls themselves asking members to attend. Shrimp saw that about forty people were at the meeting, almost as many as had heard Fry speak in Christiansburg.

Shrimp heard the members shout "AKIA!" It was the ritualistic start to their meeting. At his first meeting he'd had to ask his dad what it meant. His dad said, "A Klansman I Am. AKIA! Say it proudly and loudly, son."

Hank and other speakers referred to George Fry as an "Alien" which Shrimp knew was the name assigned to a person who was not a KKK member. The Alien's speech and the potential result of it would be a primary topic of conversation.

Shrimp saw Red Ross sitting with his family members, and made his way over to sit beside his friend. They exchanged greetings. Shrimp was happy to not sit by Big Lou. His left arm still felt bruised and he looked for ways to avoid being hit there again.

Shrimp thought a bit about the words of George Fry, and remembered what he said about women having mostly subservient roles. Shrimp had never considered this before. He had never seen a woman lead the meeting. The Klavern women provided the meals, and checked on other Klan members if someone was ill. He wondered what else Fry said that had a ring of truth to it. He almost laughed out loud at the thought of Big Lou being the Klavern leader. As quickly as that Shrimp dismissed all of what the Alien had said.

Hank started, "I call this meeting to order. Today we have two important topics to discuss, and I'm pleased so many of you are here. We'll begin the meeting with some concerns raised by those who heard the Alien speak at the town hall meeting in Christiansburg."

Everyone at the meeting had heard some version of the events previously, yet all were anxious to learn more.

"I call on Orville to describe what he heard, and Wilbur can add anything he wants as well."

Orville told about attending the town hall and how dangerous the discussion became after the Alien spoke. Toward the end, Orville told the Klavern that the Alien said he'd be identifying them to the townspeople. This elicited several gasps. This breach was unheard of in their neck of the woods. Everyone in nearby towns knew to keep quiet, to go along to get along.

While Orville was talking, Wilbur nodded his head in agreement with all Orville had to say, and had nothing else to add.

Hank and Junior agreed that the Wright comments matched what they heard from Shrimp and Red. Shrimp elbowed Red. They grinned at each other. Shrimp felt good to get this kind of acknowledgment at the meeting. It looked liked Red enjoyed it as well.

Shrimp looked around. He knew everyone here. The Wright brothers, Orville and Wilbur, were not descendants of the famous ones, but their ma and pa loved the names, and the history. Shrimp had heard them say that their family love of the Klan went back as far as family memory went.

Shrimp liked both brothers. He often laughed when Orville said the brothers "grew up lean and mean when hard times were the order of the day." He didn't know why he found that funny, but he did. They weren't that much older than him, but he thought they sometimes talked like they were much older.

Orville, at five foot five inches, often took the lead over his brother. Wilbur, five foot four inches, was the willing follower. Shrimp noticed they were in their usual attire, overalls with five-inch cuffs at the bottom. They often wore their chosen pair day after day, until someone complained about the smell. They told Shrimp and Red that they shot animals often, usually for food, but also simply for the joy of the kill. Shrimp thought that was cool. But he also thought they should change into other overalls more frequently. Tonight they were a bit fragrant.

The Wright brothers were in their mid-twenties; neither had been married, though Orville said he had "eyes for Marilyn" from the Groove Burger stand. Shrimp overheard him tell Red that it seemed like Marilyn always smiled at him, and he was sure she always gave him extra fries. Shrimp thought that made Orville a lucky guy.

Shrimp noticed that Ma and Pa Wright did not attend the Klavern meeting that night. Shrimp had learned that when Pa Wright was younger, he was a member of the inner circle of the Klavern. Now Orville and Wilbur were two of the four members of the inner circle. Shrimp knew that when the brothers got home they would only share news about the general membership. News of the inner circle was shared only inside the inner circle. Shrimp decided that was pretty cool. To him it was a secret society inside a secret society.

Shrimp looked over toward Carl and Jay Burden. They were cousins to the Wright brothers. Shrimp thought they were similar to their cousins in almost every way, except in size. Where Orville and Wilbur were lean and wiry, Carl and Jay were stout and flabby. Tonight they wore camouflage shirts with jeans, along with shit-kicker boots, their usual attire.

Shrimp was a bit surprised that Carl and Jay had not been at the meeting in Christiansburg with their cousins. The four were often seen together.

The Burden brothers were just a bit older than their cousins, but were also unmarried. The two young men were strong, but Shrimp knew they were not especially bright. Carl was the brighter of the two, and did most of the talking.

These brothers also had a long family history of Klan membership. Like the cousins, Carl and Jay were the other two members of the inner circle. Everyone in the Klavern knew it would be up to the inner circle to decide the fate of the Alien.

Shrimp looked around at other members present at the meeting. They included Ray and Ella Parker. They were older than Shrimp's parents and he'd heard both had recently retired. They attended along with their grown children Ray Jr., Buford, Elaine, Sarah, Jimmy, "Toothless" Dan, and the beautiful Belle. The family had been Klavern members for more than two decades. The Parkers were the biggest family in the Klavern, and growing bigger as the older kids got married and had children themselves.

Shrimp liked Ella Parker. She acted like a grandmother to him, and she always brought home-baked sweets to meetings, and saved one or two for Shrimp each time. He hoped she had brought her famous brownies tonight. He thought earlier about sneaking over to the refreshments table, but had been caught up in the discussion and had forgotten to check.

Shrimp saw that others attending the meeting included the local plumber Herb Smith (he always took care of plumbing issues for Klavern members), dentist Billy Dean (Shrimp hated going to see him), mechanic Ben Rover (he serviced Junior's car) and his wife Beth (an elementary school teacher, who taught Shrimp in fourth grade), and real estate agent Fran Brown and her husband Gerald (cashier at the local grocery store, who always brought packs of gum for Shrimp). These members were all around thirty years of age, and had joined the Klavern relatively recently.

There was a lively discussion about the Alien. Having been at the meeting in Christiansburg, Orville remarked that action needed to be taken. Gerald strongly agreed with Orville. Others, including Ray, Jimmy, and Ben, felt no real harm had been done. They argued that if a big deal was made out of the speech, then more people might side with the Alien. No clear outcome was explicitly stated. Hank let the discussion continue until everyone who wished to speak had the chance to be heard. He asked for more comments.

Like Shrimp, Herb said he was concerned they might be subject to attack.

Shrimp elbowed Red again and whispered, "Shit. Exactly what I thought." Junior allayed Herb's fears like he had with Shrimp.

Shrimp looked around the gathering, and thought a few looked worried. It made him a bit worried too.

Fran asked, "Shouldn't we do something about this? I can't afford to have people quit using my real estate business."

Hank told her, "I really don't think anything will come of that Fran. We'll address it later if we need to. But remember, we take care of our own. You and Herb, Billy, and Ben have nothing to fear. We will frequent your businesses, and if they fail, we'll help with mortgages, and getting food on the table."

When Hank determined everyone had their say, he turned his attention to the recruiting activities they had been planning for the past few months. This discussion was turned over to the Kleagle, Buster Ross, whose main function was to recruit. Buster was a few years older than Red. Shrimp liked Buster, but they weren't friends the way he was with Red.

Buster commented, "We've been talking about recruitment for a few months. I'm confirming our location. It's the two nearby forest campgrounds we've talked about at the last two meetings. They've been quite busy lately, filling up most every weekend. I have maps available for all the drivers."

Shrimp knew that in the past the Klavern found that campgrounds in the county were places that were amenable to recruitment. He had never been on a recruitment outing, and was not sure if he was more excited or more nervous about going this time. The process was unfamiliar to him, and Shrimp preferred the familiar.

Buster once again reminded the others that the Ku Klos Knights needed more members. He said, "Increased activity at these two campgrounds is a great opportunity to boost membership."

Buster said he wasn't sure why the campgrounds had been so busy. He guessed that it was recent improvements to the horse campground, or the nearby hunting, shooting, and horse trail options that had made them more desirable as campsites. He didn't know for sure why they were popular. He told the Klavern that the real point was that lots of people would be camping, lots of people who were potential new Klavern members.

Buster told them that everyone was expected to be part of this recruitment. They were to show up in large numbers early Sunday morning, before people might start packing up camp, and leaving to head back home. He provided a list of who should go to which campground, and suggested sharing rides.

Buster said, "I want everyone there early on Sunday, the latest around 8."

Buster told them it was best not to take the chance that people would leave before Klavern members arrived there.

Shrimp whispered to Red, "Fuck, that is too early! Are you going to go?"

"Yes, and you better fucking be there!"

"Okay. Fuck, that is early."

"You're not going to like this, but there is no Wi-Fi there."

"What? Fuck."

"Yep. But we can play Fortnite all afternoon when we get back."

"Cool."

Buster reminded them that they were to show possible recruits how great a group they were, how supportive, and family-like they were. No one was to call the campers "Aliens" or use the term "SAN BOG." When Shrimp looked confused Red reminded Shrimp that it meant that strangers were near and to be on guard.

Buster said they could use "KIGY" to show how connected they were within the membership. Shrimp knew that meant, "Klansman, I greet you."

Buster and the others were thinking their easy camaraderie would be enticing to others. It was to be a friendly, welcoming atmosphere so that people would willingly join them.

The Klavern women would bring coffee and food to share with the campers, while the men would discretely inquire about potential membership in the KKK. Decisions were made about the recruitment, and the meeting ended.

Shrimp declared, "That was a really good meeting."

Red concurred, "It felt good to be acknowledged."

Shrimp made a beeline to the refreshments table. Ella had made brownies and saved two just for him. "Thank you, Ella! These look delicious!"

Shrimp and Red helped put the chairs away. Both young men left the meeting feeling the glow of belonging to such a great group.

"I've got my car. Want a ride home?"

"Yes. Thanks!" Shrimp was happy not to be in the family car with Big Lou. There was always a chance she would hit him again, and his shoulder still ached.

As they drove home, Shrimp thought about the inner circle staying behind to discuss the Alien situation. Though some in the meeting thought nothing should be done, Shrimp had been in Christiansburg, and knew the inner circle had to act. He wondered if someday he'd be invited to be in that circle.

CHAPTER THREE

O n Saturday, two towns over from the KKK meeting, in Bluefield, was the meeting of the National Alliance. Four members had been delayed. Since their numbers had been declining in the past few years, they usually waited for all members to arrive before starting a meeting. It was unusual to wait more than fifteen minutes for late members, but today they'd waited just over an hour.

Evan Wilton, the leader of the local group, was proud of the group history. The National Alliance was primarily known for their leader William Pierce and his book called the *Turner Diaries*. Timothy McVeigh had photocopies of pages of the work in his car when he was arrested, and he had called a National Alliance phone line seven times the day before he bombed Oklahoma City with Terry Nichols. Few people would consider this a group of harmless men. Evan found that admirable.

The meeting was held in Evan's barn. It was rugged looking outside and in. There was no warmth to be found within its confines, and no seating. Meetings were usually brief, and everyone stood. Many farm implements were hung from the walls, but few were as deadly as what was located in the weapons cache Evan kept in the small storeroom. Evan knew every member had a similar cache available to him.

While they waited, the members discussed local news, and general town gossip. They would wait until everyone was there to discuss National Alliance business.

"Did you see what Missy was wearing last night? Her brother better get her in line right now!"

"Seriously. She's gonna be trouble for her family."

"Yep, that man better take care of business."

"She's young and stupid, and he needs to teach her how to behave."

"Hey, did you hear that Joe is closing the barber shop?"

"No way! Why would he do that?"

"He said it was time to get out before he lost all his savings."

"Man, this town is going to shit. How can we convince him to stay open?"

"I don't think we can. You can only get so many haircuts. If he charged more money no one would go. I don't think there's anything we can do. The economy sucks. I think we're all suffering."

"No jobs are opening up. That's the problem."

"Jobs don't pay anything."

"No one can afford to do anything is the problem."

"I have two jobs, and neither pays me enough!"

"The whole world has gone to shit."

"That reminds me, I heard there was two guys kissing at the theater. I don't know who they were."

"That's disgusting. I hope someone takes care of them, if you get my meaning."

"If I saw that, I'd put a permanent stop to it."

"I'm with you. This country has gone crazy."

The conversations continued along this line while they waited. Nothing was resolved, and there was plenty to be angry about.

Evan had led this group of men for many years, and was considering stepping down. He was getting older, and just didn't have the same energy level anymore. While he stayed engaged in this conversation, he was not sure which topic he should focus on. They all made him mad, but not as fighting mad as he used to get. Most of these guys were sounding really angry.

For the last year Evan had Duke Kent lead the meetings, after conferring with him. He knew Duke would eventually be their leader, and Evan wanted him to be experienced. He trusted Duke's opinions, and knew their group would be in good hands. Evan thought it was almost time to anoint Duke as leader.

Evan really liked Duke's style. "A certified hate monger" was what Evan proudly called Duke. Evan liked that Duke often spoke to the group with a religious fervor, citing the Bible for reasons the Aryan race was superior, and must be maintained. Like Evan, Duke had a very long and checkered history with local and state police. Evan felt Duke had proven himself worthy of leadership.

Duke and three others were the last to arrive. No one asked about the delay. They knew it had to be important. The men would not keep everyone waiting for trivial matters.

Seeing Duke made Evan remember when Duke's father brought him into the National Alliance about fifteen years earlier. His dad had Duke show everyone what an excellent marksman he was. His skill had impressed Evan.

Duke still was an excellent marksman. Duke bragged to Evan that he often hunted deer at night in his SUV, shining his bright lights in their eyes to startle them, so he could kill them more easily. Duke had also said that sometimes he took his kill home, but sometimes he simply drove away. Duke blithely commented that taking a life was just within his power, and Duke loved that power. Evan could agree with that sentiment.

Evan looked at the assembled men. They all had their own stories and different strengths they brought to the group. He looked at his son, Wendell. Like his dad, Wendell was tall and lean. Besides age, the biggest difference was that Wendell always dressed in jeans, western shirts, and cowboy boots. Evan preferred jeans, denim shirts, and work boots. Otherwise, they were the same. Both men loved horses. They also shared many of the same beliefs, but not always the same activities.

Evan had never been in the rodeo. Three National Alliance group members were active participants. His son Wendell was one of those in the rodeo group. Wendell's main rodeo events included team roping and calf roping. Evan knew that Wendell fared better at the calf roping event, because he had some of the best times recorded. He had set records at the multi-state level. His rides always thrilled the crowds.

Wendell's team roping was not quite as good. He was a great heeler, and partnered with header Dave Speller on that event. Sometimes it took Dave too long to rope the neck of the calf, thereby adding precious seconds to their time. Evan liked Dave, and thought his efforts were to be applauded. Dave gave his all; he just was not as talented as Wendell.

Every time Evan saw Wendell at a rodeo event, or most any-where, then he also saw Dave. Dave was almost always in the company of Wendell. Most people rarely spoke of one with-out mentioning the other. Evan saw that Dave was in his usual attire. It was the same as Wendell, western shirt, jeans, and cowboy boots. At least they didn't have their cowboy hats on, though their hair showed evidence of recent wearing.

Evan had met Wendell's and Dave's girlfriends, Carly and Eve, who he knew had no idea about the men's membership in the National Alliance. Membership was not talked about outside of their families.

Evan glanced over at Clark Davies. Clark was the third mem-ber of the rodeo circuit. It was a shame, thought Evan, that Clark had suffered so many broken bones over the years. He'd recently seen Clark booed at rodeo events, because people thought Clark jumped from the bull too early on his rides. Evan knew that Clark's wife, Crystal, was aware of his National Alliance mem-bership, but as a woman, she was not allowed to be a member. It was clear that she fully supported him. Clark's dad, Ethan, was also a member of the National Alliance.

Also attending the meeting that night were Adam Davies, younger brother to Clark, and life-long friend to Duke. Evan admired the way Duke had developed so many adamant sup-porters. Duke had told Evan that Adam would follow Duke any-where, and do anything asked of him. Evan knew his youngest son Steve felt the same as Clark. This was part of the reason Evan had identified Duke as the next group leader.

Evan focused next on Joe Miller. Joe, along with Edgar West, joined the group more recently than the others. They had been introduced to Evan through the Speller family. The two men had lost their jobs a few years back, and needed someone to blame. Joe told Evan that immigration was to blame, never mind that there were few recent immigrants to their region. Joe said immigrants got handed everything, and lived from the federal teat, while people like him eked out an existence with no help. Evan had to agree.

Evan knew that like Joe, Edgar was angry. Edgar was sure former President Obama was to blame for every woe in the South. Edgar was a self-proclaimed fervent watcher of *Fox News* and *Info Wars*, and his level of hate toward black people would ratchet exponentially on most every viewing. Edgar carried a lot of hate.

Like others in their group, Joe and Edgar voiced their full support for Donald Trump for the presidency in 2016, and hated Hillary Clinton. Like the others in the National Alliance, they continued to support Trump.

Also attending the meeting were people who were related by blood relations to other members in the National Alliance. Evan admired Gene Speller (grocer, and father of Dave) and Erasmus West (volunteer firefighter, and brother to Edgar). He thought they were hard-working men. He called them the "salt of the Earth." Evan also appreciated Gus Springer (bartender, he often provided kegs of beer for National Alliance meetings, and was liked by all) and his dad Bedford (butcher). Two others attending the meeting were the street sweeper Earl Graves, and his brother Leland (locksmith).

The Graves brothers were usually quiet in the meetings, but Evan knew they were constantly angry. Evan thought these two were likely to explode one day. He'd tell Duke to keep watch over those two. Maybe together Evan and Duke could help direct that explosion.

Rounding out the group were Nathan Poke (daycare worker), and two Sheriff Area Officers named Blaze Edwards and Elliott Green. Blaze and Elliott had joined the group when they were young men, long before becoming officers. Evan knew he could count on Blaze and Elliott every time there was a law enforcement encounter with a National Alliance member. Mostly they had helped smooth over parking tickets or speeding tickets. Sometimes they had stepped in to plant evidence that pointed away from National Alliance members. Neither had complained to Evan about taking care of these issues. Evan appreciated that they quietly went about supporting the National Alliance.

Duke began, "Let's get the meeting going. We have disturbing news. Gus, Elliott, and I have heard that the KKK is headed to Gopher Flats and Beggar Flats Campgrounds tomorrow. What do you think? Should we let them?"

There were resounding choruses of "No!" along with, "These are our lands!" There were a variety of swear words tossed into the mix. This was exactly the reaction Evan expected. He knew Duke expected it too.

Duke let the men voice their anger for several minutes. Evan knew it was important that they get fired up, and ready for action. He needed them to be mad. He needed them to want vengeance against the interlopers.

These two campgrounds were where the National Alliance members spent a significant portion of their time together. Some evenings, but mostly weekends, was when they gathered there, and bonded over their beliefs while drinking beer. Members of the National Alliance had been going to the Gopher Flats Campground since they were little. They would also camp at the Beggar Flats Horse campground, but not as frequently. For most, including Evan, their membership in the National Alliance was considered their inheritance from their fathers before them. In their view, the campgrounds belonged to them as part of that inheritance.

Like Evan and Duke, others in the National Alliance hated the KKK. If they saw KKK flyers up, they would paste "NA" stickers over them. Some people in town knew NA meant National Alliance, but others thought it meant "not applicable."

They had seen a few KKK signs in their own campgrounds recently. They tore them down, and burned them.

If KKK signs were found outside of town, the National Alliance members would shoot them with so many holes that you could no longer read the intended message.

Duke told the others, "I've seen evidence of KKK activity in local picnic areas and campgrounds before, but this sounds like a take-over of our land, our backyard, and our inheritance!"

Not one person thought that this was a good sign, or considered aligning with the other group.

"They better not come into our campgrounds!"

"They'll be sorry of they do!"

"They need to be taught a lesson!"

"We need to go push them out!"

"Damned KKK has gotten soft recently. Some of their members are running for political offices."

"How stupid is that? Everyone knows you should not join the scum politicians. Instead, you should annihilate them!"

"Yes! Anyone with different political opinions should die!"

"Especially those damned liberals!"

"Especially if their skin color is not white!"

Duke let the spewing of hatred continue for a few more minutes, just as Evan had advised him to do.

The National Alliance group itself was more likely to set up tables at local festivals to attract members. They sometimes used the festivals to identify people to threaten, and possibly kill. They had not used their campgrounds as their recruiting tool. It had not occurred to Evan to do so. Those were their "family time" places. Knowing the KKK planned to be there had really surprised and upset Evan and Duke.

Evan had decided it was time to show the KKK who those two campgrounds belonged to. He'd made sure that Duke got everyone riled up. Evan and Duke called on their members to send a very loud and clear message. There was no way they would let the KKK use their personal campgrounds for recruiting into the

KKK.

As the meeting progressed, the National Alliance members made no plans for sharing food and friendly interaction. They did make plans to arrive armed.

Evan was very pleased with how the meeting went. "Yes," he thought, "Duke will make a fine leader."

CHAPTER FOUR

Not a dry eye in the place. Well, except maybe a few from the law enforcement officers and investigators present. But all the family members gathered round were definitely crying. They thought this would never happen.

The flower arrangements were in place, and their scent filled the air. The piped-in music made the occasion all the more emotional. There was plenty of seating available, and refreshments would be served afterward. This was an important ritual known across the country.

Harley Fremont was weeping, and hoping it would not turn into an ugly cry. In her mind she was reliving her wedding to Augie almost 30 years previously. She remembered the record setting heat wave, and how the chapel just kept getting hotter as the ceremony and reception progressed. More importantly, Harley remembered how they promised to love and care for each other as long as they both shall live. Only Augie did not live. She had lost Augie to cancer almost a decade ago. Weddings made her happy and sad at the same time. Oh, how she wished she could go back and marry Augie again.

Harley hoped the couple would be as happy as she and Augie had been. She had been crazy for him, and he for her. It was magical.

Harley noticed that none of her law enforcement colleagues were crying, but social standards be damned, she was going to cry.

Harley's colleague and friend, Violet Carter had done all she could to be sure this wedding would be memorable and moving. She had turned her backyard in Baltimore into an enchanted place. Harley commented earlier to Violet about the yard. "Vi, you've outdone yourself. This is beautiful! The flower arrangements are fragrant, and the archway is gorgeous! I'm a sucker for those tiny white lights."

"Thanks, Harley! I so love sharing my home with other people. This is a special day for Emmylynne and Scott, and I wanted everything to be as special as possible."

"You've met your goal. I wish I'd been in the office on the day of the proposal. Bill and Woody told me she blushed a lot, and Scott could not stop grinning."

Violet responded, "Both are true. They're in love, and it's great to see. Scott showed up out of the blue. Emmylynne had no idea he was coming from Texas, and no idea he was going to propose. He got down on one knee in front of all the office staff. He was a man on a mission."

Harley laughed, "I guess he was, because that was only a few weeks ago and now we're having the wedding! You put all this together in no time, and it really does look spectacular. There are a lot of chairs set up, does this mean Scott's family decided to attend after all?"

"Last I heard only one of his brothers, and his wife, will be here. But I have enough chairs for his family should they all show up. If they would only come meet Emmylynne, I know they'd love her."

"Well, it was very short notice. Maybe they already had plans. They'll get to meet her eventually, and they'll love her like we all do."

"Oh, it looks like Emmylynne's family is here. I need to go greet them. Please wander around, and enjoy this glorious day. I may want help later with the reception, if you're willing."

"You bet. Go meet and greet. I'd be happy to assist you later."

Harley thought about her friend Violet. At five foot seven, Violet was a bit taller than Harley. Violet was skinnier as well.

Harley thought Violet was a bit of a beanpole, but she liked beanpoles. She just wished she could eat like Violet did and not gain weight. Harley thought, "Oh, I should've complimented Violet's hair." Violet usually wore it in a tight ponytail, but today she had it in a very pretty up do for the wedding. Harley made a mental note to mention it to Vi later.

Harley watched as Violet gave one of her hundred watt smiles to Emmylynne's family. While Harley was a bit of an introvert, Violet was warm and outgoing. You could see just how generous Violet was in that smile.

Harley walked to the front of Violet's house to where her motor home was parked. She wanted to give Gemma a short walk.

As she was leashing Gemma a man approached. "Hello. What a beautiful dog. What kind is he?"

"She is a Rhodesian Ridgeback."

"She's a beautiful one. I don't think I've seen her breed before. Have you had other dogs like her?"

"I had fostered another dog previously, but this one I fell in love with. She is my pride and joy. I'd stay and talk, but we need to get our walk in. Have a nice day."

"Thanks, you too."

As they walked around the block Harley was thinking that Gemma really was her pride and joy, that Gemma was nearly as much a family member as was her son Jack. Harley would do anything for either of them. Her musings skipped along to Jack. Harley was so proud that Jack had graduated college last year. He had looked so handsome in his cap and gown. Jack had looked so grown-up. Shortly after graduation he accepted an internship in a law office. Harley knew he'd eventually need to attain a law degree to pursue his dreams of being a lawyer. Jack had told her he was considering Georgetown University for law school. Harley knew he could do whatever he set his mind to.

Harley was enjoying the day, and as usual started humming while she and Gemma walked. If they were on a longer hike Harley would sing, hum, whistle, or just talk with Gemma as they moved. She would also have had on more comfortable walking shoes.

Woody Brooks approached Harley after she put Gemma back in the motor home. "Hi, Woody! Don't you look nice!"

"Thanks, Harley. You look pretty fabulous yourself. That blue dress suits you."

"Thanks." Harley had found the dress this week while shopping with Emmylynne. She didn't normally like dresses, but she couldn't pass it up. It was a dazzling blue color, it fit perfectly, and it was on sale.

"Wait until you see what Violet has done to her backyard. It looks amazing!"

"Isn't Gemma coming, too? I'm not used to seeing you without her."

"No, she'll have to wait in the motor home. Some of Emmylynne's family is allergic to dogs. Gemma will be fine. It looked like she was going to nap."

"We should get to the wedding. Emmylynne wouldn't want us to miss it."

That was how Harley ended up sitting next to Woody, with Bill Harris on her other side, and Darryl White next to Bill. These three men, plus Violet and Emmylynne, all worked together in the USDA Forest Service headquarters office in Washington D.C. They were the Law Enforcement and Investigations staff.

Harley made a few trips to the LEI office each year, and took jobs on a contract basis with their agency throughout the year. These were assignments to various National Forests across America. Hers was not an office job, unless you counted forest trails as an office.

Bill said, "Here comes the bride! Emmylynne looks fantastic! That dress is a show-stopper!"

Woody responded, "Look how happy Scott is! Harley, are you crying?"

"Bill was right," thought Harley. Emmylynne did look amazing in her beaded wedding gown, and Scott looked equally so in his black tux, as they promised to have and hold each other from this day forward. Emmylynne's cornflower blue eyes were glued to Scott's brown ones. Both wore smiles as wide as their faces. Emmylynne and Scott giggled through the vows, yet Harley was sure they meant every word.

Not long after their first kiss as husband and wife was when trouble appeared.

CHAPTER FIVE

No sooner than the pronouncement of "husband and wife" was made, Woody's cell phone vibrated. Harley watched him reach for his phone, change his mind and ignore it. It must have vibrated again, because he pulled it out, and glared at the text messages. After clenching and unclenching his jaws a few times, he got up and moved out of the aisle.

Harley watched Woody move to the far end of the yard, and put the phone to his ear. Harley had seen him take dozens of calls in her presence, and the ones that elicited clenched jaws were rarely good news. This made her curious. It was such a serene day, in a beautiful yard, it seemed like it must be that way everywhere.

Harley watched the couple start to head down the aisle, and then looked back at Woody. He was still talking on the phone. She watched as the couple made their way to the end of the center aisle, and felt her phone vibrate. Woody had sent a text message to Bill Harris, Darryl White, Violet Carter, and Harley. It was unusual for Woody to use the word "urgent," but it said exactly that.

All four quickly moved away from the wedding guests, and made their way to the fence where Woody waited. Emmylynne was quite busy at the moment, but Harley figured it would not be long before she left her guests to ask what was happening.

Woody was about to make the wedding day memorable in more ways than one.

"I'm so sorry to disrupt Emmylynne's big day," said Woody. Harley usually saw Woody with a cup of coffee in his hands, and it looked to her like he was sorely wishing he could get some java soon. His dark eyes expressed concern.

Bill said, "Woody, I have no doubt it's big news, and I'm guessing its bad news. Tell us what's going on."

"I just got off the phone with Rick Givens, Forest Supervisor on the George Washington and Jefferson National Forests in Virginia. He has been contacted twice today by sheriffs who patrol the Eastern Divide Ranger District. They need law enforcement help from us. During the first contact Rick was told a body was found with two bullet wounds, one of which was in the mouth of the male victim." Woody waited a beat while they all absorbed this information.

Bill commented, "That's awful. It's more than awful. Do they have more information about the shooting?"

"They had little information in that first call. The victim had ID on him. He was George Fry of Christiansburg. There was one bullet in him, and another passed through. They were looking for that second bullet, but had little hope of finding it."

"Okay," said Bill, "I presume Rick will continue to feed us information as he gets it. After the reception is over let's discuss who our officers are that can work on it with the sheriffs."

"Sure," said Woody, "but there's more. The second call from the sheriffs came about a different body found on the same Ranger District. This one was a black man who had been lynched."

"Oh my god!" Violet looked like she'd seen a ghost. Darryl looked ready to kill someone. Harley could hardly stand upright. It was shocking.

Bill walked over to a row of chairs, and gathered a few to bring back for the group. Once they were seated Woody said, "I'm sorry. I know this is difficult. The victim was a man named Clay Freeman. His vehicle was found just off the nearby roadway. It appeared to have broken down. Right now we can only guess what happened next, but the sheriff is sure he didn't hang himself."

Woody continued, "I told Rick that we were all here together, and would get back to him about what to say to the media. In addition to calling us, he has contacted his boss in the National Forest System. Rick knows we'll have a role in the investigation, and said we can expect calls soon to keep us up to date."

Harley saw Bill trying to think this through, so she decided to sit quietly until he had reached some decisions. She wanted to speak right up, and offer her and Gemma's services. Harley would wait to see what Bill had to say since he was the boss of this group.

Harley was particularly shocked by the lynching and could not imagine the terror felt by Mr. Freeman. It dawned on her that Darryl was probably taking this very hard. She had never thought to ask him about his family history, and now was not the time.

Harley realized she was generalizing, and that was not a good thing. Harley felt off center after this news. Then she thought about how awful this was for Mr. Freeman's family, and how awful for any compassionate human being. Harley reminded herself that Mr. Fry's family was faring no better.

Harley turned her thoughts to Bill. She met him a few years before, soon after Bill became the Director of Law Enforcement and Investigations for the Forest Service. She usually only saw him when they had meetings at his office in the headquarters office in Washington, D.C., though lately they had taken a few walks together, and had visited the Smithsonian.

When Harley first came to the Washington office Bill had told her that the staff and the office hadn't always existed. Several years before, all the law enforcement officers reported directly to forest supervisors, however after a few instances where the forest supervisor chose the side of a friend over the law, it became clear that LEI needed to be "stove-piped." Bill explained that meant they reported directly within their own internal organization made up of administration, law enforcement officers, and special agents in charge of investigations. In the current configuration, all members of LEI answered to Bill, and Bill answered only to the Chief of the Forest Service. Harley knew enough about the Forest Service to know that put him in the upper level of leadership in the agency.

Harley knew Bill believed in stovepipe reporting, he had said "it was good for the officers, and for the agency." He felt it lent professionalism to their job. Bill often spoke about professionalism, and how training would make the officers more professional. Bill tried to keep his staff as well trained as possible, including sending officers to FLETC. She had heard of this training at the Federal Law Enforcement Training Center. Harley knew other federal agencies trained there as well.

Harley rarely heard Bill complain about anything, but she had heard him complain about FLETC. It wasn't because of the law enforcement training, but because they didn't focus at all on natural resources training, which his officers needed to do their jobs well. When she asked for clarification, Bill said he meant activities such as unlawful cutting of trees, unlawful growth, or harvesting of forest products. He'd told Harley that they needed training that covered everything from issues you'd find in cities to natural resources issues. He'd said it meant FLETC training needed to be followed by on-the-job training.

Bill had told her that some officers came up from Forest Service ranks and then joined law enforcement, while others started as law enforcement officers and found their way into natural resources. Each one had a different training schedule, and Bill often said that comprehensive training took a lot of funding.

The only other thing Harley heard Bill complain about was funding. She knew he spent considerable time in meetings trying to get additional funding for LEI. Bill had told her they were already short-handed, and it looked as if no additional funds were coming their way. Harley wondered if the current situation would result in additional funding for the office. She didn't want to ask though, because they had more important things to discuss.

Harley's thoughts turned to their personal relationship. It

was clear they were physically attracted to each other. They'd flirted a bit a few times, and one time they had briefly kissed. She knew the agency had rules about dating between bosses and employees, but she was not an employee of the agency. Some day Harley would have to ask about any rules related to contractors. Since she traveled a lot, and he was located in D.C., it didn't seem like a workable relationship. She'd have to wait and see if it went anywhere.

Harley turned her thoughts back to the current situation. She tried to take stock. A shooting into someone's mouth sounded to her like an execution. A lynching was definitely an execution. She wondered what in hell was happening on that forest? Harley could hardly believe she was hearing about murders while attending a wedding.

"Oh my goodness," Harley thought. "Emmylynne's wedding." She had been so focused on the news, she felt like she had tunneled into herself and these four people. Her focus enlarged to see others having a wonderful time. She saw Emmylynne look their way with concern. Harley wondered if the rainclouds gathering overhead were a sign they should have paid attention to.

At last Bill spoke up, "Woody, you need to keep this out of the news until we know more!" Woody nodded his head. Harley was sure Woody had heard that line before. They all knew these deaths would hit the news sooner rather than later. Bill decided they should have a plan in place before that happened.

Bill told the others, "I'll call the state police and sheriff's department contacts. Woody, please start an outline of a press release. I hope we have some time before the stories break. Darryl, please call Rick Givens again, and see if he has any more information to pass along. Violet, I'll need you to gather some data on the forests including acreage, and recent law enforcement activities. Harley, I have nothing to assign you right now. Is a half hour enough time for everyone?"

Harley thought about how the public might react to either of the deaths. Woody had previously told her that he understood the need to get information into the public, but was often reticent to do so. He thought the agency "best served the public quietly when it came to crime and violence," while others, like Darryl would like "parades down Constitution Avenue" when a case got resolved. Harley could see each viewpoint, and appreciate both. She had seen these two men work together. Woody and Darryl often had differing opinions. Harley thought it was a good thing to hear from everyone. It made working with this group interesting, and challenging.

Harley spent a bit of her half hour visiting with the other wedding guests. After the half hour was over, the group met again to find what everyone learned, and to start making decisions. Bill reported that both the state police and the sheriff's department were emailing copies of their reports, but so far few clues were left behind at either scene.

"The autopsy for each victim will be performed tomorrow, and will have high priority. We're hoping the bullets removed from Mr. Fry lead us directly to the guns, and gun owners. The State Police said they've seen this type of shooting before, and have every reason to believe they're in the system somewhere. Given the bullet he took to the mouth, they think this shooting might be connected."

Bill also told them that the sheriff officers at the Clay Freeman lynching had noticed some "interesting knotting of the ropes." Bill didn't know what that meant. Bill also noted that the officers confessed they had not seen many hangings before, and the ones they had seen were clearly suicides. Bill continued by saying that the agencies would be submitting information to Forest Supervisor Givens, but they would keep Bill included in the information loop.

Bill shared that both entities lamented the lack of Forest Service law enforcement on the forest, and Bill assured them that a discussion would be had with the forest supervisor about forest budget priorities. It would not be that easy, since Bill didn't supervise Rick. Bill told them he would need to work with the Deputy Chief of the National Forest System before talking with

Rick.

Woody reported he had an outline of a press release, where blank spots needed to be filled in prior to sending it out. The question was how much information to give out. Woody was especially concerned over the reaction to a lynching in the south. It was something he thought that might further unbalance race relations. The group discussed the need to call it a hanging, and avoid using "lynching," until Woody observed it was likely that would be the headlines used by other media, and it might appear that they were trying to hide something.

They were discussing this choice when Emmylynne joined the group.

"Emmylynne, we're so very happy for you and Scott."

"Hey, did you already lose your husband? Where is he?"

"You look amazing, and the wedding was magnificent."

"Such a beautiful ceremony!"

"You guys can try to deflect, but I know something huge is going on here. What's happening? How can I help?"

Led by Bill, they gave her a brief summary of the deaths. They assured her that it was all under control, and her priority today was her wedding, her groom, and her wedding guests. Harley saw Emmylynne cast a look at Violet that suggested she would not be left out, before heading back to her groom and her guests.

Darryl reported that he had indeed connected with Rick. It seemed to him that Rick had been drinking. While all thought this was a reasonable response, it was not responsible. Darryl didn't learn any more than what Woody had learned from Rick.

Harley thought about Darryl. She had wanted to like him, but she found Darryl to be a difficult and judgmental man. Her main issue with him was his complete dislike of dogs. Each time she came to the office with Gemma, Darryl told Harley she should not bring Gemma into the building in Washington, D.C. Harley heard him tell Violet the same thing about her dog, Muffin. Since he wasn't either one's boss, they continued to bring the animals inside with them. Harley and Violet shared their dislike of Darryl's opinions. Both thought his work was great, but his disdain of their dogs made them both wary of him. Being a bit of a mama bear about Gemma, Harley found Darryl off-putting.

On one of her first office visits, Darryl had told Harley that he did not believe in K-9 officers, he'd said that they required more training than they were worth. Darryl was able to tell you exactly the cost of each K-9 officer. He compared their costs to the equipment that could have been purchased instead.

While in the office yesterday, Darryl told Harley that he was not supportive of the budding relationship between Harley and Bill. In fact, it appeared to Harley that Darryl did not want her as part of the Forest Service, even on a contractual basis. In her heart of hearts, she was not sure about a relationship with Bill either, but Darryl's reaction set her teeth on edge. There was no way she'd give up her Forest Service contract. She was good at her job, and felt she added value with every outing. Harley wondered if Darryl had mentioned his concerns to Bill. She doubted he had.

Harley brought her mind back to the task at hand. Violet reported to the group about some stats on the forest. She said that the George Washington and Jefferson National Forests had locations in Virginia and West Virginia, plus a small amount of acreage in Kentucky. The Eastern Divide Ranger District, where the bodies were found, was rural. It was about 150,000 acres in size, and was about a twenty-minute drive from about 200,000 people. Though many forests were much larger than this, no one in the group thought the size to be "small" because it was a lot of rugged ground to cover, nor did they think 200,000 people narrowed their suspect pool much.

Violet added that their database indicated that abuse of alcohol was common in this area. There were also many reports of vandalism, threats of violence, and fighting. Finally, the data showed large gatherings of people were on the increase.

They spent a few moments contemplating all they had heard. Harley found her mind wandering again. She was thinking about Violet.

Harley liked Violet a lot. They had much in common, including their love of dogs, especially Rhodesian Ridgebacks. Harley knew Violet had been with LEI for several years, and was uniformly admired.

Harley knew Violet loved her career. Violet had arrived in the Washington office shortly after Bill. Once there she had seen some gaping holes in the old data collection system, and made it better. She would say, "How did any work get done before these changes?" Violet often was heard to say, "This is my circus and these are my monkeys. Let's figure this out."

Harley had learned from Bill that in addition to her work with the law enforcement database, Violet was instrumental in the development of the electronic pad that all officers, special agents, and contractors carry. This pad gave them instant access to enter and evaluate data, plus Violet could track where everyone was located, and where every incident happened. She was always on the lookout for data and variables that would enhance her growing database, and hence the ability for LEI employees to accomplish their job. Harley could understand why so many people admired Violet.

Darryl said he appreciated Violet's information about the forest, and he'd offered to check with the National Forest System about spending patterns on the forest. He added that he suspected the data might indicate problems the forest had been experiencing. It might provide insight into what was going on.

"Tell me more about that," requested Harley. She was hoping to understand why that would be useful.

Darryl replied, "Sometimes you can see huge expenditures that seem out of line with the size of the location. For example, if you see huge costs associated with picnic tables, but only six picnic tables in a place, you can see that vandalism is likely occurring there."

"That makes sense. Thanks."

Bill thanked them all for their input. He noted there was not much more to do that evening except finish the press release, which they wanted released by 6 a.m. Sunday morning. He said he and Woody would work on that after all the wedding guests had left.

Bill requested Harley and Gemma proceed the next day to the forests, as they would be called upon to assist should the clues found at each site not pan out. Bill suggested Harley call the Forest Supervisor and the District Ranger the next morning to get background information. Bill said he'd text Harley the names and phone numbers.

Bill and Woody carried the chairs back to where they had been.

While the group had been working, the wedding guests had been enjoying food and champagne. There was plenty of laughter, and toasts to the happy couple.

Violet and Harley hurried over to assist in the wedding activities. Cake cutting time was approaching; it was time to help Emmylynne and Scott celebrate their new marriage. Harley hoped to stay busy, and clear of the wedding bouquet tossing.

CHAPTER SIX

It was early on Sunday morning. Harley was in her motor home still parked outside Violet's home. She was sitting at her dinette table, sipping a cup of coffee, and thinking about where the next few days might lead. Harley was considering the two new cases to resolve. She wondered if they were somehow related, though at first glance she thought not, as they were completely different murders. It felt to her like there were different perpetrators, yet they were found at almost the same time on the same forest. How could they not be related?

Harley knew she'd have several hours to plan her actions as she traveled from Violet's home in Maryland to the forest supervisor's office in Roanoke, Virginia, a trip of about 275 miles. She would check her GPS and see if the I-81 South route was her best option. With stops for diesel, food, and dog walks, it'd take the majority of the day to get there, and that is if everything in her motor home was running properly.

Harley was thinking about a previous road trip. She had to have the propane regulator replaced in the motor home. Then, during the installation, the repair people had accidentally, and unknowingly, kinked a pipe, and she had gone without hot water, or the generator for a few days until the next repair could be made. Because of that, Harley had to heat water on the cook top for her "showers." Her mom would have called it a sponge bath. Harley had been happy that at least the cook top and the refrigerator were working. She also had to turn off all of her electronic toys, as they were all at the end of their battery life by the time she took the motor home back in for repair.

Harley laughed at herself because she knew these were "first-world problems." There were many people who would love to have a home of any kind to live in. Still, motor home issues could be annoying. They could also get expensive. Driving a motor home meant she was driving a vehicle and a home at the same time. Things could go wrong with either or both. Still, this had been her choice and one she was happy she'd made.

Harley checked her phone. A message had arrived from Bill yesterday with two contacts that Harley needed to make before she started her day of driving. She hated to call people so early on a Sunday morning, but it could not be helped.

Harley decided to call Rick Givens, the Forest Supervisor, first. Bill had provided a bit of background for Harley. Bill told her that Rick was the latest in a string of forest supervisors of the George Washington and Jefferson National Forests in Virginia. That sounded interesting to Harley, she wondered why there were so many changeovers of forest supervisor.

Harley thought about what Violet had said, that these combined forests stretch along the Appalachian Mountains in Virginia, and cross into parts of West Virginia, and a small portion in Kentucky. The two forests contained nearly 1.8 million acres, and represented one of the largest areas of public land in the eastern U.S. Harley thought that sounded impressive.

Rick had been expecting her call.

"Hello, Harley. Bill Harris told me to expect an early morning call from you."

"I hope it's not too early for you, Rick."

"Not at all. I've already been for an early morning walk, and now I'm relaxing on the porch of my bungalow."

"That sounds nice."

"I was really lucky to find this place. It's just the right size for me, and the costs are well within my budget. Nearby I have access to a few trails, and a local grocery store. I have just a few neighbors. They're friendly people, though they have opinions about how I should manage the forests."

"I'm curious. What do they say?"

"One neighbor said I should extend the hunting season for deer since they were abundant. Another commented that the camping limit should extend beyond fourteen days, as his family wouldn't mind staying all summer long. And another told me I should ban all forest harvesting that is anywhere near old growth, because those areas are home to many threatened and endangered species."

"I cannot imagine all the details you have to attend to. I'm sure your neighbors want what is best. It sounds like a complicated job."

"Speaking of jobs, I heard you work as a contractor for law enforcement."

"That's correct. I have a K-9 partner and we've been to several national forests, either training others, or on investigations. How long have you been on the George Washington and Jefferson National Forests?"

"We find it easier to say 'the forests' as shorthand. I've been on the forests about a year now, and have learned a lot in my brief time here. Like you, I sought information before arriving on the forests. My introduction to the forests came through Walt Newman. I understand you'll be calling him too."

"Yes, after we talk, I will give him a call."

"Well, he has a wealth of knowledge, while I still feel a bit new. I have to say that I am shocked by the two deaths on our forest."

"They were shocking! Did you happen to know either victim?"

"No, I didn't. You might ask Walt when you call him. He's lived in this area his entire life."

"Have you spoken to him? Did he say anything about knowing them?"

"I did speak to him, but I didn't ask whether or not he knew them, and he didn't say so. He actually didn't say much about them at all. I guess he was shocked like I was. It might have been too difficult to address it yet."

It sounded to Harley like Rick had a story to share, so she let him speak. Rick relayed that his last appointment was in Alamogordo, New Mexico, and he had no previous experience on the forests where he was now located. Rick told Harley that Walt did his best to describe the forests, and had told Rick about the different plants and animals to be found there. Rick said that since arriving he had come to recognize the differences between the Tulip, Butternut, Loblolly pine, Chestnut oak, and Black oak trees. He laughed as he told Harley he had many more local tree species to learn.

Rick told Harley about the old growth on the forest, and how efforts were being made for saving them for future generations. Rick said there were thousands of shrubs and herbaceous plants, and the dozens of species of amphibians and reptiles. Rick recalled Walt saying he liked the salamanders and the frogs best, said they were "fascinating." Harley almost laughed at that, but didn't know if Rick thought it humorous too. When he laughed, she did too.

Rick added that there were hundreds of species of birds in the area. His favorites were the Barred Owl, Red-tailed Hawk, and Grebes. Much like the trees, he said he had many more species to learn about. Rick also mentioned there were Black Bear and Ruffed Grouse on the forest, along with many other mammals. He added that lots of visitors liked the freshwater fishing opportunities, as he did.

Harley asked what he could tell her about forest visitation, or if he had information about forest visitors. Rick told her that Walt had grown up in the area, and had good perspective on past and current forest visitation. Harley thought that was interesting, but supposed Rick's job covered so many topics that it was hard to know everything.

Harley asked Rick about the turnover of forest supervisors. "Can you enlighten me about that?"

"That's funny. I asked Walt the same thing before I arrived. He said 'Rick, don't let that concern you. Most forest sups don't like to cool their heels too long in one place, they want to work their way up the system.'

"I told Walt that I had known some supervisors to stay many years in the same place. I'd said to him 'You're at one of the largest forests in the eastern U.S., so I'm not sure where they're moving.' He made a good point. He'd said they generally left the forests 'to get in a couple of years at headquarters in D.C.' I told him that made sense to me because time in headquarters is necessary in the course of leadership careers.

"I also asked Walt what he could tell me about the employees on the forests. He'd said that many have lived near, or on the forests their entire lives, or had other family members in the Forest Service."

"Oh, then we can expect employees to be all well connected to the local communities? Maybe the employees could assist us in some way?"

"Probably. There are a number of small communities near the forests. Our employees live in many of those communities. Plus, we sometimes get invited to give short speeches at local club meetings. We also invite scout troops to assist with trail maintenance, and that type of thing."

"Is there much turnover of employees?"

Rick had hesitated, "Well, we've had a bit of turnover. Most places do, I suppose. People need to move along for upgrades in positions, and pay. Plus, one just left because he was moving away."

"Okay, so no real personnel issues on the forests?"

"None I can think of. I do have a funny story for you about my first day on the forests. Walt had told me that sometimes 'outsiders,' or people not from the local community, could get the cold shoulder from locals. Did you want to hear about it?"

"Yes, I'd like to hear it. I'll be an outsider, and it might help me."

Rick told Harley that the first day after he arrived, Rick went to the local coffee shop, as advised by Walt. Rick said it looked like almost every other coffee shop he'd seen before. He'd noticed the parking lot was full. The window coverings were up, and he could see many people inside. Most looked to be seated in booths and he could see people at some tables in the middle of the room. Before he pushed open the door, he could hear lots of talking and laughing. It seemed very welcoming. When he pushed open the door, the shop went silent. Rick said he froze in place. It didn't feel as welcoming. To him it seemed like minutes passed. Then he heard someone say, "Are you that new forest guy?"

"Yes, I am." I said, "Are you Vera?"

"Yes, I am. Come on in and take a load off. I hear you like coffee. Walt says you must try our biscuits and gravy."

By then, the noise level had returned to normal levels in the coffee shop. Rick said he had thanked Vera for being so welcoming. She'd said not to worry; everyone there loved the Forest Service. He was grateful to hear that.

Rick said that Vera took him to a stool at the front counter and introduced him to the people sitting at either side of him. Dwight was the man on his right. He'd told Rick the biscuits and gravy were known countywide, so it was a good choice to make. He hoped Rick continued to make good choices. While that seemed a bit odd to Rick, he had decided to take it as an encouraging word. Rick turned to his left and said hello to Rachel. She'd told him she always ordered eggs and toast, there were just too many calories in the biscuits and gravy. He told her he'd remember that for the next time. Several patrons stopped in for a quick hello.

When he stopped talking, Harley commented "Oh, my. That could have gone very badly."

"Vera was so nice, and still is. Now I often meet with Dwight and Rachel at the diner. They laugh at the look they said I had when I first opened the door."

"It sounds like you've made some good relationships."

"I think so. I still get lots of personal opinions about how I should manage. Did you want to hear more about the forests?"

"Yes, I would. Thanks. What do you think draws people to the forests?"

"The biggest feature is the Appalachian Trail. We call it the A.T. How familiar are you about it?"

"It's safe to say I have heard of it, but I don't know much."

"We have many access points onto the A.T. There are 325 miles of the trail located within the forests. A.T. hikers are mixed. Some people hike only a portion of the A.T., while others hike the entire trail, sometimes taking weeks, even months to do so. No horses or motorized use is allowed on the A.T. We do allow dogs and guns, except guns aren't allowed for the A.T. portions managed by the National Park Service."

"Do you have many issues with management across agencies?" asked Harley.

"No, we've really worked on those relationships. Plus, the local public's well aware of the different jurisdictions. Most people abide by all the rules, and changes in jurisdictions. When we have issues, it's usually because people didn't know better."

"Good to know. You mentioned camping on the forests. What can you tell me about the campgrounds?"

"Camping's a popular use of the forests. It occurs mostly in late spring and early summer. It can get humid, but that's about the timeframe of use. There are plenty of campgrounds, though we typically fill up. Most of the campgrounds are primitive, having few amenities. We do have several that are set-up to accommodate horses, so visitors can ride on local trails. Bear, deer, snakes, and birds are commonly seen in our campgrounds, and along our trails. For the most part, campers and hikers really enjoy seeing them.

"Many visitors to the forests think these are the most beautiful lands around. There are a lot of reasons. We have varying elevations. The colors of the trees vary from green to blue to red to yellow, and the scents of the trees are amazing. The sounds from the various birds keep birders visiting year after year. The streams and rivers are breathtaking. All of this is available to people there only for the day, and those who come to camp."

"Thanks, I'm sure it's beautiful. I look forward to seeing it. Any issues I should know about?"

"I'm not sure if it's important to the cases you'll investigate, but we have some huge costs. It seems like we're constantly replacing signs, repainting buildings, and building up fences that somehow have been brought down. Though we're not at the end of the fiscal year, we're already over budget dealing with all these issues. We simply cannot afford doing other things, like having more law enforcement officers from the agency on site."

"That sounds like a terrible problem."

"It's been a challenge, for sure. We have a few Forest Protection Officers, we call FPOs, because they cost far less than law enforcement officers. We call on them as needed to help with visitors."

"What types of visitor issues do you have, and how are they addressed?"

"We've an interesting mix of issues. We have all the land based ones you can imagine, and human ones as well."

"How about unusual ones? After the recent lynching I am wondering if you might have white supremacists on the forests."

"Well, that just doesn't seem unusual around here. As you enter the area you'll see lots of folks flying what we call the 'heritage flag.' You'll recognize it as a Confederate flag. We have several local KKK groups, called Klaverns. I don't know that the KKK members 'frequent the forest.' We really don't have many issues with them. When we do run into issues, human or otherwise, we call on our small cadre of law enforcement officers. We also have contracts with local county sheriff offices for coverage. When things get serious the state police can also be called in."

"How often have you had to call in the state police?"

"That's pretty infrequent, and usually only if the sheriff can't do it, and it's out of our jurisdiction to handle."

"Thank you for your time, and the wealth of information. This is good to know. I'll head down the road toward your office after I speak with Walt. Is it okay to park outside your offices tonight?"

"Of course. There are some external outlets if you need to plug in."

"Thanks, Rick. Please call me if you think of anything else I should know."

"I'll do that, Harley. Safe travels to you."

CHAPTER SEVEN

Harley's next call was to Walt Newman.

"Good morning. You must be Harley Fremont."

"Yes, I am. Good morning, Mr. Newman."

"Please call me Walt."

"I just spoke with your boss, Rick. He assures me you have lots of knowledge to share about your district. I look forward to learning more about the visitors to your forest, and your thoughts about the two deaths."

Walt hesitated before responding. "You probably don't know that we're closed on the weekends, so I was not at work, at least not officially."

"That has me interested. What do you mean?"

"Well, I had some time yesterday so I actually drove to a couple of local campgrounds on the district. I was just interested in how busy they were."

"Were they busy?"

"Let me start by saying it's fairly unusual for me to do that. I live a bit of distance away, but our recent uptick in numbers at the campgrounds had me curious. Usually I just see the self check-in information after the weekend, and not the actual people. I go maybe three or four times in our busy season to see how things are going. When I go, I often stop and greet the visitors. It lets them know someone is watching. Plus, we've had a bit of damage to these two campgrounds, and I wanted to see how people were using the spaces on the weekend."

"What kind of damage?"

"Well, there have been a number of broken picnic tables, we've had signs that were shot up, and some fence lines down."

"That must be some of the expenses Rick had been talking about."

"That's very likely. Some campgrounds cost more than others for upkeep, and it seemed these two campgrounds were higher in cost than they should be. I didn't see any activities that made me think these particular weekend campers were doing anything to the property while there."

"What can you tell me about your visitors?"

"Do you want visitors in general, or some specifics from yesterday?"

"Start with yesterday, and if I need to know more I can let you know."

"Are you familiar with the area?"

"No, I'm not."

"To get to the campgrounds, you need to take the state highway, turn onto some gravel roads, then drive on a Forest Service dirt road. It's not a series of terrible roads, but it's also not an easy highway drive. I have to say it is a pretty drive right now with all the green vegetation. While the rains help with the looks, it is also a bit humid. That can mean we have a lot of bugs. It might sound sketchy, but this is one my favorite times of year.

"I arrived before the clouds and rain were due to arrive, and it was comfortable outside. I always stop first at the self check-in box, and collect the receipts. Those tell me if everyone has paid fees for their campsite. Also, it gives me the names of the people there, how many people are in the site, and the makes and models of all the vehicles.

"These particular campgrounds are near Dismal Creek for trout fishing and Dismal Falls for a short hike. Plus, there are about twenty miles of horse trails nearby, and you can access the A.T. "

"You make it sound delightful."

"You'll likely be busy, but the short hike to Dismal Falls is fantastic. Though I often hike it, I didn't yesterday. Lots of campers ask me about the Appalachian Trail and the local trails. I wish I had a dollar for each time I've told horse campers about the twenty miles of local trails to choose from after they complained they couldn't take horses on the A.T."

"I'd bet that would make you wealthy," laughed Harley.

"It would indeed. The two campgrounds I went to are near each other. Both are fairly primitive, but one has access to horse trails, and has horse corrals. The other is just a bit further from the start of the trails, and doesn't accommodate horses. The horse campground is newer, and larger motor homes can fit in. The other camp is older, and really is best for tent camping or small motor homes."

"My motor home is twenty-four feet long."

"If you were to camp I'd say go with the horse camp, and the bit larger campsites. You'd have fewer options in the other campground."

"Good to know, but I don't think camping is on my upcoming agenda."

"No, I suppose not. At the non-horse camp, called Gopher Flats, the campground was full. It has only six campsites, but I only had four pay packets. It took me a bit to realize that one camper had paid for three sites.

"I drove past the first campsite, but didn't see anyone. I stopped at the second campsite because there was a family there I'd met previously. I wanted to say hello. We talked a bit about how we had previously met on the trail to Dismal Falls. They reminded me that had been five years ago. I didn't see their kids this time, but I imagine they're growing up. It's funny that some people can remember those details like when and where we first met. I didn't actually recall when I first met them, but I've met a lot of people over the years hiking to the falls."

"I'll bet you have."

"I stopped at the next site. While I had met the Vickers family before, they're the ones from the previous site; this was my first time meeting the Maxwell family. I have to say they kept a very neat campsite. They had a small motor home, and two chairs out. That was all. They told me they liked the campground, and the proximity to trails. The said they preferred to hike the Appalachian Trail. They explained that they were a bit leery of hiking along Dismal Creek because they knew about the killings committed by Randall Lee Smith. Of course I already knew the story."

"Tell me about it."

"Smith had killed two people along the creek in 1981, and he tried to murder two more people along that same creek in 2008, right after getting out of jail."

"Oh, that sounds creepy."

"It was a long time ago."

"The two recent murders weren't along the same creek were they?"

"No, they weren't. I'm sure they're not related. So, the last three families in the campground were one large group. All their chairs were in a circle. Tents were everywhere. It looked a bit chaotic, and also looked like they were having a fun trip. I've camped in that campground many times before. Some of my favorite trips there included large gatherings of family and friends. So I stopped to say hello. I found out it was their first trip to the campground. They were having a ball. They wished there were fire rings, and asked if those would be added soon. I told them I'd mention it to the forest supervisor. They jested that maybe I could work on reducing the humidity too."

""It sounds like you made some friends on that stop. Tell me about the other campground."

"Sure, if you think it'll help you understand the forest. The next campground is called Beggar Flats Horse Campground. It's about a quarter-mile away from Gopher Flats, on the east side of the road. It has two loops of ten campsites each. It's almost as primitive as Gopher Flats, but offers fire rings, and every site has a metal pipe horse corral. I've also camped there when Gopher Flats Campground was full.

"Like the other camp, my first stop was the pay box. In all, there were fifty people camped there. It wasn't a quiet camp. I saw that many people were up early to start campfires and cook stoves, or clean horse stalls and feed the horses.

"This is a larger camp, and I considered just driving on through. I decided that as long as I was there, I might as well chat with a few people.

"I stopped first at the Ledlow camp. Like me, they're tent campers. They were getting gear ready for hiking. They said they liked the campground because of the access to trails. They liked being able to hike to Dismal Falls and hike the Appalachian Trail. They said they planned to start with Dismal Falls, and then hike part of the A.T. That was going to be a lot of hiking. It's certainly more than I'd take on in a day, but they looked really fit.

"Next I met the Mann family. They said they liked the campground because it accommodated their horses. They told me they enjoyed taking their horse onto the nearby trails. Their kids were excited to meet me, and asked if I got to camp for free. I think they were disappointed that I pay just like everybody else.

"I drove past several other campsites, and then stopped at the Payne campsite because they waved me over.

"They told me they were new to camping. They also said they were new to hiking. They said they took the plunge, and bought all the gear. They had spoken with a neighbor camper who mentioned they should read up on hiking the local trails versus hiking the Appalachian Trail. But they had no Wi-Fi connection, so they asked me to explain the differences between the trails, and recommend which would be better for them. I recommended starting with Dismal Falls, thinking it'd be better to break-in hiking boots along a short trail."

"That was sound advice."

"I have met the Butler and Duvall families in the next two campsites previously, so I just waved as I drove by. Then I replaced all the camp receipts, and headed back home."

"Did you see the sheriff while you were on the district?"

"No. All was quiet while I was there. I had no idea there was a problem."

"Rick said you grew up in the area. Did you know either Mr. Fry or Mr. Freeman?"

"I'd met George Fry before. He was a quiet man, soft-spoken. It surprised me to hear he had spoken at the town hall meeting in Christiansburg. I've never met Mr. Freeman."

"I'm sorry if you are grieving over Mr. Fry."

"We hardly knew one another, but I feel his loss."

"I'm sure you do."

"Did you need to know anything else?"

"No. I do appreciate hearing about the visitors to your campgrounds. It gives me some context for the general area where I might be headed."

"Mostly our visitors are just everyday people out having a good time. Most abide by the rules and regulations."

"It sounds like it. Thanks for your time and the information. Please call me if you think of anything else I should know."

"Will do. Be safe out there."

"Thanks, Walt."

CHAPTER EIGHT

Harley thought both of those conversations were interesting. She felt like she had a bit more knowledge than she'd had just an hour earlier. She hoped it would be useful in the upcoming days.

Harley remarked, "Okay, Patsy Cline, let's go get some propane and diesel in your tanks." She had named her motor home after one of her favorite singers. Her favorite song from Patsy was: *I Fall to Pieces*. Harley started the ignition, and pressed her playlist to hear the song as she set out. Harley always had *On the Road Again* by Willie Nelson cued up next. It was time to crank up the music.

Harley often talked out loud during trips. She would say it was to keep Gemma informed of all their next moves. Harley was sure Gemma understood everything she was saying.

"Gemma, after we fill up, we'll text Jack so he knows what we're doing."

Gemma barked a response, accompanied by a wag of her tail.

Harley had a photo of Jack on her sun visor. She tapped it and smiled. Though she loved seeing the photo it made her miss her son. Harley and Jack traded text messages often. The last time he had offered some much needed tech advice. He often had questions for her too. Although she enjoyed trading messages, Harley preferred seeing Jack in person. A few times his travels would land him in her vicinity, and they could catch-up in person. Harley loved those times.

Harley stopped at the first gas station she found that had diesel fuel. She had learned to watch carefully for signs that included diesel fuel prices along with gas prices, and to watch for the green handle indicating which nozzle to use. She had heard horror stories about people who put gasoline into their motor home that was meant for diesel. That was a nightmare she preferred to avoid. This station had three islands that had diesel fuel. She liked options. She selected one, and pulled in.

It did not take long to fill up the motor home. Although she had paid outside, Harley went inside to buy a diet soda and a candy bar. She and the clerk both laughed at her diet and non-diet combination. Little did the clerk know how much Harley had wanted to purchase some cupcakes as well. She'd felt good walking away from those potential extra pounds.

Harley sat behind the wheel and typed a text message to Jack: "Hit the road, Jack. Gemma and I are headed from the wedding to Virginia. We have a fairly long day of driving. Will text you after we arrive. Love, Mom."

Harley got out and checked her tires before heading out. She had learned it was always best to be cautious. She'd put a check-it-out list on her sun visor as a reminder of things to watch for. Tires were second on the list, after diesel. The motor home was not the first one Harley owned, but it was the nicest.

Harley had grown up in a family who camped, so there had been a wide variety of camping gear they had used through the years. Her family started their camping adventures in canvas tents that leaked if you touched them during a rainstorm. They later upgraded to a tent-trailer when Harley was about six, followed by a camper shell on a truck, followed several years later by a motor home. As part of this upbringing, and subsequent travel to parks, forests, and deserts, Harley knew the various outdoor agencies, and the differences between them.

Harley grew up in an urban setting, but her parents put in a bid to purchase a lodge, store, restaurant, and horse rentals on a national forest when Harley was twelve. The offer fell through, and Harley remained a city girl.

Harley's parents would have been proud that Harley had such a nice motor home, but might have been surprised that it was her only home. There was no house to drive back to. She had never heard her parents discuss the option of no house, yet it seemed perfect to Harley.

The six tires all looked fine. They were inflated appropriately, and all had good tread.

As Harley pulled out of the gas station she saw a police car headed the other direction. It reminded her about the murders she would investigate. Harley knew she'd be thinking more about the murders in Virginia as she traveled, but her mind continued to wander to other areas as she moved down the road.

After seeing a Denny's restaurant, Harley thought about Hazel. Her sister loved to stop at those restaurants. Hazel was one year older than Harley. They were not close, but Harley visited her in Nevada about once a year. She regretted her emotional, if not physical, distance from her only sister, but Harley needed to protect herself from the hurtful words that occurred whenever they interacted. She was thinking she should travel to Nevada after this investigation was done. It felt to her like a break would be beneficial, and she'd work on being nicer to her sister. Maybe Hazel would be nicer to her.

"Gemma, do you think we should see Hazel soon?"

Gemma did not respond.

Harley continued reminiscing. She and Hazel had not gotten along well as children. Their parents always compared them to one another, and everything felt like a competition. Being younger, Harley rarely won. She'd had an almost idyllic childhood, still her parents had gotten that wrong. Harley tried to only compete with herself these days, rarely would she compete with others.

The other major flaw she thought about was that her household was blind to racism. It was not that they were color blind, and thought everyone was equal, it was that they never questioned why blacks or other non-whites had things so bad. Harley knew that many others did the same thing. It was this familial, and more widespread acceptance of racism that still ate at Harley today.

By junior high school Harley raised questions to her family about racism, and each time she was shut down. She'd bring home a friend of color, and while her parents might be polite in their presence, she was not encouraged to bring that person into their home again. These days it annoyed Harley when racist thoughts popped into her head unbidden. She'd typically give her head a shake, and tell herself to live in this decade.

Harley turned to her dog, "Gemma, I think we're going to find some racism in these upcoming cases. Let's be sure to point it out when we see it."

Gemma wagged her tail in response.

Harley passed a shopping mall. It was smaller than the one where she had worked. She thought about the twists and turns her career had taken. After her first career in banking ended, she'd moved on to retail sales in clothing. She had learned from both jobs that customer service was not her strong suit. From there Harley had tried going back to school for a degree in English. She felt much older than the other students, so she left and found a job stocking books in a bookstore. She enjoyed it, but mostly spent her money on books that caught her eye as she unpacked box after box. The books about dogs, and dog training techniques, always got her attention, and she'd bought several. Harley then tried her hand at dog training.

Harley smiled at Gemma. She thought about petting her, but Gemma looked sleepy. Harley had always had an affinity for dogs, much more affinity than she'd apparently had with numbers or customers. She started with training her own dogs, then those of friends, and friends of friends, as word spread of her talents.

Harley had dogs from the time she was a child. She'd grown up with Clumber Spaniels, the largest of the spaniel breed, and had those until she'd moved from her parents' house. Then she went several years without a dog. Her apartment would not allow them. Later, she and Augie talked about getting a dog, but never got around to it.

A few years ago Harley had stopped at a dog shelter to "look around," and found her first Rhodesian Ridgeback, Buddy. She took Buddy as a foster, who later found his forever home. Before he found that home he had accompanied Harley to some dog training camps. Harley was hooked on the breed. She found them easy to train, and very intelligent. Buddy was getting up in years, and the family who adopted him was elderly, and preferred an older dog. It was a great match, but left Harley feeling a bit broken hearted.

A friend told Harley about some Rhodesian Ridgeback rescue puppies for adoption, which is where Harley found Gemma on Valentine's Day. Harley knew her heart belonged to Gemma from their first cuddle. She started training Gemma from their first day together. Harley had not planned to partner with Gemma in law enforcement work, but that path opened up for them.

Through friends, Harley was asked to work as a dog trainer at a couple of sheriff departments. During these sessions, Harley met a few officers from the Forest Service. One of these was Wicasa Brooks, known to all as Woody. Harley was thinking that she had known Woody now for a few years. How lucky they had met. She usually smiled when she thought about Woody, but thought how concerned he looked yesterday. She hoped all was going well. Harley figured Bill and Woody had the press release out by now.

Harley continued reminiscing about her early connections to the Forest Service. Early on, as Harley and Woody got to know each other better, Woody discussed the Forest Service law enforcement tools available to them, including the older data tracking system, and the then upcoming plans, which included the addition of investigations and GPS data. Woody said he was impressed with the intelligent questions she asked about K-9 units in the agency, and about their data information system, especially in the location tracking features. Harley thought about the tools Violet had made, which were available to her as a contractor. They would definitely be used on this trip. The tools had not been available yet when Harley first worked with LEI. She was glad they were available now.

Harley thought some more about Woody. He'd told Harley often that he'd never seen anyone as good with dogs as she was. The dogs she led, and those she trained, had never made a mistake in their work. Woody said Harley brought out their skills to perfection. Woody felt strongly enough about her abilities to suggest a few local forests hire her on a contract basis when her expertise with dogs was needed. Eventually those smaller contracts turned into a contract with the Forest Service Law Enforcement and Investigations staff in the Washington office that took her to forests across the U.S. These were most typically ones that had no K-9 partners in law enforcement, but had work that called for the tracking skills that she and Gemma could provide. These were almost exclusively law enforcement matters.

Harley saw that Gemma was awake.

Harley asked, "Gemma, did we remember to thank Woody again for bringing us into the Forest Service?"

Gemma scratched her ear, and settled back in to continue her nap.

Harley stopped after a couple of hours to walk Gemma, and stretch her own legs. Harley thought Gemma was a perfect dog in every way. Gemma was thigh high in height, about seventy pounds, golden brown in coloring with a white star on her chest. She had a ridge of hair running along her back in the opposite direction from the rest of her coat. She had amber eyes with a brown nose. Two toes on each back foot were white. Her ears flopped down. Gemma was mischievous, athletic, low-maintenance on grooming, and good with children.

Harley appreciated that Gemma loved to hike, the longer the trail the better. This time, though, she only got a brief walk. There didn't seem to be many options for walking at this stop. The gas station was beside a highway, and had a small grassy area. She took Gemma there, but it could be traversed in about fifteen seconds. So they walked along the highway for a bit, and returned to the gas station. Harley got out some granola bars for herself. She gave Gemma some water in one bowl, and added food and treats to her other bowl. Then it was time to load into Patsy Cline and hit the road again.

Harley could not stop her mind from wandering back to the murders. She saw and felt the beauty nature offered, but had also seen the ugly things that people could do to each other away from prying eyes. These murders seemed heinous to her. She especially could not help but hurt for the family of Clay Freeman. How awful to know his life ended in such a horrific way. She wondered about the perpetrator. Who could do such a thing to another human being? She thought about the shooting too, but had seen this several times in her investigative career. She made a mental note to not be dismissive of the shooting death just because the other death has captured her attention. Mr. Fry's family deserved justice too.

Patsy Cline was moving down the highway pretty well, and Harley decided to send a nice note to the last repair shop.

"I think they did a great job on our repairs and I feel confident we'll get to our destination with no problems. What do you think, Gemma, should we send a nice note?"

Gemma responded with a bark, and turned her attention to her chew toy.

CHAPTER NINE

The alarm had activated early Sunday morning. Shrimp had hoped it had the time wrong. He didn't, it was time to get ready. He was trying to psyche himself up, and look forward to the day. Early mornings were not his thing.

Red called. "Hey, Shrimp, you ready for today? My dad says it'll be cool."

"Fuck, man. It's early! Yes, I'm up, and we're about to head out already. Too bad we're going to separate campgrounds. My mom told me we got assigned the smaller campground, and your family got assigned the bigger one. We're supposed to finish up at our campground, and go to where you are. We're leaving now. We have to stop and pick up coffee and donuts for people in the campground. I need some too."

"Yeah, we'll be stopping too. I think we'll be getting fruit, bagels, and coffee. I'd rather have the donuts you're getting. Don't forget Fortnite this afternoon."

"Cool, dude. See ya later."

"Later, man."

By agreement, nine of the Ku Klos Knights parked along the Forest Service dirt road near Gopher Flats at 8 in the morning. They included Orville and Wilbur Wright, Rose and Junior Kendall with Shrimp and Big Lou, Herb Smith, plus Ben and Beth Rover. Also by agreement, fourteen members parked along the dirt road by the Beggar Flats Horse Campground. They included Carl and Jay Burden, Hank and Melba Ross and their sons, Red and Buster, Ray and Ella Parker and their adult children Ray Jr., Buford, and Elaine. Billy Dean, along with Gerald and Fran Brown rounded out the group.

Each of the groups carried food and drink to share, having stopped at the local coffee shop for coffee, donuts, bagels, and fruit. The ones who brought weapons left them in their vehicles.

All nine visitors to Gopher Flats stopped at the first campsite, and said, "Good morning!" to Joe Beck.

Shrimp saw they were tent campers. It was a large tent. So it seemed possible it held a large family. Then Shrimp saw the Jeep, and decided it was probably only one or two persons in camp, since they'd have to fit people and camping gear inside the vehicle.

In a quiet voice Joe responded, "Good morning. Please keep your voices down. My wife is still sleeping."

All but Orville and Wilbur moved to the camp road to wait for the others.

Orville whispered, "We're here to offer food and coffee as a sign of our goodwill."

Joe replied, "Thanks, I have coffee going already, and we'll pass on the food. As I said, my wife's asleep, and I don't want to disturb her."

"We'll be back in an hour or so. Maybe we can stop by then?"

"Sure. Yeah. See you then."

As they watched, Joe went into the tent. Shortly after, Joe and Jen exited the tent, got into their Jeep to drive out of camp.

Shrimp heard Wilbur say, "Hey, look, they're leaving. Should we do something?"

"No," replied Orville, "Let them pass. I don't think they want to join our Klavern."

Wilbur added, "Yep. Looks like they won't be joining us."

Shrimp was disappointed, and it looked like other members were as well. That was not the start he had hoped for.

Shrimp saw mixed reactions from the other campers in the Gopher Flats campground.

The Vickers family looked like they enjoyed the visit. They ate some food and the adults talked while the kids played with their dog, Doofus. The Vickers family had little interest in joining the KKK, but said they appreciated the coffee, food, and good company. Shrimp enjoyed the dog, and wished he had dog treats to share.

Shrimp was bummed they would not join the KKK. He'd like to get to know them better. Plus, they had a large trailer, and Shrimp would have liked to see the inside. He was not a camper, but found it intriguing that people would leave their comfortable homes to do it. Maybe that trailer was really comfortable too.

After leaving the campsite Shrimp asked, "Dad, why do you think they decided against joining us?"

Junior commented, "Well, son, not everyone is a good fit for our group. They seemed nice enough, and I thought they liked us. But who knows what is going on in their lives? Maybe they're too busy. They weren't rude to us like some people can be. So I think they support us, they just can't join us. It's not right to pry too much into their reasons."

"I liked them, too. Maybe they'll reconsider. We should stop in again before we leave."

"We might do that," said Junior, "but that might seem too rude on our part. They've given us a decision, and we should abide by that, don't you think?"

"Okay. I guess I'd prefer to hear an outright 'yes,' rather than a 'no,' or a 'we'll see.'"

"You've always been like that son. Sometimes it feels like you're pestering us when you insist on a clear answer. I don't think our plan today is to pester people."

Shrimp didn't think he pestered too much, but maybe his dad was right. They probably wouldn't stop in again.

Shrimp could see the next family having a different reaction than the Vickers family. He had seen them looking at all of them in the Vickers campsite, and saw them start packing while glancing their way. He figured they would not want to talk. He was right. They wanted nothing to do with the visitor group. They said were busy, that they had made plans for the day, had to finish packing, and be on their way. Their kids were moving fast, taking things from their tent to the vehicle. The parents kept yelling "Daisy, be quiet!" as their dog barked incessantly.

As they moved away, Shrimp uttered, "Well, dad, looks like we got the rude response after all. Even the dog didn't like us."

"Yes, I'd say it was pretty clear they want nothing to do with us."

"I hope the next group wants to join. We're already halfway through, and no one has said yes."

"All we can do is be friendly, and talk about the benefits of group membership. We hope for a 'yes,' but even if all say no to us, we have tried. That's what we're here to do. Success may come today, or maybe next time."

"It'd be a lot more fun if people said yes to us," insisted Shrimp.

Klavern members quickly figured out that the next three groups were traveling together. They got to meet everyone, and the dog Buddy, who was thrilled with all the attention he got. They spent the most time with this group, and shared stories of all the good times families could have in their group. The Klavern members talked about how many years their families had been a part of the group, and assured the Armstrong, Carpenter, and Magee families that they would be welcome, and could also be lifetime members. For their part, the three families were quite taken by the friendliness and camaraderie of the visitors. It sounded like something they might want to join.

Shrimp thought it was pretty cool that these families might be joining the KKK. He said to his dad, "I do like hearing a 'yes.' And all three families want to join. This campground thing is turning out to be pretty cool."

The Klavern members headed back to their vehicles to drive a short distance away, stopping just outside the entrance to the Beggar Flats Horse Campground. They parked behind, and across from their fellow Klavern members on the roadway.

Red saw them arrive and raced over to chat with Shrimp. The others gathered round to hear how things had been going.

"We're making some good progress here. We met the Mann family, and we think they're going to join us. That's cool, right?"

"Yes!" declared Shrimp, "We had three families offer to join us, too. It was kinda cool to do this. I thought it'd be boring."

"Klavern outings are never boring!" said Red. "There was one family we didn't get to meet. They loaded up kids and dogs, and left before we approached their camp, but they didn't take any of their things."

"Sounds like they won't be joining us," laughed Shrimp. He was still buoyed by his experiences in the other campground.

"There were two more families I'm pretty sure won't join us. They acted scared of us. I left before that ended, but it didn't look promising."

"Maybe we'll have more luck with some of the other campers. Let's go join them."

As they headed to meet the others, Shrimp declared, "More cars are arriving! Were we expecting more people?"

CHAPTER TEN

Bill Harris was chatting with a neighbor when a call came in on his cell phone. He was just finishing a brief conversation about her garden. Bill had been admiring her basil, rosemary, and sage. He told her he wished he'd had time to grow his own herbs.

"I'm sorry, Sharon. I need to take this call. Hello."

"Good morning, Director Harris. This is Rick Givens."

"Good morning, Rick. Did Harley call you this morning?"

"Yes, she called me, and she called Walt Newman. I called Walt to learn what they talked about."

"Did you have concerns over her calls?"

"No, not at all."

"What can I do for you, Rick?"

"I thought I'd better check in with you. I was kind of expecting Darryl to call me this morning. I'm embarrassed to admit I'd had a few drinks by the time he called me last night, and I think my conversation with him was a bit muddled. I wanted to see what I might be able to do today, or if you might have questions for me."

"We've all been there Rick. I think Darryl didn't call because Harley was going to call you."

"Okay. I guess I feel the need to be more helpful than I think I've been. We're all pretty shaken up over the deaths."

"What did Walt say? Was Walt upset?"

"Now that you ask, he really didn't say anything about the

murders. He mentioned that he had driven out to his district yesterday, and had not seen anything amiss while he was there. Walt said he'd met some nice campers, that everyone seemed to be having a good time."

"Is his district office open on weekends?"

"No, but I know Walt sometimes checks out a few campgrounds each year during our busy season. He knows a few campers because they're regular visitors. It wouldn't be unusual for him to do that.

"There was something I didn't talk with Darryl about last night, but Walt and I talked about today. We talked about supremacist groups being active in the area."

"Tell me more about that."

"I told Walt, 'You know we've had the KKK on our district, and we think some of the damage to our sites was caused by them, and you know we've had people complain about the possibility of the National Alliance in our campgrounds. Do you think either group were involved in some way with the murders?' Walt said he felt people were 'getting excited over nothing.' He said we'd hear from lots of people in the campgrounds, and local communities, if white supremacists were really active."

"Is that what you think?"

"I'm pretty sure this is something we need to make the investigators aware of. It may turn out to be nothing, but it might be important."

"I agree; it's more data. What it means, we don't know yet."

"There's a bit more on the topic. I hope I'm not breaking confidences with Walt. Walt says he has known about these particular white supremacy groups for a while. He knew there had been a few clashes recently in local towns, but he thinks the clashes were overblown. He says that these are all 'good ole boys' that had family in the area for generations.

"Even though Walt has had to help replace fencing, and signs, and rebuild picnic tables in the campgrounds, he still feels that it is fairly harmless stuff, just guys blowing off steam. He said there has been no real, or lasting damage, and certainly they haven't hurt anyone.

"Walt's been camping on the Jefferson National Forest forever, even before the inclusion of the forest with the George Washington National Forest. He said he knows every trail, road, and campground on the forest. He said he has never felt intimidated by others at the campground, and doubted other people were intimidated either. He said he continues to camp there with family. That it's a family tradition. He thinks I worry too much over supremacist groups."

"What do you think?"

"I think maybe I haven't worried about it enough."

"There you go. It's always better to listen to what your head is saying to you."

"It wasn't a negative conversation. I think Walt's entitled to his opinion. I did offer to send an FPO over to Walt's district. We have a few FPOs on our other districts, but none on Walt's. Jimmy Wilson has expressed an interest in moving around. Jimmy's had forest protection training more than a year ago, and he seems to have a good head on his shoulders. Walt thought that would be a good thing to try. I know Walt would prefer a law enforcement officer, but my funds are too limited this year."

"I understand. Darryl was going to look into forest expenditures to see where all your funds are going. He thought it might give us more insight into the forests."

"We don't know why we've had such high costs this year. It could be supremacist groups at our sites, and it could be other people. We just don't know. Walt did mention the KKK had been really active lately in Pearisburg where he grew up, and also in Pembroke and Bland. But we still can't connect that with forest use, or destruction of our property."

"It sounds frustrating."

"It's a bit frustrating. I know if I had more law enforcement coverage I could get some answers, but because of the costs, and my overruns, I can't afford the coverage."

"Let me look into what we might do for you. I can certainly ask around and try to get more funds directed. I'm making no promises though, because I'm having funding issues myself."

"That would be great. I appreciate it. Bill, there's something that's bothering me. I've been thinking about the murders almost non-stop, but when I asked Walt, he said all he knew he'd heard on the news. He didn't bring the topic up again."

"Rick, I'd be careful. You can't expect other people to process things the way you do. This may be his way of protecting himself."

"Thanks, Bill, you make a really good point."

"There's something I can do. I'll ask Violet Carter to look in-depth into your district law enforcement data. It might lend credence to examining the supremacist groups further, or playing it more like Walt suggested."

"Does Violet have data that measures supremacy groups?"

"No, nothing like that. But maybe a combination of camper receipts, data we have on violations, GPS data, and other variables Violet collects can be weaved together."

"That's certainly worth the look."

"You mentioned the calls with Harley this morning. Was there any discussion with her about supremacy groups?"

"I don't think so. I talked to her about the forests, and Walt said they spoke about forest visitors."

"Okay, thanks. Was there anything else Rick?"

"No. I appreciate your time, Bill."

CHAPTER ELEVEN

Later that day Bill Harris was just returning home from taking his neighbor's dog for a walk. Bill did not have a dog of his own, but enjoyed their company. He was away from home for many hours every day, and felt it would be unfair to a dog to be alone so much. Bill had three neighbors who loved that he took their dogs for walks when he could. As he opened the front door, his cell phone started to ring.

"Director Harris, this is Rick Givens."

"Well, hello, Rick. To what do I owe the pleasure of a second call today?"

"Director, this is not about the two murders. I have a new topic. Sorry to disturb you with another call on your day off."

"I think my 'day off' must be a bit like your 'day off.' Tell me, what's happening?" Bill flipped on the entry lights and made his way to his couch in the front room and sat down.

"I just spoke with the local sheriff's office in Christiansburg. They had a visit from the Athey family, who said they'd been camping in Beggar Flats Horse Campground on the Eastern Divide Ranger District. The Athey family said a large group of people approached their neighbors in camp, and also stopped in at other campsites. They heard them tell the campers in the next site that they were there to befriend them, and offered food and coffee. It felt odd enough to them that they drove to the district office, which was closed. They then drove into Christiansburg to see the sheriff.

"In addition, the sheriff got a call from Mr. Joe Beck, who said he and his wife had been camping at Gopher Flats Campground when a group people approached them. They got frightened enough to leave their gear behind. The Beck's took some photos of the cars, and license plates of those folks, so we'll know more about them soon enough.

"We don't know if the same group of people visited both campgrounds, or if we have multiple groups of people. I thought you should know about this. And before you ask, the sheriff sent an officer to check the two campgrounds. You should also know the campgrounds are proximate to each other on the district."

"Thanks, Rick, for the head's up. This does sound very strange. There's not much we can do about people visiting others in the campground, but I think we should pay attention to the people who were bothered by it.

"What the heck is happening on your forest, Rick? No, don't answer that. I know none of this is your fault. Could this just be a coincidence or might something bigger be brewing?"

"I'm getting a bad feeling about this. I'm thinking I should send Walt out to the campgrounds, and I may go as well. I'll call you back after we hear from the officer."

"I'd appreciate that so I can pass along news as needed to my staff."

After the call, Bill stayed seated for a few more minutes, trying to absorb the news, and then plan his next steps.

After a few other calls, Bill called Rick back.

"Rick, it's Bill."

"I was hoping to talk again. I just got a call about a meeting at the Sheriff's office in Christiansburg tomorrow. I've been instructed to attend it."

"So I heard. I'm contacting a few other people about the meeting, and wanted to keep you informed. I wanted to let you know who is coming, and invite you to join a video teleconference call late tonight, possibly after 8, if you're able."

"Thanks. I'd like to hear more. I'll plan to make the call."

"Okay, Woody Brooks will send you the call-in information.

My first call was to Law Enforcement Officer Gray Wallace. I've asked him to join you at the meeting in Christiansburg."

"Okay, I'm familiar with him, of course. Gray's been on the job with the forests a few years longer than I have. He does a good job of keeping me updated on law enforcement activities. I know that's not unique, but I also know some officers report up the stovepipe, and not much with the forest employees. That can be dangerous for forest personnel. I'm glad he'll be there."

"My next call was to Richard Golden."

"Yes, I'm also familiar with Patrol Captain Golden. Richard oversees the entire Southern Region, and he's a busy man."

"That he is. As you know, he's a pretty serious person. Richard has been on the job just over twenty years. He does not appreciate small talk or people who shirk their jobs."

"That sounds about right. I look forward to reconnecting with him at the meeting tomorrow."

"I have also instructed two officers from the Monongahela National Forest to join in the investigation. They are Wesley Lexington and Brian Calvin. Brian is an officer completing his training with Wesley. They won't be there in time for the morning meeting. They'll likely arrive by early afternoon."

"Okay. I don't know them, but I look forward to their assistance. Is there anything I should know about those two?"

"Wesley has been an officer for years, and is very well regarded. That's why he was assigned the training position with Brian. Brian's young, and new, but with Wesley there, I have every confidence in both."

"That sounds encouraging."

"Later, I'll speak with Harley. I know she was headed to your office in Roanoke, but she'll be sent to Christiansburg instead."

"That makes sense. I appreciate you sending so many people on this. Those two deaths are going to keep us very busy."

CHAPTER TWELVE

Shrimp asked, "Who are they? They're not Klavern."

"Hey you, stop!" yelled one of the men. He was addressing the group from the Klavern. They paused, but saw him pulling a gun from his car. This was not going to end well. "SAN BOG!" screamed Orville. "They have weapons!"

"Run, Wilbur!" yelled Orville to his brother.

A shot was fired into the air. That did not stop the running, except for the younger Ross men, who Shrimp had seen skirt around the camp to head back toward their vehicles, and their weapons.

Running after the KKK, the same man shouted again for them to stop. This time he added, "Get out of our campground! This is our land!"

Another shot was fired into the air. Then there was more yelling. The men said again said this was their land. The anger in their words was emphasized by the shots fired into the air. They were not here to talk, they were here to scare, and maybe to kill.

The shots were heard clearly by all. There was chaos in the campground. People were yelling, dogs were barking, and the horses were snorting and stamping.

The Kendall parents were trying to move Shrimp and Big Lou along, but both seemed frozen in place. Then Shrimp moved, but just into the nearest campsite. Now he had no idea where his parents or Big Lou were.

Shrimp watched a man light Orville Wright's car on fire. It was toward the front of the line of parked cars on the roadway. The windows were down and the man had some gas in a gas can, and matches. The car lit well. He then moved clear of the cars, and went to join the others in his group.

Shrimp did not see where Buster and Red had gone. He hoped they weren't near the fire.

Other members of the Klavern heard the "SAN BOG!" call, and shouts of "Aliens!" and began running back toward the first campground loop. They wanted to help their fellow members.

Shrimp saw a fistfight had broken out. He could see Ray Parker knock a weapon from another guy's hand, and there was a scuffle for the weapon. But others including Ray Jr. and Buford got into the fight too. Shrimp could not see who had the weapon.

Shrimp was torn. He didn't know whether to yell, "Stop it!" or join in the fray. Still frozen, he simply looked around and tried to make sense of it all.

Shrimp saw his mom and dad; they were trying to get the female Klan members away from the melee. He supposed they already got Big Lou to safety. He stayed behind the tent to see what would happen next.

Shrimp saw that Orville Wright had picked up a metal pipe, and was going to swing it on another man, when the guy who had first yelled at them shot him. Orville was shot! Shrimp wanted to rush into the fight, but was unarmed, and he was scared.

Wilbur saw Orville fall, and Shrimp watched helplessly as Wilbur ran to him, catching bullets in his back. Shrimp was shocked. Everyone in the Klavern depended on Orville and Wilbur. He prayed they would be okay. There was a lot of blood. He wanted to yell at everyone to just stop it. He knew they had to fight. He didn't see anyone running to help Orville or Wilbur.

Shrimp was having trouble processing all that he was seeing. He thought, "This can't be happening! We came here to make friends, get some new members, and enjoy some food." This did not make sense. "Who were these guys? Why were they so angry? Why were they shooting people?" He realized, these were not just people; these were his friends, and were practically family.

Shrimp saw more shots land, hitting Herb Smith and Beth Rover. Herb had glared in the direction of the shooter, almost as if daring him to do that again. Shrimp hoped that didn't happen. Beth had yelled out. It looked to Shrimp like she was badly hurt.

Shrimp didn't know where to look next. It felt like Klavern members were all being shot. He was scared. He knew the tent was not much cover, and he could hear people sobbing inside the tent. Yet he stayed where he was.

More bullets were flying, but as far as Shrimp could tell, none hit other people. These bullets were shot into the air. Shrimp tried to make sense of that and supposed they were worried they'd shoot their own people. There was the possibility that could happen.

Then Shrimp saw Buster and Red headed away from the vehicles. He saw that they were able to retrieve a few weapons. He'd like to get a gun, and take care of these bastards. As Buster and Red headed toward the melee, Shrimp was about to call out, but stopped when he saw a camper vehicle drive away. "Look out!" he yelled.

It almost hit several people as it left, including Buster and Red.

Shrimp strained to see what was happening. Finally, he saw the vehicle had not hit Buster or Red. Shrimp wanted to cry with relief.

Shrimp glanced around, but saw no other vehicles leaving. If he'd been camped there, he'd want to get out. He wasn't camped there, and wanted to get away.

Others in the Klavern and the other group had watched the vehicle too.

Someone shouted, "Hey, the police might soon come! They probably went to get the police!"

Shrimp heard a call for retreat. It wasn't a voice he recognized. He heard other calls of "Retreat!" Most people from the other group ran back toward the vehicles on the roadway.

Soon after that, Carl gathered everyone around. He addressed Klavern members about what happened. Carl had been crying, and so had Jay. Shrimp was still crying.

"Wilbur and Orville are gone. Those bastards killed them! They killed them!"

"Let's move our cousins to our cars, and leave," wailed Jay.

"I'm sorry, Jay, there's not enough time to do that. We need to get away before the police come."

Hank added, "First, we need a plan. But Carl is right we need to leave soon before the police get here.

"Herb, you've been shot, and so has Beth. You'll need treatment, but be careful of what explanation you give."

"Mine is a scrape really, and I can attend to it at home," responded Herb. "If anyone notices, I'll say it happened on a plumbing job."

"Mine is a bit more than a scrape. I think the bullet is still in me. I'll need to seek medical attention. I plan to say I had a hunting accident on my property," said Beth. Shrimp thought she was being very brave. Her wound was still bleeding, and it looked like it hurt.

Carl spoke up. "Gerald told us some people were seen in the second loop leaving on horseback. It could be people who shot at us, or even people who killed Orville and Wilbur."

"It might just be campers," replied Herb.

"We can't be sure until we check it out. Jay and I have ridden these trails before. We're going to grab some horses, and go after those bastards!"

"I understand," said Hank, "please be careful. I don't want anyone else in the Klavern hurt."

"We'll be careful. We know what we're doing. Right, Jay?"

"Right, Carl. We'll make them pay!"

"Sorry, Gerald, but your car burned," reported Red. "It caught fire after Orville's car. But it might be drivable."

Hank replied, "Leave your car, Gerald. You'll need to take Carl's car, so it's not here when the police arrive. Carl, hand over the keys. Call us when you need someone to pick you up."

Shrimp watched as Carl handed over the keys, and Red handed over a weapon to Carl.

Red told Carl, "Me and Buster got this from your car before the flames grew too strong. We're sorry we couldn't stop the fire."

"I'm happy to have my weapon, Red. Thank you! If we find the bastards, then I'll need this."

Carl and Jay hugged Red, and told everyone to head home, and lay low.

Carl told the others, "We'll just be out today and maybe tomorrow. It should not take long to hunt down other people on horseback."

Gerald asked, "Do you think that's a good plan? What will you do if you're out overnight?"

"We've been on these trails before. We know some good hiding places. We'll be fine. Someone has to try and make these guys pay for what they did. We're the Inner Circle, and we've got this."

"What about your phones? Can the police track you?"

"There's no service out here, but we'll turn them off just in case."

Shrimp watched as they turned off their phones, and headed off to find horses to take. Shrimp had never heard Carl or Jay talk about trail riding before.

Shrimp could not fathom how the Burden brothers could formulate a plan so quickly. His mind was reeling. He'd never seen death up close like this. He was thankful for everyone who had made it out safely.

The Klavern members started toward their vehicles. Carl and Jay had turned down the second campground loop in search of horses.

Hank said, "Let's move now, people!"

Red and Buster had their weapons at the ready in case the other group would not allow them to leave alive. It was a tense time.

Shrimp and the others heard a car explode, and they saw

someone fall down, but it was hard to tell whom it was. The fire was too hot to get close. Doing a quick check of Klavern members they decided it was someone from the other group.

The other men were in their cars, and had just started down the Forest Service road by the time Shrimp and the others got back into their cars. The Klavern followed a short distance behind down the same road. They all saw the Sheriff's vehicle, and no one stopped.

CHAPTER THIRTEEN

Rick called Bill again, as promised, after speaking with the sheriff area officer on site at the campgrounds. Bill was at home watching television when the call came in. Rick sounded flustered.

Rick told Bill about a melee in the Beggar Flats Horse Campground, and the deaths of three more people. Of all the things Bill thought Rick might say when he called, three more deaths was not among them. Bill was very concerned. Now there were five deaths in a span of days.

Bill sat at his kitchen table, his water untouched. He had to wonder if these three newest deaths were in any way related to the first two. He was not sure how they could be, yet didn't think the timing was a coincidence. He sat and contemplated a bit about how to best assist what must be chaos on the George Washington and Jefferson National Forests. He considered the people he'd instructed to report to the sheriff's office in Christiansburg. He knew they were the right people, with the right skills, but he'd not known there would be five deaths to investigate. Bill decided to learn more before directing any more resources to Virginia.

Bill determined the best course of action he could take was to look at the data. With all the data officers had collected on the forests during stops and investigations, he knew there had to be something that would enlighten them. Bill could not do it alone, and needed answers soon. He thought the best way to accomplish that was to call in his most of his staff. Together they would see what information they had that might inform any or all of the five deaths.

Bill drained his water glass, got up, grabbed his keys and headed out the front door. He waved a greeting to one of the neighbors. His plan was to walk to the Metro stop about a half mile away. Later, Bill realized he had not seen much on the way to the office, he'd been thinking about all he had heard, and all that needed to be done.

In less than an hour Bill arrived at the Forest Service headquarters office in Washington, D.C. It was located at 14th Street and Independence Avenue. The entry was near the visitor center on Independence. After he passed through security, he took the stairs on his left for the second floor. He preferred stairs to the slow elevator, even though it landed him on the complete opposite side of the second floor from the law enforcement office location.

The LEI offices were on the northeast side of the building. There was not much to see outside their windows, but other buildings and alleyways. That was okay, since they rarely spent time gazing outside.

Bill liked their space that included offices for Bill, Darryl, and Woody. Their three offices had desks with few personal memorabilia, locking filing cabinets, and chairs for visitors. There was a small conference room that housed the video teleconference equipment. That was located beside the room that served as their break room. Another office was the computer center that belonged to Violet and Emmylynne. Their office had lots more computer power than found in the other offices. It stayed locked whenever Vi and Em were away.

The entry area had a counter spanning the length of it, and you had to get buzzed in by the receptionist unless you were LEI staff. Photos on all the walls were mostly the usual Forest Service posters of Smokey Bear, Woodsy Owl, and trees and flowers. Like most of the other furniture found in headquarters, the furniture was wood, as was the countertop at the entry area.

It was all built to last, and the envy of those with metal desks and cabinets.

Unlike many of the other deputy area spaces in headquarters, the LEI space had no cubicles. When Bill first started working there, he was surprised at all the cubicle spaces throughout the vast building. It was mostly along the outer building edges on the north and south ends of each floor where you could find offices; the centers were almost all cubicles. Bill felt that cubicles provided little privacy for individual employees. He had argued for offices since he felt privacy was needed for law enforcement work. He was pleasantly surprised when offices were made available to his staff.

From his office, Bill called Violet Carter, and requested she come into start analyzing every piece of data they had from the entire region. He wanted to know what types of crimes and acts of violence had been previously reported. He told her he would need this today, as tomorrow the investigation began in earnest, and he wanted the officers and investigators to have every bit of information available at the meeting in Christiansburg.

It was late afternoon when Violet arrived at headquarters. Already at the office were Director Harris and Woody Brooks. Bill greeted her, and apologized for the weekend work. He rarely felt the need to gather the staff on the weekends.

Vi replied, "No worries, Director. I was binge watching *Stranger Things* and downing too many of the party leftovers. I brought a bag of food, thinking we might get hungry tonight." Woody said he could use a snack, so they headed to the break room. Each item she brought out smelled wonderful, and made Woody even hungrier.

Arriving soon after were Emmylynne, and her newlywed husband, Scott. Director Harris was surprised to see them.

"I thought you were on your honeymoon Emmylynne and Scott. I'm pretty sure these offices do not qualify for honeymoon accommodations." Everyone laughed.

"I made Vi promise to call me if any work needed to be done. I couldn't hear about those two deaths and do nothing. Scott agreed we could stay and work on this crisis. Someday we'll look back and know it was the right thing to do."

"What about your honeymoon plans?"

Scott responded, "They're postponed. The hotel said they would keep our information on file, and to call them when the emergency is over."

Emmylynne added, "We felt like the honeymoon could wait. There's a lot to do and I want to help. Besides mayhem does not appear to be taking a holiday."

Bill told her, "We're sure to have many more crises during your career, so you can skip this one if you'd like. Still, I'm happy to see you both!"

Emmylynne said they would stay. She had been noticing some patterns in Virginia and West Virginia data, and wanted to verify those.

Bill told her, "Wait until you see your office."

Vi had brought some of the wedding decorations, and already installed them in the office space she shared with Emmylynne. Bill could see this delighted Emmylynne. This showed what Bill knew about Vi, that she was truly a thoughtful person, in addition to her amazing computer and analysis skills.

Bill said, "Okay, sorry to redirect us, but its time for the UCR report."

Bill knew that Emmylynne, though the newest member of the team, had already learned about the FBI Uniform Crime Reporting guide. The Forest Service, like most other enforcement agencies, record law enforcement incidents based on the UCR guide. Part I of the guide includes categories such as criminal homicide, forcible rape, robbery, aggravated assault, motor vehicle theft, and arson. Part II includes categories such as other assaults, stolen property, vandalism, weapons violations, drug sales and use, driving under the influence, and such. Part III includes assists with the other agencies, like assisting the Forest Service. Emmylynne told Bill that she and Vi would be examining data from all three parts of the guide. She told him they'd analyze all the data in the categories as best they could.

It reminded Bill that Vi and Em had a specific gripe about the guide. While these types of information can be made available to other agencies, the agencies do not specifically tie the data to incidents on Forest Service lands. Instead, all the data are combined. So while the sheriff could inform you of the number of murders they had processed, they could not tell you how many occurred on Forest Service land. This was an inefficient system for interagency sharing, and one that Bill heard that Vi and Em hoped to someday bridge.

Bill walked with them as Vi and Em went to their office to get started on analyses. Vi had already booted up the computers, and had accessed the law enforcement data systems.

Bill commented, "I'll leave you both to your work. Call me when you have items to report, or ideas to share."

Vi started with looking at Part I crimes on the forest in the past ten years. Murders were rare in that time period, with only one reported. There were a few suicides over the ten-year stretch. Several rapes were reported each year, while arson was almost unheard of. Only three vehicles had been stolen on the forest in the last decade, and very few robberies were reported.

Both women thought these data were interesting. Em decided to look back at the details to see if anything matched the recent murders, and to look into the rapes. Em had been seeing an increase nationwide, which either meant rapes were increasing, or reporting was more frequent. Either way, Em had previously noted this to Bill, and at staff meetings, thinking officers might need specific training on the topic. Em asked if the rapes might be related to the white supremacy groups.

Vi replied, "We won't assume anything, but let's figure this out!" Bill had been called back in for the brief discussion. He said, "Your idea is worth further investigation, if your data allows you to address it."

Vi told them she'd move on to the Part II crimes. She found few altercations and a few dozen reports of stolen property, mostly from campgrounds. Where she found plenty of reports was when she examined vandalism, weapons violations, and arrests for driving under the influence.

After discussing this with Bill, Em decided to look for patterns among the vandalism reports. She was looking for similar types of vandalism, similarity on locations where this happened, and anything else that might stand out. After that, she would move on to the weapons violations, and the DUI data. Again, her sense was these were increasing on the forests and elsewhere. Important to her was finding patterns in combination. She'd think nationally, but focus locally, as her analysis needed to be on the George Washington and Jefferson National Forest, and especially on the Eastern Divide Ranger District.

Vi and Em took a short food break. Afterwards, they asked Bill to meet with them and Woody to go over what they had found so far. They believed they were starting to see some items worth mentioning. If their counterparts in other agencies were seeing something similar, it might change the way they conducted law enforcement in the next few years on the forests.

Everyone met in the conference room. Bill had brought in a coffee pot, and slices of cake for everyone. They took a few moments to eat and drink, and then Bill turned the meeting over to Vi.

Vi reported, "There appear to be clear ties between locations of reports of alcohol abuse, rapes, and vandalism. It's almost as if what started as a small group gathering turned into a free-for-all on the district."

"That's interesting. Tell us more," said Woody.

Vi observed, "Many of these activities were in, or proximate to campgrounds and picnic areas. The groups of people contacted by law enforcement were not overly large, like a rave. That threw us off a bit, but we looked deeper, and what we found was enlightening. It was almost always more men than women in the groups, the women were often quite impaired, and in some cases they did not recall giving consent for sexual activities. Some of the men ticketed were repeat offenders.

"Not far from where DUI stops were made were sites with vandalism, and sometimes sites with dead animals, regardless of hunting season. This appears to tie in shootings, though there were few tickets given for shooting on the forest."

Bill added, "In general, these activities are even more frequent than the numbers we have in the database. What we know is that there's little enforcement coverage over a very large area, and we think that makes it difficult to find activities in progress. Officers are more likely to find evidence after the fact."

Bill summed it up. "The data appear to suggest rather frequent gatherings by small groups of people who engaged in unlawful activities, sometimes including abuse of alcohol, and women. Sometimes the issue is shooting and alcohol. Vandalism caused by gunfire occurs almost constantly. In my opinion this is not an ideal use of public lands. Vi and Em, did I miss anything?"

Vi replied, "Em and I noted that there isn't a UCR category for membership in a supremacy group. This is important on these forests, and on this district, because the KKK was mentioned, as well as the National Alliance. It could be that these 'parties' on the forests were there because the area has become 'home' or comfortable to one or more of these groups."

Bill said, "It's a stretch to be sure. This'll require much more work to verify, but I think it's worthy of consideration."

Vi added, "We're the first to say personal opinions do not weigh much against data, but our data did not specifically address white supremacy. We think it would be worth evaluating with the other agencies." Vi and Em were also quick to point out that alternative groups could be at work here as well. Everyone should keep his or her options open.

In the meantime, Vi thought it seemed reasonable to ask officers to note on their reports if they suspected membership in a supremacy group. Bill knew it would be the subject of much discussion, because race was not a proxy for belonging to a supremacy group.

Vi offered, "Perhaps we could refocus on hate crimes. That's a distinction that carries merit across various law enforcement agencies."

Vi and Em had mapped the reported incidents on the smart board. They color-coded them by type of activity. Bill could visualize a fairly clear picture of what Vi and Em reported as a pattern. There was nothing to indicate group membership. Nor was there anything to indicate crimes of hate.

Bill expressed concern that by discussing white supremacy groups, perhaps they were giving too much credence to information that had been gleaned from a few of the campers. Woody argued that maybe not enough credence was being allocated since one of the victims was lynched. This back and forth discussion was a hallmark of the group. Nothing was taken for granted. Every assumption was addressed. Bill liked it that way.

Bill felt they had enough data for his video teleconference and to present at the meeting the next morning.

Bill told them, "Vi and Em, thank for your diligence. I can always count on your expertise when we need it most. I give my thanks to each of you. I really appreciate you being willing to come on a late Sunday afternoon to work on this.

"I enjoy your thoughtful critique. I hope you know that not every group's willing to work with each other in this way. I think of it as a hallmark of our group. And before I get too sappy, I wish you a great evening."

As the meeting ended, and people started to head out of the office, Bill also thanked Scott for joining them, and delaying the honeymoon. He also thanked Vi for bringing in the food.

Woody said, "I need to stay a bit longer, Bill. I have two press releases that I'm working on. Both will require your approval before they go out. I think another half hour will do. Will you have time to do that before the video teleconference?"

"Yes, I'll make the time. Did you leave the video teleconference information for me?"

"Yes, the room's ready and the details are on the desk. It looks like three of you will make the call."

While Bill waited on the press releases, he focused on the upcoming call with Harley, and the video teleconference.

CHAPTER FOURTEEN

Harley was traveling down I-81 South. She was musing about how she'd woken up in a funny mood that morning. Not funny in a bad way, she meant in a humorous way. She'd had a few laughs at her own expense.

After dressing that morning, Harley had peered into the mirror. She remembered that she had once been concerned about aging, but decided that age fifty-two looked well on her. She'd declared out loud, "It sure beats not getting older!" Her teeth were straight, and she smiled into the mirror. She knew those smiles hid fierceness within, a stick-to-itiveness that was admirable. When a task seemed too large, she broke it down into component parts, and trudged along until it was resolved. Then she'd said, "Mirror, mirror on the wall, I'm not seeing perfection here. But I'm seeing a damn fine woman!" She'd laughed, and stepped away from the mirror.

At five foot, four inches tall Harley was usually shorter than those around her. That didn't bother her. Harley said that she was often underestimated because of her height. She'd laughingly told her friend Vi that "women her height were often overlooked." After Vi had groaned at her remark, Harley said she tried to use this to her advantage. Harley laughed when she recalled that conversation.

Harley had cleaned her glasses and put them on. "Baby's got four eyes," she sang as she prepped her day. She could have sung, "Baby's got blue eyes," but today she was poking fun at herself, and enjoying it. In general, though, Harley was not happy about having to wear prescription glasses and sunglasses, but they were necessary. If she went without, the world would be blurry to her. She'd also be ticketed for driving without her required eyewear. She did not want that to happen.

Just two months ago, Harley had to buy new glasses and sunglasses, since her eyesight had worsened since her last trip to the optometrist. He'd blithely told her that she was, "The age where she could expect her eyes to get worse with each passing year." He'd also told her that condition precluded laser eye surgery. Harley thought, "Well, isn't that just peachy. Time to eat more carrots!" Still, she was alive, and she could see. She'd always taken extra care of her glasses, like cleaning them often, and being careful where she placed them so they did not get lost or broken.

That morning Harley had been glad her motor home did not carry a weight scale. She did not particularly like her weight, today or most any day. She'd tried a joke, "A wiggle when I giggle, and a jiggle in the middle," but it didn't make her laugh much. She carried her extra weight in the middle, and wore what she called "comfy clothes" to disguise it. Typically that involved jeans and long-sleeved t-shirts, sometimes that meant sweat suits. She was not a wearer of makeup or jewelry. Today she had donned her "traveling" clothes, loose jeans and a long-sleeved t-shirt. The t-shirt had an outline of a dog that reminded her of Gemma. It said, "Will wag for swag." That always made Harley laugh.

Harley's clothes choices reminded her of growing up, and being considered a tomboy. In later years, she'd been called a ball-breaker, because she stood up for herself. She'd told Vi that, "People didn't know how to label independence and intelligence in women." Harley thought the joke was on them. She was smart enough to understand herself, and their attempts to belittle her. This morning she'd joked, "I'm little enough, people. Give me a break!"

Harley shared with Vi that people thought Harley was intimidating to others. She could not see why people would think so. "Whom would a short, heavy, white, older woman intimidate?" Both had laughed then, and Harley did again this morning.

Harley's good mood had dissipated when she had to make her early morning calls to Rick and Walt. The thought of the deaths, and the investigations, took the wind out of her sails. She had work to do, and it was time to get serious.

Harley continued driving down the road in Patsy Cline. She was in control; she took breaks when she or Gemma needed. Harley was headed toward the unknown, but had handled that before, and she would this time too. The worst time had been handling Augie's cancer diagnosis. She'd been in tough situations before, but nothing prepared her to lose the love of her life. Unless something happened to her son, Harley now knew she could take on any task. The task might not be easy, but she knew she had the skills.

Harley thought about Bill and her work. She figured that so long as she enjoyed being a contractor with the Forest Service, she would continue to do things like this trip. It was not her forever plan. In a couple of years she planned to retire to a small ranch, where she could raise a dozen dogs, and train many more. She knew her affinity for dogs would never waver.

Harley drove through rain several times during the drive. She was glad it was not the heavy rains that had been predicted, because those rains could slow her down. Harley felt it was good for the soul to have rain. If she had more time, she might dance in it with Gemma.

As she was driving Harley had heard some text messages ping on her phone. It sounded like several. She decided she'd stop at the next rest area, have some Diet Coke, and find out what was happening. Perhaps her son was replying back from her earlier message to him. Maybe she could give him a call, and not just exchange text messages.

Harley stopped at a rest area. It looked like a pretty one. There were a few semi-trailer trucks parked there, as were about a dozen motor homes and cars. The rest area looked clean, there was a place to walk Gemma, and some vending machines likely held sugary delights Harley might be tempted to buy.

Before Harley investigated though, she checked her phone. There was a message from Jack. It appeared that he was much too busy having fun with his friends to take time for a call right now. That was okay, but she'd try before bedtime tonight. There were also messages from Bill, Woody, and Violet. Violet's message was about the wedding, and made Harley smile. Bill and Woody's messages suggested much more was happening, and she needed to call in to Bill as soon as she was able.

Harley took Gemma for a short walk in the dog walking area. She had seen all kinds of rest areas in the course of many journeys, and often the dog walk areas left something to be desired. They were often dirt, covered with ant and gopher mounds, or had multiple signs warning about rattlesnakes, coyotes, or other deadly creatures. This one was a bit higher on the dog walking area scale, and even had a grassy, weedy area. They had even provided bags for cleaning up after your pooch. It looked like most dog owners had kept the area clean. Harley hummed a couple of songs as they traversed the dog walk area. She was pretty sure Gemma walked to the beat of the music.

Harley returned to the motor home, and sat at the table to call Bill. Harley guessed he'd tell her the clues led them to the killers, and she could head on to Hazel's house. She was wrong.

Bill said, "Hi, Harley. How's the drive going?"

"We're doing okay. The rains aren't bad so we're making good time. Do we need to keep heading to Virginia?"

"Yes, you definitely are needed. We have three more murders to add to the other two you know about."

"Oh my god! I cannot imagine. Are these all on the same forest?"

"Yes, all on the same ranger district. I had a few calls today from Forest Supervisor Rick Givens. On the last call, he'd just heard from a sheriff area officer named Dexter Dreyfus. Dreyfus was the officer sent after the sheriff learned that several unexpected people showed up at two campgrounds in the district.

Seems this group was the KKK, who were there to recruit new members."

"Do they usually recruit at campgrounds?" asked Harley.

"We're not sure, and we're trying to learn more. As Dreyfus approached a campground, he saw several cars departing the area. He made notes about car makes and colors, but didn't recognize people. Anyway, in the campground he found several very shaken campers, and three dead men. Actually, one of the men was by a burned car at the entrance to the campground, and two other men were shot in the first loop. The men had identification on them, and you'll hear more about that at the meeting I need you to attend in the morning in Christiansburg at the sheriff's office."

"Okay, I'm trying to catch-up here. There are three more dead men, and a meeting tomorrow. I don't even know what questions to ask, except what time is the meeting?"

"The meeting begins at 8. You're expected to be included in all aspects of the investigations."

"Okay, so the investigations include Mr. Fry and Mr. Freeman, and now three more."

"Yes. Sorry, I know this sounds bizarre. If it is too much you can always wait for another case to come along."

"Why would I do that, Bill? I'm fully capable..."

"Yes, I know. I apologize. Guess I just want to protect you from this."

"Apology accepted. How about you tell me more, and if I feel the need to bow out, which is quite unlikely, I'll tell you so. Let's start with the dead men in the campground. Were they campers?"

"No, they weren't. We presume they were KKK members. It appears more men arrived after the KKK, and a fight ensued between the two groups. We don't know for sure, but since the National Alliance is active on the forest, one or more of the dead men could be one of them."

"Wow. You have the KKK and the National Alliance fighting in a campground? Am I the only one who thinks this is crazy?"

"No, Harley, we all think this is wild. We don't know everything yet, or really I should say we don't know much of anything."

"Okay, sorry to keep interrupting. How about you tell me what is known so far. I'll stop you if I have pertinent questions."

"Great. I'll start with the campers. Givens and Newman went to the area, and went through the check-in box at two different campgrounds. The campgrounds are close to each other, on the same road. It took some time to determine, but it appears that one campground was not a part of the melee.

"Campers in the melee campground are now accounted for. One family drove away. Most families sheltered in place while the shooting was going on. A few, mostly on the loop away from the action, took their family and horses onto the nearby horse trails. Another family tried to walk to Dismal Falls hoping to find a cell connection so they could call the sheriff.

"The campers all returned back to camp, but two horses were missing. Their owners were a bit upset by that. Someone had to open their stalls and remove them, and none of the campers did that. So it appears the bad guys, whomever they are, may've done it."

"We don't really know about that do we?"

"No, it'll be part of the investigation is my guess. The state police will likely lead the investigations, with the sheriff department involved, and we have several officers headed there as well.

"Oh, and let me mention the two cars burned just outside the campground entrance. The fire crew reported that an accelerant was used to start a fire in one vehicle, and the fire appeared to have spread to the next vehicle. It was the first car's gas tank that had exploded. It was likely the victim was simply in the wrong place at the wrong time."

Harley was worried. Bill, who was usually calm, was unsettled. Harley could tell by his speech cadence, his voice was a bit higher, and he was speaking more quickly than usual. This case was the first time he had questioned whether she should be involved. She took a deep, calming breath.

"Bill, what're the next steps you're taking?" She figured this would put him back in control since he would focus on what he could do.

Bill replied, "In about ten minutes I have a video teleconference with Rick Givens and Gray Wallace to tell them what I told you. Woody's been here working on press releases. Plus, Violet has been here scouring the dataset to get as much specificity on crimes and violence in the past on the forest and the district. Would you believe that Emmylynne and Scott were here, too?"

"No...they should be on their honeymoon."

"Yes, they should. Yet here we were enjoying leftover food and cake from the wedding. Violet brought it with her, and even brought in decorations for the computer lab."

"Oh, I wish I could've been there too. It sounds festive."

"Woody is still here, and Darryl started to come in, but I told him we had it under control. We'll need someone fresh here tomorrow morning."

"What did the data indicate?"

"Our data analysis didn't show any previous shootings like Mr. Fry's. I specifically mean the shot into his mouth. The data suggested several large group gatherings that could be related to use by supremacist groups. But it could easily be some other large group. The data also indicated alcohol abuse, and abuse of women. None of our data match these five deaths, though we have lots of evidence of shootings on the forest."

Harley asked, "Do you suppose there's any connection among all these murders?"

Bill said, "Well, that's the $64,000 question, isn't it? I don't really believe in coincidences, but there appears to be quite the puzzle ahead to figure it all out."

They discussed a few more details, commiserated about how the Forest Service was going to be perceived, as if this was somehow tarnishing, because it happened on Forest Service lands. Bill asked if Harley would check in frequently with him and Violet. She agreed this would be a good idea. Harley carried the data pad provided by the agency so she could be tracked. It would hurt nothing to check in, as she was able.

Harley and Gemma had several miles to go yet today to get to their new destination of Christiansburg, so they ended the call. She thought, "Well, at least I'm still traveling down the right highway, just a bit further than I'd planned." It was time to continue driving.

At long last Harley and Gemma arrived at the Wal-Mart parking lot in Christiansburg. It looked like she'd not have the hoped for electrical option tonight, and would have to rely on her generator. She found that some Wal-Mart stores were more lenient about letting people stay there overnight and use generators, while others were less so. Two other motor homes were parked in the lot, so she parked in their vicinity.

Harley located a nearby county park to take Gemma for a walk. They spent about an hour hiking the trail. Harley thought it felt good to really stretch her legs, and imagined Gemma did too. Harley noticed how green it was, and how everything smelled fresh. The trail had some muddy portions, but Gemma did not seem to mind. They'd heard a few birds as they walked, but didn't see any. Nor did they pass any people on the trail. Harley thought maybe it was too close to suppertime for trail hiking for most folks, or maybe just too humid for comfort. She enjoyed hearing the birds, and tried singing their notes back to them. Some of her earlier good mood was returning.

Harley and Gemma returned to the Wal-Mart and the motor home. One of the neighbors was outside. They exchanged hellos, and Harley commented how great his food smelled. He was barbecuing some steaks, and it made Harley's mouth water. It was time for Harley to cook some dinner. After dishes she'd get in some reading.

Later that evening, while relaxing at her table, Harley called Jack. Her son said he'd had a great time with his friends, and was preparing for a meeting he had in the morning. She wished him a nice evening.

Harley closed out her evening as she often did, by thinking

about all the reasons she had to be grateful. As always, she was grateful for Jack. She was grateful that Gemma was such a good traveler. Harley had taken Gemma on the road since her "gotcha" day. Harley adopted Gemma as a young pup on Valentine's Day. Gemma was now two and a half years old.

Harley hoped Gemma knew how much she adored her. Every morning Harley sang to Gemma (tune to *"Oh My Darling, Clementine"* with apologies to Percy Montrose): *"In an RV, on the roadside, contemplating their long drive, were a driver, and beside her, her darling doggy, Valentine. Oh my darling, oh my darling, oh my darling, Valentine! You are home and loved forever, faithful precious Valentine!"* Tomorrow morning, like every morning Harley would tell her, "My Gemma is the best dog ever!" And now, just like they did every evening, they went for a quick walk at 9. Harley called it "pees and cheese" time, since their brief sojourn was followed by a chunk of cheese for Gemma, and then bedtime.

Considering all she was grateful for, Harley added that she was also grateful for her position as a contractor, and that Patsy Cline had done well, covering a lot of miles, and having no problems.

CHAPTER FIFTEEN

Harley and Gemma were up by 6. They walked the county park area again. Harley thought it was lovely. Everything was so green. It had rained more during the night and the fresh scent was intoxicating. Harley wondered how much stronger it was for Gemma's sensitive nose. Harley smelled flowers and trees, the dirt on the trail, and the grasses nearby. It all smelled so good. She thought it would be a nice memory to hold on to, but it'd be better if she could bottle it and take the scents with her.

Unlike the previous evening, this time they passed a few morning walkers. They wished them a good day, and Gemma sat for them, and shook their hands.

Since they were out, Harley decided to do more training with Gemma. When Gemma was first being trained she had required a lot of treats. Harley was glad a simple, "Good job, Gemma!" or a pat on the head sufficed for her these days.

A few people stopped to watch as Harley and Gemma went through their training exercises. One young child asked if she could try it too. She looked quite delighted when Gemma sat, laid down, and rolled-over on command. Harley was thinking the girl might be a budding dog trainer.

After the family had moved along, Harley continued their practice. She held up one finger over Gemma's nose. Gemma sat quietly, and watched Harley carefully. She used to have to re-mind Gemma to "Watch me," but those days were long gone.

Gemma always watched her.

"Good job, Gemma!"

Harley twirled one finger in a circular motion, and Gemma backed up. Harley approached her, and patted Gemma's head.

Harley put a finger down in a swipe motion and walked a distance away. Gemma waited in place until Harley called her. When she did, Gemma came running to her. Harley had Gemma circle around Harley, and then sit.

"Gemma's a good dog!"

Harley held her hand out with all five fingers stretched. Gemma stayed in place until Harley returned to her. Harley patted Gemma's head again.

They did each of these commands multiple times. There were other commands they could not practice in this setting, such as tracking, containing a person in place, and attack.

To finish up, Harley had Gemma shake hands, high five, and rollover. Gemma pranced back to the motor home, with Harley close behind. Harley loved these training sessions and it looked like Gemma did as well.

Once back in the motor home, Harley added water to one bowl for Gemma, and food and biscuit treats in another. It was time for Gemma to eat.

Harley turned on her computer to locate the nearest animal hospital, and any local veterinarians who serviced dogs. She'd take screenshots, and have this information on her phone in case it was needed. Once she had that, Harley made some breakfast for herself. It was cool enough outside, so she had oatmeal and a hot tea. Cleanup did not take long.

Harley moved with practiced steps around the motor home. In the back of the motor home was her queen-sized bed. She kept a sleeping bag on the bed for herself, and a dog bed for Gemma. Both were easy to pull off and launder as needed. There were storage cabinets over the bed that held jackets and sweats. Her closet was located next to the bed, and just a bit further down the hallway was the bathroom. It had been cleverly designed so she had plenty of room for a toilet, the sink, and the shower. The shower space also housed her laundry bag and some cleaning supplies. Just outside that area was the dining area, which was across from her two-burner cook top, double sink, and refrigerator. A television was above the sink, but Harley rarely turned it on. Over the cab of the vehicle was another queen-sized bed. Harley used that space for storage containers. Some held extra food for her and Gemma, and beverages; others held extra towels, bedding, and clothes. She had installed a cargo net so all those containers would stay overhead while she drove. Once the dishes were done, Harley took a fast shower, and dressed for the day.

Harley decided it was late enough to call Bill. He probably had a late night the previous evening, so she hoped she was not calling too early.

"Good morning, Harley."

"Good morning! Not too early for you, I hope."

"I was up for all of five minutes or so. I was just getting ready to head in to work. I suppose you and Gemma have been up a while already."

"Just over an hour. I called to check in, and see if you learned anything on the video teleconference I'd need to know about before heading to the meeting."

"There was not much beyond what we talked about already. How would you feel about a human partner, along with Gemma, on this investigation?"

"Are you still concerned I can't handle this?"

"No, not at all. Sorry to give you that impression. These are bad men, and you don't even carry a weapon. Well, one beyond Gemma, but she can't outrun bullets, and neither can you."

"I was thinking about safety myself. You've seen the vest I wear. I have a knife in it, and pepper spray. I carry a water filter so we can drink from springs. I carry extra snacks. I plan as much in advance as I can so I don't get into bad situations. Plus, I have a satellite phone, and the data tracker. All this is supposed to make you feel better. Besides, you know that supremacists aren't all killers."

"I know, Harley, but these particular ones have proven themselves to be killers."

"Well, I still won't carry a gun, but I will consider a human partner who carries a gun. Sound okay to you?"

"More than okay. I'm greatly relieved. I'll call the Sheriff's office right away and make that happen. You know, this goes beyond the need to protect you as if you were just another contract employee. I do care about you, you know."

"Me, too, but I don't know about the long distance romance kind of thing, and I'm not ready to settle in any one place."

"I promise not to tie you down. Just don't rule me out."

"Deal. I need to pack my vest, and Gemma's, so I'm hanging up now. Bye."

"Be careful out there."

As she prepared for her day, Harley thought back to the conversation with Bill. She could again sense his discomfiture over this investigation. She did not really know if she could attribute it to a gender bias kind of thing, or a romantic interest kind of thing. Either way, she needed to let go of all those thoughts, and focus on getting the bad guys, while staying safe.

Harley packed her vest with her usual items, added granola bars and lip-gloss. She tied her long dirty blonde hair into a ponytail and put it through the hole in her baseball cap. She packed another vest for Gemma, so she could carry some water and food herself. Then Harley checked Gemma's collar to make sure her tracking device was operating.

Harley drove to the sheriff's office, locked up Patsy Cline, and she and Gemma headed to the meeting.

CHAPTER SIXTEEN

S tone Stevens was in the break room at the sheriff's office. He had arrived early for the meeting, and was enjoying coffee and pastries. He had brought a couple of boxes of sweet treats in with him only to discover a few more boxes already in the room. Stone was a Senior Special Agent of the Virginia State Police. He was a man who believed in authority, law, and order. Right now he was a man thoroughly enjoying a cream cheese croissant. Between bites he was catching up with Jacey Jenner, an investigator with the Christiansburg Sheriff's office. The two had been friends for years.

Stone declared, "Important weekend for me! I asked Genevieve to marry me."

"That's great news, Stone!"

"Yes, it is. This last year has been a whirlwind. First dad had his stroke, and we had to move him into a one-story house, but I got to meet Genevieve in the process. Why am I telling you this? You met her first, and recommended her as our real estate agent. She's amazing!"

"I heard she's been taking you shopping for new furniture lately. It is about time you upgraded from frat style."

"Very funny, Jacey. It wasn't frat style. I wasn't sleeping on box springs on the floor."

"Okay, you were just a step up from frat then. Have you two set a wedding date?"

"Yes, we'll marry in December. Then we plan to have three

kids as soon as possible. We're not getting any younger, and we both think three kids is perfect."

"Well, I'm blown away. Also, I'm very happy for you both!"

"Happy about what?" asked Carver Grayson as he entered the room.

"Oh, nothing boss," replied Stone. "Good to see you, sir. I brought donuts, and found that Jacey also brought in some pastries. Guess we both know your weakness for anything sweet."

"There might be enough that I'm willing to share with others," joked Grayson. "I'll be setting up in the conference room downstairs if you'd care to join me, Stone." Stone watched as Grayson picked out three donuts, and poured some coffee.

"Yes, sir. I will clean up here, and then join you."

The building they were in had been home to the county sheriff for years. It had a brick facade, but large clear glass entry doors. Though it seemed to mix a modern touch with a more traditional look, it somehow worked together. There were actually two buildings, with one housing those under arrest, and the other being the hub of law enforcement. The latter was a two-story building with a basement. On the first floor there was a check-in counter, then a security pass-through. A long hallway led to the interview and conference rooms. The carpeting in the hallway looked well used, and would benefit from an upgrade. Photos along the hallway depicted years of sheriff photos, and several photos of local community members shaking hands with the sheriff. On the second story were offices, a bullpen area, a break room, and at the end of the bullpen was the office of the sheriff. This office had large glass windows with blinds. The basement held all the computer and investigation labs.

Stone and Jacey walked downstairs from the break room toward the largest conference room. This building was Jacey's workplace, but Stone had been here several times before, and knew his way around. If their work turned into a complicated or long-term investigation, the sheriff made some offices or desks in the bullpen on the second floor, and small conference rooms on the first floor available to visiting law enforcement officers.

Usually when the state police were called in that meant they would be the lead agency on the investigation. "What have you heard, Jacey? Is French or Grayson leading the charge this go round?"

"French dearly wanted the lead after he heard about the two deaths, but more came up, so he decided your boss should take the lead. My guess is they'll find a way to collaborate, and work together. I heard that the Forest Service has sent people as well," said Jacey.

"Guess I'm one of the Forest Service contingent," said Harley, "I'm Harley Fremont, and this is Gemma, another Forest Service asset."

"Hello to you both," said Jacey. "Hey, Gemma, what a good dog."

Stone asked, "What is she? A mutt?"

"A Rhodesian Ridgeback," said Jacey.

"Very good. How'd you know? It's not a breed many are familiar with," said Harley.

"I'm a huge fan of dogs. I have to confess I also heard from Woody Brooks that you were coming. He speaks very highly of you and Gemma. He told me you have resolved a few law enforcement cases for the Forest Service. It's a pleasure to meet you. I'm Jacey Jenner, and I'll be partnering with you and Gemma. This 'uninformed about dogs' man is Stone Stevens from the state police."

"Pleasure to meet you both. I look forward to working with you, Jacey. Gemma, shake." Gemma sat and greeted both people, and they all moved into the conference room together.

Stone noticed the conference room carpet seemed in better shape than the hallway carpet, though not by much. The room had not changed much since the last time Stone was here. The draperies covering two windows were closed. The fluorescent lights were on, and one bulb was flickering. Unlike the hallway, this room had six posters of the Blue Ridge Mountains. There were two long rows of tables, about three feet separating them down the middle of the room, with two chairs at each table. A table and dais was at the end of the two lines, along with a computer setup, and a smart whiteboard. The sheriff's emblem on the dais was black, with a thin blue line, and a gold star shaped shield. There was an American flag was in the corner.

After several minutes waiting for everyone to enter and get settled, Rolland French called the meeting to order. "Let's take just a few minutes for introductions. For now, your name, position, and agency will suffice. I'm Rolland French, Montgomery County Sheriff."

"Jacey Jenner, Lead Technician in Investigations, Montgomery County Sheriff's Office."

"Stone Stevens, Senior Special Agent, Bureau of Criminal Investigations, State Police."

"Harley Fremont, contractor with the Forest Service, and this is Gemma."

"Sami Foster, Homicide Investigator, Montgomery County Sheriff's Office."

"Christopher Wray, Trooper, State Police."

"Blaze Edwards, Area Officer, Montgomery County Sheriff's Office."

"Elliott Green, Area Officer, Montgomery County Sheriff's Office."

"Rick Givens, Forest Supervisor, Forest Service."

"Carver Grayson, Deputy Superintendent, State Police."

"Jeff Langley, Special Agent, Bureau of Criminal Investigations, State Police."

"Richard Golden, Patrol Captain, Forest Service."

"Gray Wallace, Law Enforcement Officer, Forest Service."

"Thank you all. The Medical Examiner, Hal Quinones, was unable to attend today. I understand two additional Forest Service officers will arrive later. Richard?"

"Correct. Both are from the Monongahela National Forest, Law Enforcement Officers Wesley Lexington and Brian Calvin."

Stone looked at Jacey. Jacey appeared as surprised as Stone felt. To Stone it seemed like a lot of people.

French continued, "You are probably wondering why we have so many people on the case, so we'll explain more in short order. First, let me say that Carver Grayson will take the lead on our joint efforts. I will partner with him and Richard Golden as the oversight team. Everyone else will get an assignment, and report back here to Stone or Jeff as assigned, and they'll report to Grayson."

Stone nodded at Jacey as if to say, "Yes, Jacey, you were right."

Grayson stood and turned to the smart whiteboard. He cued up a file he had prepared.

Grayson began, "We have several deaths to investigate. According to the medical examiner, the first death occurred on Thursday of last week, between 2 and 11 p.m. It was the shooting death of Mr. George Fry on the George Washington and Jefferson National Forests. On Saturday, Mr. Clay Freeman was found hanged in the same forest. This was followed by three deaths on the forest yesterday. Mr. Orville Wright and Mr. Wilbur Wright were shot, and Mr. Joseph Miller appears to have died from injuries sustained from an exploding gas tank."

Stone saw a surprised look on most faces and imagined his face mirrored those. He'd known about the first two murders, but had not known about the other three. Stone had taken a break from work and media the day before. It looked like he wasn't the only one.

"As near as we know, only one murder has occurred on this forest in the last ten years, and now we have five in less than a week. Later we'll need to determine what happened to cause all this. First, I will lie out the evidence we have so far on each death. I expect anyone with additional information or questions about any of these to speak up during the discussion. Following that, we'll start assigning duties for follow-up, and discussing additional assistance needed for our investigations. Any questions or comments before we begin?"

Hearing none, Grayson continued, "Mr. George Fry was shot twice at close range. One shot was in the chest, but the killing shot was into his mouth. We've all seen or heard of these types of deaths before. The shot to the mouth generally is a message for others not to talk. We'll need to see if that's true for this case.

"According to his family, Mr. Fry was well respected in the community, and generally kept to himself. They had no idea why he was shot, or what he was doing on the forest, as he was not known by his family to frequent the forest. The medical examiner has extracted the bullet to the chest. The bullet to the mouth exited his head, and was found in a nearby tree. Both bullets are being processed to see if we know the weapon used. There were no other clues. Does anyone have anything to add?"

Golden asked if there had been similar deaths in the county in the past few years. Grayson responded that there had been none in the county, but five in the state in the last decade. Those had been tied to drug trafficking, so it brought up the possibility that Mr. Fry had been in the drug trade.

"Moving on to the hanging of Mr. Freeman. The family reported that everyone loved Mr. Freeman. He was due to be married, and was, in fact, on his way to a family celebration Saturday when he was murdered. His vehicle was not operational, so it appears to have broken down in the forest.

"The medical examiner reports death was due to strangulation by hanging. The rope used is in our possession. So the perpetrators, and I'm using plural here because this is not the work of one person, either caused the breakdown or happened upon Mr. Freeman after the car stopped working. The perpetrators were carrying rope, which indicates some type of premeditation, or they typically carry rope. We'll need to examine those assumptions.

"We have a few tire tracks, but that is a well-traveled portion of roadway, so the tracks may mean nothing. Also of note was the way the rope was tied. We have had suicides before, but haven't seen these types of knots. Does anyone have anything to add or have questions?"

Wallace asked if the rope was special in any way.

"Not that we have discerned so far," responded Grayson.

Wallace asked what exactly made the rope knots so interesting.

Grayson replied, "All I know right now is that they were 'unusual knots.'"

Then Wallace asked if the tire prints were used to identify a particular model of car. He was told that they were tied to the Toyota RAV4, but there were so many in the area, the actual vehicle could not be traced, though it might prove to be useful information later.

Grayson mentioned that his office had received several calls about this death, or more to the point, about lynching. In almost equal measure, people were incensed, or said he had it coming. Grayson said his concern was race relations, and they needed to reach out to community groups to determine what kind of blowback this was causing. They did not want another Charlottesville disaster. French concurred and said their office had fielded similar calls. They all would spend time examining this death carefully in hopes of a quick resolution; no one wanted a race war in the area. French mentioned that the state police public affairs office would keep them informed about public comments. He asked that if anyone received calls about the lynching to forward the calls to that office.

Grayson put up a map showing the area of two Forest Service campgrounds. It indicated distance between the campgrounds as well as the configuration of each campground. He had marked different spots on the map to correspond to different things he wanted to point out. He used a laser pointer to indicate different areas as he mentioned them.

Grayson said, "Yesterday saw three more deaths. All were located at the same campground on the forest. Two were inside the Beggar Flats Horse Campground on the first of two loops, and the third was on the road just outside the campground entrance. The two victims inside the campground died by gunshot. Those were Mr.'s Orville and Wilbur Wright. We did not locate weapons near either body, though a metal pipe was near the bodies.

"The third body, Mr. Joseph Miller, likely died from being

proximate to an exploding gas tank. There had been two cars on fire, and one was hot enough for the gas tank to explode. A weapon was found near his body. That weapon is being checked today.

"We also have a few shoe and boot prints, a dozen shell casings, but few useable tire prints. We also have some food containers not belonging to any of the campers being evaluated for fingerprints. The medical examiner is processing the three deceased today. We have made notification to their families.

"We have evidence that an accelerant was used to light one car on fire, then the other car likely caught fire next. The second car barely burned, indicating the accelerant was used only on one vehicle. Both vehicles are being investigated. We have tied the car tags to one of the deceased and the other to Mr. Gerald Brown. Brown had not reported the vehicle stolen."

Grayson said, "It appears two opposing groups came to the campground. One group is thought to be the KKK. The other group is unknown at this point, although Forest Supervisor Givens has noted that the National Alliance has been active in this area, and specifically in these campgrounds. We don't know that they were the second group for sure, but it seems likely. Any questions or comments?"

Wallace asked when they might have more information from the medical examiner on the three most recent deaths. He was told Quinones worked quickly, and they hoped to have more information by the end of the day.

Golden wanted everyone to know there were two missing horses from the campground. He said that it was not known if the horses were set free, or if they were taken. Both horse owners had filed complaints. Golden mentioned that all campers at the horse camp had been accounted for. He also discussed the need to track down campers from the nearby campground to determine what they had seen or heard. Golden told them that Rick Givens had campground check-in information on each campsite to help with the process.

French said, "We were contacted by two campers from the Gopher Flats Campground, and they had taken photos of the cars of the visitors to the campground. The cars in their photos belong to Mr. Orville Wright, Mr. Junior Kendall, Mr. Herb Smith, and Mr. Ben Rover. We originally thought that the campground visitors at Gopher Flats were not related to the incident at the horse camp, but now it is clear that at least one car and person from that group moved toward the other camp, and the person was killed.

"We had additional contacts from the public. A family who'd left Beggar Flats Campground also contacted us. They were concerned over people they called 'unexpected visitors.' Lastly, Sheriff Area Officer Dexter Dreyfus was on his way to check on these two complaints when another family stopped him on the road to the campgrounds. They reported a melee at Beggar Flats Horse Campground. The officer proceeded directly to that campground, and located the three deceased. Any more comments or questions?"

It had been fairly quiet in the room as the officers absorbed all the information. Stone could see concern etched on many faces. All had been aware of the first two murders, but he could see that three more deaths were making them rethink the work ahead.

Golden noted that all five murders were in the same district on the national forest within the same week. He asked if there could be any link between Fry, Freeman, the Wright brothers, and Miller. Grayson replied that it was much too early to make any assumptions, but they should all be looking for evidence they could be linked, as well as evidence against. Givens commented that the deaths were possibly linked to hate groups, but said they did not have enough information to make that call.

The group spent the next half hour discussing similarities in crimes they had investigated in the past few years, and the current incidents. Each group had gaps where the previous crimes were not a match to recent events, and had some instances of similarities. None of the data sets were equipped to measure extremist groups, but some had noted an increased level of activity in hate crimes the last two years.

The next task was to assign resources. Grayson revealed that state police representatives would take the lead on each breakout group. He said they would begin by separating into two teams. One team would investigate the deaths; Stone would lead that team.

Stone saw Jacey nod at him in approval.

Grayson informed them said that Jeff Langley would lead the team conducting research and interviews of family members. Additional interviews would be divided between teams depending on the topic of the interview.

Stone looked over at Jacey to discern her reaction to that announcement. Jacey appeared to be okay to not be the leader of any group. Stone decided to ask her about that later.

The oversight group, Grayson said, was to look at evidence that the deaths were interconnected, as well as evidence that they were not. He told the assembled that each of the investigative teams would have members from the state police, sheriff's department, and Forest Service.

Golden mentioned that Harley Fremont and her K-9 partner were under contract with the Forest Service to work on the homicide investigation. He gave Fremont an opportunity to briefly describe how she might best engage with them. When she finished, Golden told the Sheriffs that the Forest Service understood the limited contract the sheriff department was under, and all budgetary questions for overages on that contract would go through Woody Brooks in the D.C. office.

Once all discussion was completed, Grayson reminded everyone that what they heard in the meeting was to be kept within these agencies. There would be no one except the public affairs office of the state police making statements to the press. He added, "So, keep this close to the vest, and be very careful out there."

"Your investigations will begin today, and the first report out will be at 5 today. We plan to have a 5 o'clock report each day of the investigations," said Grayson. "If you cannot be back here at the office, then provide your report to your team leader before that. In the meantime, you'll have a meeting with your team leader to plan your next steps. Stone's team will meet in conference room B and Jeff's team in conference room D."

Stone and Jacey stayed seated as others moved to join their assigned groups to plan the next actions. Stone asked, "Are you okay not leading a group?"

"Yes," replied Jacey, "Jeff has more seniority, and will be an excellent leader. Plus, he's state police. Besides, I get to partner with Harley Fremont, and the amazing Gemma."

"Good to know you're okay. It was great to see you. Let's plan to get dinner soon."

"Yes, let's do that, so I can congratulate Genevieve in person."

CHAPTER SEVENTEEN

Evan Wilton's phone rang as he was walking toward his barn. It was Duke Kent calling.

"Damn it, Evan. Did Blaze or Elliott call you first? Or did they just start calling people themselves?"

"Easy, Duke. No need to yell. Blaze called me just a few minutes ago. I believe he and Elliott had made all the calls to everyone already."

"Blaze should have called me first."

"I don't see the problem. With the two of them making calls it went faster than you or me calling everyone."

"Well, you and I should have been the ones to call. We're the ones in charge here."

"I still don't see the problem. They had all the information, and could answer questions best, given the topic."

"I don't like it, Evan!"

"Well, I'm okay with it because I know how people reacted, and what they asked about. Plus, I know what Blaze and Elliott planned to do about interfering with the investigation."

"What? Blaze didn't say anything about that to me."

"If you want to be leader someday, you need to learn that you can call on other people to lead if they have expertise. If you'll calm down a moment then we can talk about what I learned."

Evan waited a minute while Duke pulled himself together. Evan admired Duke for many reasons, but his temper was not one of the admirable skills. Evan knew Duke was still young, and more control would come with time. He'd hoped Duke had that control already, because Evan was hoping to have Duke take over the National Alliance. Evan was ready to step down. Evan might have to readjust his plans a bit and give Duke a bit more time.

"Yeah, okay. What did you learn, Evan?"

"Obviously, the police know about people dying in the campground. Blaze heard the KKK was responsible for killing that Fry guy. He told me those rumors were out there because Fry had bad-mouthed the KKK at some meeting."

"I heard about that meeting. It was in Christiansburg."

"Blaze said the police have not done enough investigating to be sure it was the KKK. He said they didn't identify us for Freeman or the campgrounds, although we came up as a possibility, and they'll look into us.

"So, Blaze and Elliott went into the evidence area, and got an "AKIA" coin. They will plant it near where Freeman was found. Then they'll offer to go to the site, and 'discover' the coin. It'll look like the KKK was responsible."

"Okay, that's good thinking on their part. Why didn't Blaze tell me that?"

"Maybe you were too mad to listen."

"That could be true."

"Did you ask about Joe Miller?"

"No. Guess I really was mad, and not thinking."

"We don't think they can link Miller to us, but we don't know what Miller has in his house that might indicate he was a member. How about you drive by there, and if no police area around, see what you can do."

"Sure, Evan. I can do that."

"You should know that most people Blaze and Elliott called were really anxious about being found out. We might need to have a meeting to calm nerves, and direct people what to do next."

"Okay, did you want to set that up, or do you want me to?"

"I'll make a few calls myself, and see if a meeting is even

needed. I'll let you know if we'll be meeting. We also need to figure out how to help Joe's family. Why don't you think about that?"

"Yes, I'll take care of Miller's house, and think about what we can do for his family."

"Duke, remember to keep cool. It's hard to think of options when you are angry."

"Got it."

CHAPTER EIGHTEEN

Harley headed to conference room B. It was not far, just the next room down the hall from the large conference room they had just left. She and Gemma settled in to wait for Stone to appear.

Harley looked around. This room did not look much like the larger conference room. This room had a single row of tables, with enough seating for six people. The tables were clear of paperwork, though a coffee cup and plate were at the far end of the table. There was a window, with the drape left open. Harley could see cloudy skies outside, and figured more rain was on the way, or at least more humidity. There were two photos of birds on the walls. One was a red-tailed hawk, and the other a pileated woodpecker. She thought about her walk that morning. Though she had not seen a woodpecker, she had heard one. She had not seen a hawk, and hoped she would get to during her time in the area.

Stone entered a few minutes later. He commented that he was ready to discuss team activities.

"Everyone go ahead and sit down. I don't expect this to take much time, but we can be comfortable.

"Several of you know Jacey Jenner, or just met her earlier. Jacey and I have worked together on cases for several years. This time out she'll be partnering with Harley Fremont, along with Gemma. For today, your assignment Jacey and Harley is to gather as much information as you can from the medical examiner's office."

"Okay," said Jacey, "looks like my list right now would be to get any additional information on the Fry and Freeman murders, information on the death of Mr. Miller, and see if the M.E. is ready to confirm cause of death. Next, learn what more I can about the specific causes of deaths of both Wright brothers. What else?"

"Thanks, Jacey. Yes, those are the items we need from the M.E. Also, please check with the lab on the status of the ballistics tests related to Mr. Fry. If the weapon used matches one in the system already, it would make our job easier."

"Yes, we can do that. We'll have all reports to you before the 5 o'clock deadline."

Harley added, "Before we go to the M.E.'s office, I'd like to get a look at the rope and knots. I understand those are here in the lab."

"Good idea," responded Stone. "I'm curious myself about what makes them unusual. The materials themselves might provide some clues."

That was exactly what Harley had considered. Seeing the materials, and asking about any evidence they might contain, could provide them a direction for further investigation.

"Sami and Chris, we're going to split some interviews with Jeff's team. I need you to talk to the Wright and Miller families."

"Okay. We'll find out what was already learned from the notification visits, and head over immediately. I'm thinking we'll go over what we know from them already, and see if they remember more. Since we may be talking with KKK and National Alliance members when we go, we'll keep dispatch informed about each move we make."

"Of course," responded Stone. "Be quick to request backup if you feel the need. Don't take any chances."

Harley thought those interviews might be interesting, but she was not sure she'd enjoy interacting with potential extremist group members. She was happier with the assignment she had.

Stone continued, "Gray, I'd like your assistance on-site at the campground, along with Rick. I have two tasks in mind for the two of you that I think best fit your Forest Service experiences. The first is to go to the campground to look for any clues we may have missed. The second is to contact the horse owners, and get us descriptions of those horses."

Rick nodded at Gray. Gray said, "Yes, we'll take care of those items today."

Stone asked the group, "Does anyone else think of items we can add to our list for today, or have need of additional officers to conduct your work?"

"No," said Chris, "I don't think Sami and I need more officers with us, but I'm wondering if we need more people for the on-site visit?"

"Are you thinking people might come back to the camps while our team is there? Or that we missed a lot of things?"

"I'm thinking we have two campgrounds that may be tied together, we have the road between them, and the nearby trails may need to be looked at."

"Good point. Gray, Rick? What do you think?"

Gray responded, "We'll accept the extra help. We could use another two or three officers."

"Okay, Let me talk with Jeff. He's just down the hall. If he can free a couple of people we'll use them, or I'll go request more officers. I want to get this settled, so please wait here, and I'll be right back."

As they waited, talk turned to the potential of supremacist groups on the forests. Like the others, Harley was interested to hear Rick discuss the damage on the forests, and especially to the two campgrounds they had discussed in the large conference room. She found the social milieu in this part of Virginia to be very interesting. It sounded like most people considered supremacist groups and activities just a regular thing in the local communities, and it appeared to have spilled over into the forests. Harley had not been to other places that seemed to openly accept extremists.

Stone returned, and said that two sheriff area officers had volunteered to assist on the forest. They wanted to go to the sites of the original murders, and then to the horse campground.

Rick commented, "That's a bit of ground to cover, but everything is on the same district, so it is possible. We'll see them at the horse campground."

Stone told the team that he'd heard a few of the other assignments for Jeff's team. They were mostly research types of activities. His personal opinion was the area officers were probably best used in the field. He thanked Chris for recognizing that need and speaking up.

Stone remarked, "Forest Service Law Enforcement Officers Lexington and Calvin have just arrived, and Carver Grayson will update them on what is known so far. After that they'll likely be assigned interviews to conduct, unless we need them in the field.

"Okay," said Stone, "let's get started. I look forward to seeing you at the report out at 5, or hearing from you in advance. I will be here working on a plan of activity for tomorrow. This will serve as my office for the duration, so you'll know where to find me. Stay safe out there."

Harley did not think it was much of an office space for someone with such an important position. She knew Stone didn't work in Christiansburg often, but thought the sheriff could find a better space for Stone. After all, there was no good place for a laptop, few electrical plus, and no filing cabinets for storage. There was a landline phone available. Harley suspected the "office" would look a lot different the next time she saw it. She was pretty sure there would be a lot of paperwork that Stone would need to handle and file. Harley figured Stone could handle it all. She headed out the door with Gemma and Jacey.

CHAPTER NINETEEN

J acey and Harley, with Gemma, headed down to the basement, to one of the labs located there. Harley was surprised
at how much natural light there was along the hallway. She
thought of basements as dark. This one was not dark. Jacey used
her pass code to allow them entry into the second lab they came
to.

The room itself looked large to Harley. It was probably similar in size to the large conference room overhead, but that was
where the similarities ended. There was a very long counter
with a steel countertop, and lots of storage below. On top of the
counter were myriad machines that Harley could only guess as
to their purposes. There was a distinct odor in the room, and
Harley looked to see if Gemma was reacting to it. It did not appear to bother her.

More storage cabinets lined one wall, while sinks and refriger-
ators were along another wall. Red tape on the floor and blue
tape on the floor indicated where guests could and could not
stand. There was an eye flush in the corner. Harley hoped they'd
not need to use it.

They were here to look at the rope and knots they'd heard
about. These were in evidence bags in this lab.

"Carla, this is Harley Fremont and Gemma with the Forest Service. And this is Carla Wiley, head of this lab."

Carla smiled, "Great to meet you. I heard you'd be here to see
the rope and knots from the Freeman murder. I have them ready

for you." She handed the lasso, in a sealed bag, to Harley.

Harley could feel the weight of the lasso.

"Jacey, feel this. Does it feel heavier than you think a rope ought to?"

"Yes, it does to me. But I'll admit I'm not an expert on it."

Carla said she thought it was heavy too. It weighed more than the ropes they typically had processed.

"Who needs a rope this heavy?" asked Jacey. "Is there a job that would require it?"

"I hope we find out," said Harley. "Maybe moving cattle requires it? Maybe you tie it to a super duty truck?"

"Were there any fibers on it that you could identify?"

Carla told them it was apparently a new rope. She had not found any fibers beyond those from the victim.

Jacey guessed, "Perhaps that tells us the people who used it wore gloves."

"How about the length," asked Harley, "anything about it to help us identify who would use it?"

Carla told them she'd seen varying lengths, and strengths of ropes used for suicides that she had previously processed. She said there was not one size fits all. She doubted there was a specific one for lynching either.

Jacey asked to see the knots more closely. Carla told her that they had identified the knots as a honda knot, and a stopper knot. She'd had to look up the honda knot, but had seen stopper knots before. The honda knot has a round shape that helps it to slide freely along the rope it is tied around. The stopper knot typically did the job of stopping the rope from slipping out of the knot.

Carla commented, "When tied correctly the stopper always works."

Harley gulped a little at that comment. She was thinking the stopper did its job too well, and Mr. Freeman had died as a result. "How awful," she thought, "to have died that way."

It occurred to her that Mr. Freeman must have fought hard when she realized his fate. She asked Jacey, "Do we know yet if Mr.

Freeman had scrapes on his hands or skin under his fingernails?"

"That'll be our next stop. We'll need to ask the M.E., Hal Quinones."

"Carla, what do we know from the ballistics tests?" asked Jacey.

"They're still being conducted, so I'll have to get back to you."

They thanked Carla for her assistance, and went back upstairs, and then outside to head to Jacey's vehicle. There were far fewer vehicles there now. Jacey saw the Navion, and asked if this was Harley's motor home. She told her yes, "it was home, sweet home." Jacey said she'd looked at those motor homes herself, and they were impressive. She thought the workmanship was in a class by itself, and wished she could afford one. Harley pointed out that she had no brick and mortar home, and that was how she could afford the motor home. She observed that everyone had choices to make, and that was her choice. Harley also told Jacey that she'd like a small ranch in the future, so eventually she'd be back in bricks and mortar.

On the drive, Harley mentioned Carla's lack of specificity about the rope weight and length. Jacey told Harley she'd worked with Carla for years, and trusted her to conduct superior work. She said Carla was never one to simply concur with the opinions of others. She waited until she had facts to share.

"Okay," said Harley, "then we know, based on Carla's work, that the rope was heavy, and there were two knots that were used. The stopper and the honda."

"Yes, and we know there were no fibers," said Jacey.

"I am wondering who uses rope like this, and knots like this."

"I have an idea, but I need an expert to weigh-in. Okay, we're here now, let's see what Hal has to say. Maybe I can get some support for my idea that is brewing."

"Care to share that idea yet, Jacey?"

"Not yet. I really prefer to be more cautious."

The Medical Examiner's office had not been a long drive. Harley saw it was another two-story building, with a brick façade, and glass doors. It looked like it and the sheriff's office had been built around the same time period. Like the sheriff's office, there was a check-in counter, and a security area. Once they passed through security, Harley could see the similarities ended. It was quiet as they walked along the corridor. Harley could hear a slight squeak in her shoes, and the light tap of Gemma's paws. They headed to the second floor, and approached the receptionist. He told them it would be a bit of a wait, and to please be comfortably seated.

"We have time, you sure you don't want to share your ideas with me?"

"Hey, tell me about that ranch plan, Harley."

"Okay, I'll take that as a 'no.'"

"Sorry, it's far-fetched, and I'd rather wait."

"Fair enough. I hope I don't have to wait a long time to learn it. I'm not good with being patient."

"You're kidding, right? You must have endless patience to train animals as well as you do."

"Oh, I'm not kidding. With dogs I have lots of patience, with people, not so much."

They chatted amiably while they waited. It was about ten minutes until Hal breezed in the reception area.

"Jacey! It's so wonderful to see you. How're your mom and dad?"

Harley was expecting someone distant, someone who spoke in scientific terms. She smiled about that preconception. Harley instantly liked the M.E.

"Dad is doing well, Mom is a bit more frail than I'd like. I know they'd love to see you soon."

"I look forward to seeing them. Maybe the four of us could go to dinner soon. My treat. Who's this?"

"Where are my manners? This is my partner, Harley Fremont, and her working dog, Gemma."

"Lovely to meet you. That's a handsome dog. Let's head into my office to talk."

Harley had not anticipated such a nice office. The floor was wall-to-wall plush carpeting. The desk was a mahogany wood, with a glass cover over the top. All the filing cabinets matched the desk. A matching credenza held dozens of books. On the top were several small statues; which upon closer inspection were various tasteful awards. On the walls were various degrees, and photos of the M.E. with other important people.

"Ted, can you bring some coffee, and a bowl of water?"

"Yes, sir. Right away," responded the receptionist.

"Here we are," said Hal, "please have a seat. We have lots to go over. Thanks, Ted. We really appreciate it."

"Thank you for considering Gemma's needs. That is very kind."

"You're welcome Ms. Fremont. May I call you Harley? Call me Hal."

"Thanks, Hal. Yes, Harley is fine."

Hal spent some time going over the specifics of Mr. Fry's death. He described manner of death. He described the few clues they had. He also mentioned they were still conducting some tests.

Once again Harley shuddered a bit. She wondered if Mr. Fry knew his death was imminent. He must have since the shooter was facing him. Harley imagined looking down the barrel of a gun. It made Harley think about the type of weapon used. She knew the bullets were still in the process of being tested. Carla from the lab would call if they identified the weapon, and weapon owner.

Hal described the death of Mr. Freeman. He told the pair that Freeman had skin under his nails. They were testing if they had DNA in the system to match. Again, there was no answer yet. Hal had confirmed this to be murder by strangulation, caused by a hanging. Hal told them Mr. Freeman had his hands zip tied behind his back. That was not something they had heard before.

Harley wondered if Jacey was as disturbed by this method of death as she was. Then again, she was an officer, so maybe not. She'd have to ask her later. Harley reminded herself to give as much care to Mr. Fry's death as to Mr. Freeman. But it was Freeman's death that she felt in her gut. She thought that perhaps it was because it seemed race-based to her, and she was sensitive about prejudice and racism.

After they left the office, Jacey asked if they could stop for a bite to eat, and talk through the next steps. The "Quick Bite" was quiet on this late afternoon. They had almost stopped Harley from bringing Gemma in, but Jacey flashed her badge, and they were seated. They placed their orders.

To Harley, it looked like most every diner she had been in before. There was the long counter with various types of desserts displayed. There were tables in the middle, and booths down the side. The seats were covered with vinyl. Harley could attest that they'd just cleaned them, because her booth seat was still a little damp. Gemma laid her head on Harley's feet, and settled in for a nap.

"I'm thinking about the rope weight," said Jacey, "and the knots. I have a friend I'm going to text the photos to, and ask him a question. When he responds I'll share my theory."

Jacey sent her text. Right away she had a phone call. It was Carla. They had matched the weapon to an owner. That information would be sent to Jacey's email at the Sheriff's office. Then before Jacey could eat another bite, a text response came in. Jacey smiled, and told Harley, "We have a lead!"

"I have a friend who is a well-known rodeo photographer, named Ross Morgan. Ross tells me our photos are of a weighted lasso, a honda knot, and a stopper knot. He has seen these many times on the rodeo circuit. This may be the break we need on the Freeman case."

"That's fantastic! What do we do next?"

"For now, we head back to the office and attend the meeting. Let's hear if anyone there confirms this, or sends us in another direction. Sound okay?"

"Yes. Great idea you had there, partner!"

Jacey actually blushed a bit. Normally her partners were not as effusive as Harley. She remarked, "Remember your 'cattle' comment earlier? That's what made me think of the rodeo."

CHAPTER TWENTY

During his afternoon in the office, Stone had familiarized himself with the campground locations and forest information. He mused over how quickly his "desk" was being covered in paper.

As he looked over a map he was a bit stunned to realize he had camped before in one of the campgrounds being investigated. It was only on one occasion, but it struck him that it could have been him at the campground when the three murders happened. Stone reminded himself that although he sometimes went to remote locations on the forest, he was never unarmed. Still, this might serve as a reminder to be extra careful on future trips, especially since Genevieve would be along on them. Stone again worked to organize the paperwork he'd collected so far, but he had no filing system in place, making his attempts futile. He'd have to figure out how to fix that issue. He thought to himself, "The cases are a big puzzle, but that doesn't mean my office has to look the part." He thought about what he might need to help. Perhaps he could find filing cabinets, a bulletin board to post the maps, and whatever else he could find to get organized. He knew he worked better when he could lay his hands on the right paperwork at the right time.

When it was time, Stone made his way back to the large conference room. He'd arrived a little early, and watched as several people from the earlier meeting arrived for the closeout of the day. He nodded to Jacey as she and Harley entered the room. Stone cast an admiring glance at Gemma. She was a good-looking dog. He'd have to look into the breed, maybe consider one for himself. "I wonder what Genevieve would think about that?"

Carver Grayson called the meeting to order. He pulled up a file onto the smart whiteboard screen. On it was an outline of the murder of Mr. Fry, which included facts known so far, inquiries under way, and a timeline. Carver requested a report from Jeff and Stone related to Mr. Fry.

Stone listened as Jeff spoke. Jeff mentioned that although a few members had been unable to attend, they had called in with information. As Jeff relayed findings, Carver added those items to the electronic file. Carver told everyone he was doing that so findings would appear on the board, and could be confirmed that he was writing exactly what he was told.

Jeff continued, "The Fry family was still quite distraught, and did not have much more to report beyond what they'd said during the notification. They said they were quite certain Mr. Fry would not willingly go to the forest."

Although the team was not ready to confirm this conclusion, it appeared Mr. Fry was taken to the forest against his will. That meant he'd been picked up from somewhere else. They would need to look into that. There could be video evidence of who had taken him.

Jeff also said that Mr. Fry's social media posts displayed his increasing activism. His family confirmed Fry had been talking more about the state of affairs in the nation and the local community. The family had not known he'd spoken up at a town hall meeting, but agreed with all he'd said.

Stone declared they'd had a big break on the case. The lab had information about the bullets extracted from Mr. Fry.

"The bullets matched to a weapon in the system. The weapon belongs to Mr. Toby Burden."

Stone explained that the weapon was in the system due to a shooting incident five years previously, a hunting accident that had wounded his son, Carl Burden. It had not been a life threatening wound, but had required reporting by the hospital where Carl had been treated.

Jeff added that a just completed interview with Mr. Toby Burden at his home indicated the weapon was not currently in his possession. He'd claimed it was "not missing," so he had not reported it stolen.

Jeff continued, "In fact, Mr. Burden reported that his sons left for a camping trip yesterday, and probably had the weapon with them. He said no one else would have had access to it. The weapon was not where Mr. Burden thought it should be, so he figured the sons must have it with them. The father didn't know exactly where his sons went, or when they would return from the camping trip.

"Mr. Burden said he 'knew his sons,' and they would 'never shoot anyone.' He was sure they were home the day of Mr. Fry's murder, and would vouch for them. He claimed his family were not members of any supremacist group, nor did they know any supremacist group members."

Jeff said that he would also like to report on some related research from his team.

"Yes," replied Carver, "go ahead."

"Our research indicated many active supremacist groups in the ten-county area served by the forest. The most frequent activities were reported for the Ku Klux Klan, and also the National Alliance."

Jeff reported a decline in the membership of the National Alliance over the past twenty years. He also noted that the National Alliance had tended to recruit at local events, such as fairs, and they had been known to recruit at campgrounds, but their information could not confirm the National Alliance had recruited at Gopher Flats or Beggar Flats Horse Campground.

Jeff also reported the KKK recruited actively, but was not known for campground recruiting. "But it seems like that was actually the case on Sunday in the forest. The KKK was probably there to recruit new members. I know Stone has information to add to this discussion."

"Well, I have some new information that needs investigating. It ties into the KKK discussion. Two officers today found a coin near the location of Mr. Freeman's death. It was not seen during previous trips to the site, but we have it now. It says 'AKIA,' which means 'A Klansman I Am.' The saying is associated with the KKK. We'll be processing the coin to see if we can link the coin to the Freeman murder, or the KKK to the murder. Should this evidence be linked, then it is possible the murders of Fry and Freeman were committed by the Ku Klux Klan."

After checking on any other new information or any questions, Carver pulled up the file on the Freeman killing, and asked for Stone to report out.

"We may have a lead in the Freeman case. The lynching was done with a weighted lasso. On the lasso were two knots: the honda knot, and a stopper knot. Our team confirmed the knot types to be typical for some rodeo events. If so, the perpetrators may have a link to the rodeo. Two team members will be following up on that. We have also learned Mr. Freeman had some skin under his fingernails, and it's being analyzed. In addition, we learned his hands had been zip tied behind his back."

After checking for additional information and questions, Carver asked to move along to the murders at the campground.

Jeff began, "A camp visitor had taken several photos of cars parked outside the Gopher Flats campground on Sunday, and from those photos, several cars were identified. As mentioned previously, these vehicles belonged to Mr. Orville Wright, Mr. Junior Kendall, Mr. Herb Smith, and Mr. Ben Rover.

"We have requested a search warrant for the vehicles, and the homes of the vehicle owners. The burned vehicles at the campground belonged to Mr. Orville Wright and Mr. Gerald Brown. The Brown vehicle has not been reported as stolen. A warrant is being sought for the Brown's residence."

Stone added to the reporting. "We heard from the M.E. that Mr. Miller died from the results of an explosion of the gas tank of the Wright vehicle. Our lab reports that the weapon located near Mr. Miller was registered in his name, and wasn't fired recently.

"Both the Wrights died as a result of gunshot injuries. Orville Wright took two bullets to his chest and died instantly on-site. Wilbur Wright was shot in the back twice, and bled out on-site. The bullets indicated these shots were fired from the same weapon, a semi-automatic pistol, from about ninety feet away. The bullets could not be traced to a particular gun; it was not in the system.

"Additional evidence is still being examined, including shell casings for fingerprints, bullets for fingerprints, and plastic ware for fingerprints."

Stone went on the mention that the horses reported missing from the Beggar Flats campground continued to be missing.

"The first was a bay, it was light reddish brown with black points, also called a mane for non-horse people. The other horse was a chestnut, which is reddish in color. Both owners have produced evidence of ownership, and provided photos to our team."

When Stone finished, Carver requested questions or additional comments. Hearing none he move on to the oversight team.

Carver noted, "The oversight team has added this new chart to indicate how these murders might be linked, as well as places they seem to have no overlap."

Carver had pulled up a file with a couple of columns. The first was titled "Support/Commonalities," and the second "Lack of support/Differences."

"There were a few items you have reported that support the idea that the murders were linked. The first is supremacy groups. It sounded like the KKK would have reason to want to kill Mr. Fry, and we believe two supremacist groups, the KKK and the National Alliance, frequent one or both of the campgrounds. Plus, we think these were the two groups who clashed at the campground. We are unsure at this point, but Mr. Freeman's lynching might be linked to a supremacist group, possibly the KKK. It is still too early to confirm, but so far supremacy groups would be in the 'support' column."

Carver continued, "Camping is a second possible commonality. The campers were at Beggar Flats and Gopher Flats, and the Burden sons were camping. Maybe this linkage applies only to the third set of murders. It remains to be seen.

"The third commonality is recruiting by supremacist groups. Recruiting in nearby counties included some recruiting in campgrounds, but more often at local events. Again this is a loose connection.

"Another commonality was horses. Again, this might be for campgrounds only, but the rodeo linkage might prove interesting, and link Mr. Freeman's murder to horses, and maybe even the three deaths in the campground. It is possible, but not probable.

"Finally, the key difference is the different types of murder. Gunshot deaths are wildly different from a lynching. Plus, one person died as a result of an explosion. Those differences may prove difficult to overcome. There is a lot of work ahead of us still."

Carver thanked everyone, and said the next day should bring more clarity.

Stone was impressed with how much information was gathered on the first day. He felt that it was quite a break with the bullet matched to a weapon already. Once the Burden sons were located they'd likely have the killer or killers of Mr. Fry, despite the unlikely alibi provided by Toby Burden.

Stone had hoped his team would catch a similar break with matching bullets to weapons for the campground murders, but no results were in yet.

Stone planned to stay a bit late that evening, and type ideas for next steps for his team members. He knew Jeff would be doing the same thing.

Stone was hoping a donut or two were still in the break room upstairs. Add a little coffee or a coke, and he'd be good to go.

CHAPTER
TWENTY-ONE

Shrimp was in the family room and heard his dad on the phone. He heard the tremor in his dad's voice. Whether it was from fear or anger, Shrimp could not discern. He gave a quick rundown of his own deeds lately. He was fairly sure he had done nothing wrong, so maybe this was not about him.

Junior yelled, "Family meeting in the kitchen. Now!"

Hearing his dad yell did nothing to settle Shrimp's nerves.

Upon entering the kitchen, Shrimp watched his mom lower the flames on all the burners on the stove. The aroma of bacon, grits, and gravy was making Shrimp quite hungry. It took a few moments for the import of his dad's words to wander through his food aroma-infused brain.

Junior revealed that the Burdens were in real trouble.

"Apparently Carl or Jay used Toby's gun when the Alien was shot. The police came to interview him, and told him it was his gun that killed the Alien. They had asked Toby for an explanation, and asked him questions. It was all Toby's fault, according to him. Toby said he'd cleaned the weapon, and rather than putting it in the gun safe inside the house right away, he'd been distracted. He left it in the garage with the other weapons. When his sons picked up a weapon Sunday morning, they must have picked up his registered gun."

In his mind, Shrimp could picture Red handing the gun to Carl at the campground. He figured Red was feeling terrible.

"To make matters worse, when Carl and Jay took the horses out on the trail, they had the gun in their possession, thinking it was unregistered. That means they'll use it for protection. Or they would use it against the Orville and Wilbur's killers, should they find them on the trail. If they do, there'll be even more evidence against them.

"If the brothers are found by the police, they'll have the weapon on them. Toby is really worried because he can't see a good outcome for them."

Junior reported that Toby wanted a few of the Klavern members to meet and talk about options for getting the Burden brothers to safety.

Junior added, "Toby provided an alibi for Carl and Jay to the police, and said that they were simply away on a camping trip. But he had the clear impression the police did not believe him.

"Toby also told the police that the boys were home on the day Mr. Fry was killed. But again, he did not think the police believed him. He thinks his boys are looking at serious time in prison. He feels terrible, and wants help."

Shrimp looked at his family. They had been mourning the loss of Orville and Wilbur, and now their cousins Carl and Jay were in trouble. It was more than they should have to bear in a short period of time. He could see the weariness and sadness etched on their faces. But he also saw determination in his dad's face. Junior looked like a man with a plan.

Junior told them that a handful of Klan members would meet to discuss their options later that night.

"The Ross family wants to lead the meeting. But they don't want the meeting to be held at their house. So, we'll have the meeting at the Parker's house.

"It's to be a small meeting, so I'll represent our family."

Junior noted, though, that he had time to eat before he left.

Shrimp considered requesting to tag along, but his dad had already laid down the law. It did not include Shrimp. Shrimp didn't know what to make of that. Didn't his dad think he was old enough to contribute? Maybe he had some ideas the older men might not have thought of. Maybe it was time for young people to take over the Klavern. He'd have to talk to Red about that. Maybe Red was old enough to be included. Maybe only the men got to go.

Shrimp ate and ate. It seemed like that was most of what he did lately, beyond gaming and sleeping. After his dad left for the meeting, Shrimp wandered to the front room, while his mom handled the dishes. Shrimp sat on the couch and started to think about the situation with the Burden brothers. He wondered why they couldn't just call or text them to warn them not to come home. They could tell them to hide the weapon. Then he remembered that he did not have a connection at the campground, so the trails weren't likely to have connection either. He wondered if they did have a connection if they could hear over the sound of the horses walking along the trail.

Shrimp texted to Carl's number, but it looked like the message was not delivered. It was a bit later that he got scared thinking that if the brothers got caught, would his text message appear and get him in trouble too? "Fuck! How stupid am I?"

Shrimp also considered how self-centered he was being right now. He'd seen Carl and Jay head off to the horses. They didn't have camp gear, and what about food and water? How long would they stay away? Where were they sleeping? How were they feeding the horses? Shrimp hoped they knew what they were doing. Maybe they had supplies, and Shrimp just had not noticed. They acted like they had a solid plan.

Then Shrimp went to his room, and lay on his bed. His room was small, but it held the essentials he needed, including his bed, a dresser that fit inside the closet, and a desk made up of cement blocks with a board across it. That desk held his gaming and computer set-up.

Shrimp got to thinking about the Alien, Mr. Fry. Shrimp had not agreed with what Mr. Fry had to say, but he was not sure killing the man was a good thing. One day he had seen Mr. Fry, and told his family about it, and then Mr. Fry was dead. Was that his fault? Well, it was done, and he had not pulled the trigger. Shrimp wondered if the entire Klavern would be blamed for the actions of the inner circle. Would he end up in jail? That thought made Shrimp exceedingly uncomfortable. He looked around his room and tried to imagine an even smaller space in jail, housed with criminals. He was horrified at the thought of endless days in jail with no gaming system.

Shrimp thought of the Klavern as extended family. But now that prison might be an option, he was reconsidering. Is this how he wanted to live his life? He was not sure killing people was the answer. What, then, was the answer? Shrimp did still believe in many tenets of the Klan, but doubts were creeping in. He'd have to think about what kind of life he would have without the Klavern. That was scary; his whole life was with them.

By late morning, Shrimp had drifted off to sleep. He was sound asleep when he heard knocking on the front door. He heard the announcement, "Police, open up!"

CHAPTER TWENTY-TWO

Harley and Jacey had made an early morning appointment with the Southern Rodeo Association. The headquarters was in Four Oaks, North Carolina, but Jacey had called the manager there, who said it would be better to try the local contact at Felts Park in Galax, Virginia. He'd told Jacey that the local contact would know rodeo riders in the state, especially those in the local area.

Jacey and Harley were to meet Cliff Bronson at his office near the rodeo grounds at Felts Park. It took just over an hour to drive there. They had time to talk about themselves a bit, particularly their histories in law enforcement. Harley was impressed by Jacey's career, especially since Jacey was about fifteen years younger than Harley. Jacey admired how Harley had moved from her husband's death to where she was today. Jacey said she loved hearing about the dog training and tracking adventures that Harley had been on.

Once at the park grounds, Jacey and Harley passed through a huge parking lot of compacted dirt. They exited their vehicle and walked past several buildings, most of them were small storage sheds. Harley wondered what was in them. The park looked like it was home to many activities, and that the rodeo was just one among them. Harley imagined the sheds held items for various recreation activities, and perhaps grounds keeping.

The largest building in the row, which looked like an office, had the door open.

"I think we're here," said Jacey.

They could see a few desks and office chairs, some computers, and dozens of rodeo photos on the walls.

"Welcome, please come in!"

Right away Harley saw photographs of past rodeos.

"Is that you I see in some of those photos? Do you still participate in rodeos?" asked Harley.

"Well, I may have been a bit younger then. I haven't been in a rodeo event for many years, unless you count the opening fanfare. Then, I'd say I ride all the time. That's a gorgeous dog! Is it friendly?"

Harley introduced herself, Jacey, and Gemma. She had Gemma sit, and then shake hands with Mr. Bronson.

Jacey asked, so Mr. Bronson explained what his current position entailed. Then he asked, "Can I get either of you a fresh cup of coffee?"

Neither accepted, but Harley requested water for herself and Gemma. Once he provided water, they all settled in. Jacey and Harley sat on one side of a desk, and Mr. Bronson sat on the other.

They showed Mr. Bronson some photos. Mr. Bronson confirmed the weighted lasso was one he was familiar with. He commented that several rodeo events included the weighted lasso, but the honda knot and stopper knot, were not as consistently used. Mr. Bronson told them that the knots were most often used in roping events, more specifically, for calf roping.

Jacey told Mr. Bronson about the lynching. He was appalled. Once it dawned on him why these two were asking him questions, Mr. Bronson asked, "Do you think a rodeo rider did that to that poor man?"

"We're not sure yet, Mr. Bronson," said Jacey.

"You'd better call me Cliff, my dad is Mr. Bronson."

Harley replied, "Thanks, Cliff. What can you tell us about the rodeo circuit, and about the calf roping event?"

Cliff spent a little while explaining what the header and heeler do, the timing, how events were tracked over different locations, how points and winnings were accrued, and other specifics. Then he remarked, "Rodeo riders are just good ole boys. They're not racists, and they're not murderers. I'm sure our guys weren't involved."

"We appreciate that you think so. Help us prove that. Let's talk about all the calf-roping teams on your circuit. How many teams are we talking about? We'd like your thoughts on these folks as we talk through the list. I think we can start with who is currently around, or has been nearby for the past week or two."

Cliff provided them a long list of pairings for the calf roping events. Most were not local, and some who were local were recently or currently away for riding events.

Jacey told Cliff they would follow-up with trying to contact all the people he identified as local. She asked Cliff to not contact them himself. Then Jacey walked a short distance away, and called Stone so she could provide the names. Stone would work with Jeff to compare those against a list the team had developed of possible supremacist group members. Jacey said they'd be back to the office in an hour to look over the results.

They thanked Cliff for his time and cooperation, and started driving back to the office. It was a somber ride back until Harley couldn't take it anymore. "Is this a good time to say this isn't my first rodeo?"

Jacey laughed. "Woody said you had a sense of humor. I was wondering when we'd see it."

"Well, it's a long drive so we have to keep entertained."

Jacey wanted to know more about the commands Gemma knew, and how Harley taught them, so they spent the remainder of the drive on the topic. Gemma slept all the way back.

Once at the offices, Harley took Gemma for a walk. Then they went into the motor home for food for Gemma. She left Gemma inside the motor home so she'd have time to eat.

When Harley joined Jacey, she learned they discovered only

a few names overlapped between the rodeo list and the alleged supremacist list. Four of these people had been contacted, and had verifiable alibis for the time of Mr. Freeman's murder. These would be investigated, but they appeared to be solid.

There was one team they were unable able to contact. The two members were Wendell Wilton and Dave Speller. Cliff had spoken very highly of these two, having known both for many years. Still, Jacey and Harley decided to set off to try and locate the pair. Harley got Gemma, and they all loaded back into Jacey's vehicle.

Jacey told Harley, "We're headed to Poplar Hill. Both men have homes in the same housing area."

The homes were small, but each had enough outdoor space for horses, and a small barn. As an outsider, Harley thought the area looked bucolic, and a wonderful place to live. It looked like most of the neighbors had the same type of set-up.

They arrived first at Wilton's home. His vehicle was there, but no one answered the door. They drove a short distance away to Speller's house. Again, they found a vehicle, but no one answered the door. At Speller's house they saw a neighbor outside. The neighbor, John Whitman, said he'd seen Speller and Wilton getting ready to take their horses for a ride.

Whitman said, "It's not unusual to see them do that. They ride their horses often together."

"Was there anything different this time?" asked Jacey.

"Well, I did notice something different. Both had lots of gear on the horses, and their guns. It was unusual, so I asked Dave about that. He said they were going to ride the Appalachian Trail for a few days, and would be camping out. He said they weren't sure what kinds of animals they might encounter so they were taking guns too."

Jacey asked, "How did they seem to you? Were they anxious?"

"No, not at all. What I saw were two buddies, who were happy to be going out for a ride."

"Are you sure they said the Appalachian Trail?" asked Harley.

"Yes, I've never known them to camp out, and take so much

stuff, but I'm sure of what they said. They said 'Appalachian Trail.'"

"Well, that trail doesn't allow horses, so that's why I ask."

"I don't know anything about that," said Mr. Whitman. "Just seemed like they were trying something new."

"Anything else, Mr. Whitman?"

"Nope. That's all I know. Them fellas haven't done anything wrong have they? It'd be a shame, them being rodeo guys and all."

"Nothing we know of, just checking in. Thanks, Mr. Whitman."

Harley found herself wondering why Wilton and Speller would head to the A.T., and not a local trail. All she could come up with was the thought that the A.T. led to other states, while the local trails did not. Maybe these were the guys they were looking for, and maybe they were trying to escape on horseback via the A.T.

Just after the interview of the neighbor, Jacey received a call with alarming news.

CHAPTER TWENTY-THREE

"Jacey, this is Stone. We have a problem that I think Harley and Gemma are best to help resolve. Can I speak with her?"

Jacey handed the sat phone to Harley.

"It's Stone, and he needs to speak with you."

"Hello, Stone. This is Harley."

"Hello, Harley. We have a job for you and Gemma, with Jacey. Jimmy Wilson, the FPO sent to the Beggar Flats Horse Campground, made his first check-in call today, but missed the second one. We're concerned about his welfare. It's possible he just forgot the time, but his boss said that was very unlikely. He said it was not like Jimmy to forget. Can you head out to Beggar Flats Horse Campground to see what you can do?"

"Of course, we'll leave right away. I sure hope he's okay.

"Stone, we just found out the possible suspects for the Freeman killing, Wilton and Speller, are on horseback headed to the Appalachian Trail.

"We're going to my motor home so we can pack for the trail. It won't take long. We'll check on Jimmy, give you a call, and then hike the trail a bit to see if we can confirm the suspects are headed that way. We'll call when we have more information."

"Thanks, Harley. We're anxious to hear about Jimmy. Stay safe out there."

Jacey, Harley, and Gemma drove back to Christiansburg to make a short stop at the motor home. Harley added more food to the supply she already had on her, added to Gemma's pack, picked out a few more pairs of socks, and her bedroll. Jacey commented that she'd like to drop by her house, but that was too far in the wrong direction, so she'd make do with the clothes she had on. She borrowed a backpack from Harley, and added some supplies, and a bedroll.

They arrived at the Beggar Flats Horse Campground about an hour later. They walked both loops, and did not spot Jimmy. Gemma stopped at a trailhead at the end of the second loop, and sat down. She barked at Harley.

Harley explained, "Gemma scented someone on the trail going this direction."

They headed down the trail, with Gemma leading the way. Less than a half-mile away they heard someone calling for help. It was Jimmy Wilson. He had seen them and called out.

Jimmy was hurt. He had a sizable knot on his head, and he had a gash in his leg. There was quite a bit of blood. They rushed to his aid.

"Jimmy, are you alright?"

Jimmy responded, "Sort of. I'm pretty sure I passed out. I don't think I've been here all that long, but I can't be sure. I tried to stand and walk out of here. Then I got dizzy, and I was not completely sure what direction to take. So I ended up just staying here. I'm so glad you're here."

"You did the right thing, Jimmy. It's best not to move until you get examined."

Harley took out her satellite phone and handed it to Jacey.

"Jacey, call for help while I attend to Jimmy."

Jacey moved back toward the campground to a more open area where she had a good signal. Jacey called to request medical assistance.

While Jacey did that, Harley dug some things from her vest. She had a few medical supplies with her, and did what she could to clean Jimmy's head and leg wounds.

Harley and Gemma stayed with Jimmy. Jacey told them she would walk back to the campground to meet the paramedics.

It looked to Harley like Jimmy had either been left in a sheltered spot, or he scooted over to have cover over his head. He was off the trail, but would be easily seen, or could easily see people on the trail. Unfortunately, it had not been a busy trail that day, with the campground closed.

"I'm really grateful you guys came looking for me."

"Everyone was concerned about you. I'm relieved to see you. It looks like Gemma is happy too."

Gemma took an instant liking to Jimmy, and leaned her body into him. Jimmy said he felt stupid to get hit like that, but Gemma made it worthwhile. He stroked her ears and muzzle, and hugged her.

"This is a really good dog. Gemma, you're a good dog."

As they waited, Harley showed Jimmy several photos that she had downloaded. He passed through several photos before he said, "This guy, and this one here."

Jimmy had identified both Wendell Wilton and Dave Speller as the men who had dragged him down the trail. They had warned Jimmy not to follow them.

"This guy hit me with his gun, and I think he knocked me out. I don't know how I hurt my leg, but possibly when I fell."

Harley said, "That was Wendell Wilton that you identified."

The longer they waited, the angrier Jimmy got. He said, "I was on the far loop of the campground, and when I got back toward the first loop I saw those two guys walking the area where the Wrights were shot. So I approached them, asking if I could help, and they overtook me."

Jimmy was quiet for a bit, and then said, "I have been thinking about my FPO status, and I don't like always being unarmed. If I had been a law enforcement officer, then things would have gone differently. Now I'm convinced I need to complete the training at FLETC, and become an officer. I don't ever want anything like this to happen again. I'll request the training, and I hope the forest supervisor will approve it."

Harley could understand how that might feel to be exposed to danger like Jimmy had been. For Jimmy's sake, she hoped Givens would approve the training. She thought perhaps she'd mention the idea to Bill. Harley didn't know if Bill could help or not, so she didn't mention it to Jimmy.

Jimmy told Harley, "It's really likely that the two men continued down this trail, but I can't be sure. I didn't see them leave. I'm sorry I'm not more helpful."

"You're doing just fine, Jimmy. You've given us lots of information to go on. Did you see their horses?"

"Yes, sorry, didn't I say that? They each had a horse, with lots of gear on them. I know for sure that Wilton had a gun. I don't know about the other guy."

"You didn't see another weapon?"

"I don't think so. I should have paid more attention to detail. I was focused on how they were searching the area."

"You did your job. I'm sorry you got hurt in the process."

Jimmy paused then said, "I was surprised. I was not expecting to see other people in the campground because the signs all said it was closed. I should have known they were up to no good. I should have radioed for assistance."

"Where is your radio?"

"I had it. Those guys must have taken it from me."

"Did they take anything else?"

"No, I only had the radio with me. Everything else is in my vehicle."

"How does your head feel? And your leg?"

"Both are throbbing."

Medical assistance arrived for Jimmy. It looked like he'd need to go to the hospital, possibly for overnight observation. Jimmy said he'd rather help locate the men, but he could barely stand and walk. The medics used a gurney to move Jimmy.

Everyone went back to the campground. Jimmy thanked Jacey, Harley, and Gemma, as he was loaded into the emergency vehicle. He told Harley to give Gemma a treat for her good work.

Harley and Jacey went to Jacey's service vehicle to get their supplies, and that treat for Gemma.

Jacey told Harley that she called Stone while she was waiting for medical assistance to arrive. While Stone knew what they were doing, Jacey wanted the team to know what trail they were taking, and what direction they were headed.

"Jacey, I have a device that lets the Forest Service know where we are. My friend Violet developed it."

Harley pulled out her data pad to show Jacey. She explained that it had a tracking device so that the Forest Service staff could track her movements. Except, if no satellite connection were nearby, it would lose track of them until it picked up again.

"That's impressive. I like knowing we have that along. So, rather than a general idea of our direction, people can find us if we need help."

Harley sent a message on her sat phone to Violet. Harley needed to know if the trail they were taking connected to the Appalachian Trail. Violet responded that they were about four miles from the connecting point.

Jacey called Stone again after Harley filled her in on what Jimmy had relayed.

"Jimmy confirmed it was Wilton and Speller who had hurt him. He said he'd been on the second loop of the campground, and when he came back, the two men were searching the location where the Wright brothers had died."

They decided it was looking more and more like these two were involved in some way. It might also mean they were in the campground when the melee happened. They speculated the men were searching for bullet casings.

Jacey asked, " Do you think Wilton and Speller could be responsible for Mr. Freeman's murder and the murders of the Wright brothers?"

They all knew it'd take more work to get those answers. It made Stone reconsider the "AKIA" coin the two area officers had found. Now it sounded as if the National Alliance might be involved. Stone said he'd step up the analyses of that coin. He would also speak with Carver Grayson, and ask about the two officers who'd found the coins.

Jacey, Harley, and Gemma set out on the path.

Harley was not sure how Jacey felt about all the walking they'd been doing already, and would continue to do, but for her and Gemma, it was like coming home. This was what they knew; they were in their element. Finding Jimmy and tracking Wilton and Speller was how they could assist the investigations. Harley thought it was time to be a resolver. She and Gemma set a fast pace.

CHAPTER TWENTY-FOUR

Evan called Duke Kent. He needed to update Duke, and find out what Duke had been doing. He had reason to worry, and reason to think Duke was responsible.

"Duke, have you heard from my son or Dave?"

"I called them both again, but now neither one is taking my calls. I went by their houses, and they didn't answer the door. They have some explaining to do! They should know a call from you or me means National Alliance business. And they should always answer the door to us."

"Before we talk about that, tell me what you found at the Miller house."

"Oh, that did not go well. I went over, but a police car was there. I tried again, but it was still there."

"Did you try calling Miller's wife?"

"No, I figured she had her hands full."

"Maybe you could have kept her calm. Maybe you could have reminded her to tell the police nothing."

"How come I'm the bad guy here?"

"I didn't say that Duke. I'm trying to relay how to handle things for when this all gets turned over to you. You'll need to remain calm and reasonable. You'll need to think about different actions you could take."

"Maybe I'm past calm and reasonable. Tell me, Evan, did you hear from your son?"

"Wait. Did you say earlier you went by to see Dave and Wendell?"

"Yes, I did. They did not answer at either house, though both their cars were there. I saw their horses were gone, so maybe they're on trails that have no Wi-Fi."

"Good, now you're giving them the benefit of the doubt."

"I'm not concerned about that right now, or how you think I ought to lead. I'm concerned your son screwed up. You didn't answer my question. Did you hear from Wendell?"

Evan paused a moment before answering.

"Yes, I spoke with both before they took their horses out riding."

"Why the hesitation, Evan? What are you hiding?"

"I found out they were leaving. Not for just a trail ride. Leaving for good. I tried to stop them. They said you had really upset them with your calls. That your anger had made them think you would blame them for Freeman's death, even though it was all your idea."

"Leaving where, Evan? For how long?"

"Maybe you're not hearing me, Duke. Your anger alarmed them."

"Maybe you're not hearing me, Evan! Where did they go? When will they be back?"

"They left for the Appalachian Trail. They know the trail leads out of state. They went into hiding, Duke. They wouldn't tell me where exactly, or who they might turn to. I tried to talk Wendell out of it."

"What? Why didn't you stop them?"

"I told them to stay put. I told them that no one was going to identify them as Freeman's killers. Just like I'm telling you, no one is going to know you were responsible."

"So they just left?"

"Yes, Duke, they're gone. They had made up their minds before they even called me."

Duke practically shouted, "They should have stood their ground! You should have told your son he cannot leave!"

"I told them that National Alliance members would provide rock solid alibis for them. I asked them to remain calm and think things through. They're men, Duke, and can make their own decisions."

"Evan, their leaving only makes them look guilty. What if the police find out anything? This will confirm their suspicions about the National Alliance, even after Blaze and Elliott tried to redirect them."

"Blaze will keep us informed if anyone is searching for them."

Duke was sputtering obscenities.

Evan let Duke go on for a while. "Do you feel better yet, Duke?"

"No! I do not!" yelled Duke.

"Duke, I tried very hard to talk them out of leaving. I told them they had the support of the entire group. But they said they had participated in the killing of the black man, and were truly scared for their lives.

"They said they didn't think that Edwards and Green could do much to slow down law enforcement. So they were going to take care of themselves.

"They were packed, and on the way, before they even called me. There was not anything I could do to change what happened. Do you think I want my son to go into hiding?"

"What I think is you did nothing. I think you let your son get away."

"Now that Wendell has made a decision, and has left, I'll tell you that I support him doing so. I have to take his side. He's my son."

"Well, Evan. I have to do what I have to do. I'll be calling a meeting. Our entire group needs to know about this. They also need to make a decision about group leadership. I think it's time for you to step aside. I suspect others in the group will agree."

"Oh, and you think you're ready to lead? We'll just see about that, Duke."

Evan ended the call. His hands were shaking. He had decided

it was time to hand things over, but that didn't mean he'd make it easy on Duke. The others needed to hear that Duke's actions were probably what led to where they were now. Evan thought this might be the end of the National Alliance. Only time would tell.

Evan walked into the kitchen for a beer. The Formica flooring and countertops were well past their use date, but he did not notice. He yanked the refrigerator door open, grabbed a beer, and realized he was still shaken. Evan downed the beer, and then had another. He grumbled about Duke being an ingrate. Evan used harsher adjectives too.

A short while later Evan's phone rang again. This time it wasn't Duke calling. It was Evan's son, Jack.

"Dad. What in the world is going on? Are you okay? Is it true that Wendell and Dave left?"

"I take it that Duke called you."

"Yes. He was angry! He's calling for you to step down as leader. He's blamed everything on your 'lack of leadership.'"

Jack told Evan he would vote for him to continue leading. Jack also said he was worried about Wendell.

After they hung up, Evan considered having another beer. Then he decided getting drunk was not the answer. He would need his wits about him if and when they had a group meeting. He had not thought to ask Jack when and where the meeting would be, but since Duke was so angry, it might not be at Evan's barn. He wasn't sure how he felt about that.

The next call came from Blaze Edwards. He told Evan that Duke had just screamed at him and Elliott. He complained that it wasn't the first time Duke yelled at him.

Blaze reported, "Duke said we screwed up by calling everyone ourselves. He said we were to blame for scaring people. That was the first time he yelled at me. Then he called again and said we were to blame for Dave and Wendell running."

"Looks like he's spread the blame to you. Earlier he told me that I was to blame for Wendell and Dave leaving."

"Evan, you need to know that Elliott and I are doing what

we can to deflect away from the National Alliance. There's not much we can do without risk of losing our jobs."

"I'm sure you two are doing all you can. No one is asking you to risk your careers."

"Actually, Duke said just that. He told us the National Alliance was more important than anything else, including our careers. I don't know what else he thinks we can do. I can tell you that Elliott and I don't like Duke's attitude at all."

"I'm sorry to hear that. Duke is very likely the next leader of our group."

"I think that's a mistake. We're all covering for the lynching and now we're all covering for the two people he shot in the campground. Usually, I'd say we need to have each other's backs, but he's almost single-handedly caused our problems. Plus, the investigations are going faster than we thought they might. They have a lot of people working on them."

"Well, you'll need to speak up in the meeting and let people know where you stand. Duke might still get the leadership position. The others will also need to know about the investigations, and how they're going. A lot is depending on you and Elliott."

"Well, we're worried."

"I understand. Let's see if this starts to blow over. We can all talk about how to protect you and Elliott. By the way, when and where is the meeting?"

"It's at your barn tonight at 8. How come you didn't know that?"

"Duke probably forgot to call. Thanks, Blaze."

Evan knew he had some thinking to do. The National Alliance ranks had been dwindling. Duke was interested in leading. Maybe it was time to hand it all over. Maybe it was time for someone younger to be the leader.

CHAPTER
TWENTY-FIVE

The pressures of the investigations were being felt all around. Bill Harris felt it.

In the Law Enforcement and Investigations office in Washington, D.C., Bill received news that was unexpected. Violet and Emmylynne reported a disturbing discovery. In reviewing all the photos being sent in from the various investigations, they discovered Walt Newman, the District Ranger, had been camping, or at least in the Gopher Flats Campground, with people thought to be members of the National Alliance.

Bill looked at multiple photos in which Walt was pictured in Gopher Flats with suspected National Alliance members. In one he was enjoying a beer, in another he was laughing with others, while in another he and Duke Kent were shaking hands.

Bill contacted Forest Supervisor Rick Givens and Patrol Captain Richard Golden. Richard was as incensed by the photos as Bill.

Rick took a different approach.

"Listen, Bill, I know it sounds bad, but being in the campground is related to Walt's job as District Ranger."

Bill replied, "I described the content of the photos to you. These don't look job related. I'm sending a text with each of the photos so you can see for yourself."

"Fair enough. I'll take a look, and decide what to do."

"Look, Rick, I cannot tell you what to do. If this were my employee, I would show them the photos, and ask them to explain. I think the least you can do is talk with him."

It did not look good to Bill, and he guessed it would not go well for Walt. Bill was having trouble finding an innocent explanation. He hoped for Walt's sake that there was one.

Not long after hanging up Woody knocked on Bill's office doorframe. He had two cups of coffee with him.

"Hey, Bill. Do you have a few minutes? We may have a problem."

"Hello to you too, Woody. You brought me coffee. You usually do that when there's a problem. What has got you worried?"

"We were asked to let the state police in Virginia handle all the press releases, right?"

"That's correct."

"I'm seeing others, but perhaps they're simply picking things up from other sources," observed Woody.

"Okay, better give me a list so I can give Carver Grayson a call. We want to be sure he knows about this."

"Okay for me to sit? I think we'll be a while."

"Sure. Which murder are you referring to?"

"All of them."

"Okay, you'd better walk me through this," uttered Bill.

"The earliest releases were only about Mr. Fry's murder. At first, many of the details were incorrect. But later releases talked about both gunshots he received. Then, later versions reported he had been shot once in the mouth."

"That was not supposed to be released."

"You're correct, but it's out there. People were starting to call Mr. Fry a drug addict, or a gang member. They were associating the shot to the mouth as a 'code of silence' kind of thing," said Woody.

"This must be really difficult for his family to read."

"I know it bothers me, and I'm not even related to him."

"Anything else about Mr. Fry?"

"Yes, word got out about the town hall meeting he spoke at, and what he'd said. Then the narrative switched to white supremacy groups, particularly the KKK," commented Woody.

"This could turn ugly rather quickly."

"It already has. Some people are coming out in support of white supremacy, and others are against it.

"Once the Freeman murder information was released all kinds of sources picked up the stories. They're making it sound like all white people are white supremacists. Or maybe closer to what I read, that all white Virginians are supremacists."

"Tell me what they're saying about the lynching," requested Bill.

"As you might guess, it's really ugly. There are a couple of sources that found information about a couple of suicides in the forests, and they are suggesting that Mr. Freeman did that. Most though, are saying our forests are not safe for black people, and to stay away."

"That doesn't sound good. Are they saying anything specifically about the Forest Service?"

"Yes, most of it isn't good. We're being portrayed as supremacists. They're talking about our white staffs, and how we're doing nothing about these murders. They have a few photos of white employees on the George Washington and Jefferson National Forest that they're using as 'proof' of our white staff. These include Walt and Rick."

"Maybe later we can change the messaging, but now we need to let the state police continue doing the press releases. Is there more?"

"Others are saying they are quite surprised the lynching happened in Virginia, saying they expected this maybe in Mississippi years ago, but not Virginia now. Some are placing blame on our current politicians."

"I'm sure that's not being well-received. What's being said about the murders in the campground?"

"Here's where it gets crazy. Five murders on one national forest within a week have got them all speculating. There are lots of suppositions about why, including the alleged white supremacy, and about the current administration fomenting hate, but others are saying these five murders must be linked. No one seems to have proof, but the idea is out there. So far the state police in Virginia are neither confirming, nor denying that."

"I know you're not adding to any of these sources."

"No, I'm passing all calls, and messages to the state police. But I think you calling Grayson is probably warranted."

"Good to know, Woody. Have you called state police public affairs in Virginia about addressing some of the charges against the Forest Service?"

"Yes, I did Bill. They said all communications about any of the murders include all agencies involved in the investigations. They prefer to have nothing at this time that addresses only our agency."

"Got it. Thanks for letting me know.

After Woody left, Bill thought about what he should do next. He'd call Grayson, but then he needed time to consider what might happen next. It made him worry that messages of fear and hate were being released. They had enough to do related to the murders without the added pressure of media and social media opinions. He was worried that staff on the forest might get targeted in some way. Bill was glad Woody brought it to his attention, but it required more than attention, it required planning.

CHAPTER TWENTY-SIX

Harley was feeling good about their progress. They had long ago left the local trail, and had taken the Appalachian Trail. The A.T. had taken them on varying elevations; up, then down, and up again.

Jacey had described some of the different trees and shrubs they passed along the way. She'd shown Harley Pitch pine and Loblolly pine, then Chestnut oak and Black oak. Harley doubted she'd remember all the differences in the many types of trees. Her level of expertise was minimal, and mostly could discern if it was an evergreen or deciduous tree. Jacey was much more knowledgeable. Harley was grateful that Jacey was willing to share her expertise. Harley had not known Jacey knew so much about trees.

Jacey also knew about local birds. She had pointed out various birds as they hiked. Jacey would see them, and point them out to Harley. Harley had trouble picking them out among the dense foliage of the trees. Harley joked that Jacey was making it up, that the birds weren't really there. Harley knew they were there because she could hear the different sounds they made. Jacey had been telling her which birds went with which sounds. At least she had done so for several miles, but Harley had noticed she was much quieter now. She hoped she was not pushing

Jacey or Gemma too hard.

"Jacey, do you need a break?"

"Yes, I'd like to stop for a short while. I could use some water. Come to think of it, I wouldn't turn down a granola bar."

Harley apologized. "Sorry if we set a fast pace. Let me know any time you need a break. Chances are we need one too."

They found a log and checked it for insects before settling in. Gemma lay down right away, and Harley poured some water into Gemma's collapsible bowl.

Jacey took a long drink of water and remarked, "The pace is fine. I am wondering at our progress. The two suspects are on horseback, and we're on foot. Kind of seems like taking a knife to a gunfight."

"Well, we're the law, and the law says we cannot be on horseback on the A.T."

"I'm just saying we're at a disadvantage here. How do we even the playing field?"

"We hope they don't know their way around. Plus, we have the amazing Gemma. She's our secret weapon. We also have the data pad so we can be tracked and our colleagues can find us. I doubt the men have any of these."

Harley watched Gemma cock her head, and look at Harley. She'd heard her name. Harley got Gemma a small bowl of dog food, and opened a granola bar for herself.

"Tell me more about that."

"Gemma and I work as a team. She has good scenting abilities, and I watch for clues along the trail. See over here are a few hoof prints. No one else is likely to be on horseback, so if we follow these we should find Wilton and Speller. Gemma will show us if they go off-trail."

"So, I have a couple of questions. First, what if it rains again and the footprints go away? Second, how can we possibly catch them? Third, how do we know their destination? Fourth, are we going to go off-trail?"

"If it rains hard enough, we lose the hoof prints to follow. But sometimes Gemma can still scent them. I can watch for broken twigs, or horse droppings, or other clues.

"Catching them is admittedly tough. They will stay ahead of us, but they don't know we're on the trail so quickly after them. This might lull them a bit into taking their time. So rather than a granola bar, they might be enjoying steak cooked over an open flame. Oops, sorry if that made you hungry.

"I have to say we don't know their destination. You're a police officer, where do you think they would go?"

"Well, I know there are more than three-hundred miles of A.T. in Virginia, but I have to guess they'll make their way out of state. Maybe they have family they are headed toward."

"Okay," Harley replied, "then we'll have to catch them before they get so far away. Are you concerned about going off-trail?"

"A bit. After having walked part of this trail with you, I've noticed the terrain off the trail looks rough. I wonder how anyone could locate us if we go off the trail."

"Suspects don't always take the beaten path. If Gemma points us, then we'll follow. Our safety comes first, so if we hit really rough areas, or anything that makes us uncomfortable, we'll see if we can find another way around. So, speak up when you want to."

"Okay, that sounds reasonable."

"Finish your granola bar. And when you're ready, let's keep going for another hour or two before it gets too dark.

"When we reach a point where I have a connection again, I will ask Violet to contact authorities along the trail entrance points to be on the lookout for Wilton and Speller. We should request they look for family or friends out of state where they might be headed.

"It might be more likely they get caught after they leave the A.T., rather than by us. But my preference is to catch them ourselves."

"That is my preference too. For one thing, then we'll have horses."

Harley laughed at that, and they continued walking. She laughed some more and commented, "We still can't ride them…"

CHAPTER TWENTY-SEVEN

Stone was once again gathering up the many papers on his tabletop, and trying to keep organized. Earlier that day he'd found a rolling file cabinet that had two drawers. He'd also found hanging file folders, files, and labels. Stone had started files for each of the deaths his team was investigating. Then he found some freestanding bulletin boards. He'd made files for the smaller maps he had, while others went onto one of the bulletin boards. He'd also found some plastic magazine holders. At least that was what he thought they were meant for. They would fit additional file folders or other things as needed. He'd find a good use for them. He placed them on top of the filing cabinet that he had put into a corner. So long as his desk wasn't strewn with papers, he'd feel more prepared for whatever came next.

Stone needed to chat with Jeff, so he went upstairs to the office Jeff had been assigned. Jeff was on the phone, and offered a shrug to Stone. Stone looked around Jeff's office. Jeff's desk was metal and huge, taking up most of the space. There was barely room for a file cabinet in the corner. Jeff's small window allowed light into the space; Stone wondered if it had ever seen drapes or blinds. Jeff had added an old-fashioned green desk lamp on one corner of the desk. The desk was overflowing with paperwork. His trashcan, located by the door, was full of wrappers from previous meals. Jeff shrugged again, and made a hand motion to indicate the other person on the line kept talking.

Stone decided to go back downstairs to his office, but he'd stop again at the supplies room to see what else he might find. He picked up some writing tablets and pencils. He mused that he was nowhere near the administration goal of being paper free. Some of his colleagues did a better job at that, but he liked writing things down. His happiest find was a round cup where he could put pens and pencils. It surprised Stone how much these few things could make him feel better.

Toward the end of Stone's organization spree, Jeff had knocked on his door.

"It's looking better in here."

"Thanks, I almost feel like I have a handle on this."

"You stopped by my office earlier. Sorry, that was a long call. I thought I'd see what you needed."

"Thanks, I came by to let you know that Jimmy's been found. He has a concussion, and a nasty cut on his leg, but he's going to be fine. He's at the hospital here in town."

"Thanks, Stone. That is truly great news. Will he get released?"

"We don't know yet. It sounds like he blacked out after getting hit on the head, so I'm guessing they'll keep him overnight. I'll take a break soon and go visit him."

"Have you met him before?"

"No, but he's a team member, so I'll go see him."

True to his word, Stone spent an hour on a quick trip to meet Jimmy at the hospital. The hospital was not a long drive from the sheriff's office.

Stone used to dread going to see people in hospitals until his dad had a stroke. During that time Stone came to respect all that hospital staff did for their patients and for the families. Stone was glad Jimmy hadn't needed the intensive care unit, like Stone's dad. He hoped it meant things weren't too serious. Stone wandered down a few hallways to find Jimmy. Stone made eye contact with all the people he could, and sent them supportive smiles and waves.

Jimmy told Stone that he needed to stay the remainder of the day, and likely the evening, to be sure he was okay. Jimmy told him all that had happened in the campground, and on the trail. Jimmy said he was grateful to Harley and Gemma, who took care of him.

Stone enjoyed meeting Jimmy. Despite all that Jimmy had been through, he was in good spirits. Jimmy shared his career goals. Stone agreed that Jimmy should try to become a law enforcement officer. To Stone, it was a worthy goal.

Seeing Jimmy made Stone remember his frustration earlier that day. He felt he should have helped locate Jimmy. That should have been priority one for each of them, even over the deaths they were investigating. All he could do was send the right people to help. He had also been frustrated that the judge had not had time to attend to the warrants right away. He needed the information those interviews might provide. He was frustrated that none of the deaths were close to being resolved. He had wanted progress, and he had wanted it right away.

Stone was feeling a bit less frustration now. He thought about Jimmy's attitude, and decided it was a great way to view the world. Stone figured if Jimmy could go through all that, think about his future, and know what his next steps were to get there, then he could too.

After seeing Jimmy, Stone returned to his office to pull together the information on all that had happened that day. It had been a busy day. He noted that there were still pieces missing, and things that were worrisome. He'd need to think about what steps he could take to make them less worrisome.

In the meantime, Stone needed to be ready for the closeout session. He knew it would be an interesting meeting. Stone was waiting for one more call from team members before stepping next door to the large conference room.

The closeout session had just started when Stone arrived.

When he entered the conference room he saw Carver at the smart board with Mr. Fry's murder notes on the screen. He felt a bit guilty about being a few minutes late, and he would make sure that didn't happen again.

A table had been set up along the back wall. It had some pastries and a large coffee pot. Someone had brought in crackers and cheese, grapes, and cookies. There were stir sticks, sugar packets, small plates, and some napkins. Stone felt he'd been disruptive enough, and did not stop as he passed the table. He deliberately selected a different chair to sit in this time, hoping it would help him keep an open mind.

Carver Grayson had started the meeting with an update on Jimmy Wilson. He noted that Jimmy was very grateful for the team of Harley and Gemma. Carver said that Jimmy reported he was "ready to return to work," but the doctors advised more time to heal. Carver said, "I heard a few of you made time to visit Jimmy today. Thank you for that."

Carver glanced at Stone, and continued. He asked for Jeff's report.

Stone glanced at Jeff, hoping his face expressed an apology for his lateness. Jeff nodded his way. It was a simple move that Stone appreciated.

Stone noticed the drapes were open today, and he could see stains on the carpets that he had not noticed previously. A bit of sunlight made the star on the dais shine a little. Stone hoped that was a good sign.

Jeff said he had several items to report related to Fry's murder. First he explained they had used a combination of interviews, a confidential informant who was a Klavern member, and research. He told the gathered officers that he and Stone had worked together on all the investigations throughout the day. He'd report out on Fry, and Stone would lead discussion of Freeman and the campground murders.

Jeff remarked, "I will try to keep my focus on Mr. Fry, but I'm seeing potential for overlap among the cases, especially between Mr. Fry and the campground murders. Stone and my discussion will likely overlap in places, but we'll be clear about which murder we're addressing."

Stone nodded at Jeff. He and Jeff had talked about the local Klavern being involved in Fry's murder and the campground melee, where two Klavern members had met their death. Some of what they learned applied in both places. Plus, there was the question of the AKIA coin at the Freeman murder, and the tie-in to the KKK.

Jeff continued, "We had two team members look into the possibility that Mr. Fry was involved in the drug trade. They spoke with family, friends, and work acquaintances. Not a single one supported that idea. They said that beyond coffee, Mr. Fry had no bad habits, and said he certainly was not into drugs. We also checked for arrest records, and spoke with a few confidential informants who were known drug users. Based on what we learned, it's safe to discard the idea that Mr. Fry was involved in the drug trade. We're concluding that Mr. Fry's death was not drug related. It's much more likely the message being sent by the bullet to his mouth was for people to keep quiet."

Jeff again mentioned the confidential informant that had assisted them. He told the officers gathered that the informant had been a member of the Klavern for many years. He knew many of their names, and he had provided some photos of group gatherings. The informant had not been to a Klavern meeting for a few weeks, so he had not known about the weekend recruitment plans. The informant said that Klavern had been discussing recruitment a lot recently, and these specific campgrounds were mentioned along with other possible venues.

"So far we have not been able to locate the Burden brothers. Our teams have combed several district campgrounds, and the brothers are not camped at any of them. We have a few people watching the Burden home, but they feel it is more likely that the brothers are still away. There have been no sightings of them."

Stone noticed that his fellow officers were riveted by what they were hearing. All were watching Jeff carefully; there was no shuffling of papers, no picking up of coffee cups, no shifting in their chairs.

Jeff added that the search warrant for Mr. Burden had been signed and served. Mr. Burden was not in the home, but his wife had answered the door when they served the warrant, and begrudgingly let the officers inside.

Jeff said, "Mr. Toby Burden's assertions that they weren't members of a supremacist group were meant to misguide us. We have confirmed their membership in a local Klavern of the Ku Klos Knights of the Ku Klux Klan. Indeed, our informant told us that the Burden sons, Carl and Jay, were members of the 'inner circle' of that Klavern. The informant said there were four inner circle members, the Burden brothers and the two deceased Wright brothers.

"In our search of the Burden household, we also found additional evidence of KKK membership. Once we locate Mr. Toby Burden he will be arrested as the weapon owner. He is likely to be released, because we cannot tie him to the murder of Mr. Fry. My guess is when we find the sons and the weapon; we'll have an arrest that will stick.

"Also, we did get approval for tracing the phones of the sons, but the phones were turned off on Sunday, and there has been no activity since then. The last time they were turned on was about five miles from the Forest Service road into the campgrounds. This means it's possible the sons are tied to both the murder of Mr. Fry and the melee at Beggar Flats Horse Campground."

Jeff answered a few questions and turned over the discussion to Stone.

Stone reported on progress related to the murder of Mr. Freeman. He told them a break came in the case after Jacey and Harley confirmed a link to the rodeo. Stone described the work of comparing the list of suspected supremacist group members with calf roping teams in the rodeo circuit. There were several names on the list. He noted only two men, who were known to be local, were unaccounted for. These two were on the Appalachian Trail on horseback. "As we speak, the team of Jacey, Harley, and Gemma are tracking the two men, Wendell Wilton and Dave Speller, on the A.T."

Stone described the distinct disadvantages of being on foot while the suspects were on horseback, and the many miles of trail to cover. "We have every confidence that Jacey, Harley, and Gemma will succeed, but it will not be easy.

"In addition, Jimmy Wilson identified these same two men, and reported it was Wilton who assaulted him. This places two suspects in Mr. Freeman's death to the campground where the melee occurred.

"We also investigated the tire tracks near the Freeman murder. Jeff's team has been researching suspected local KKK and National Alliance group members. Among the items they looked into were the vehicles owned by the members. We all admit it would be quite a stretch, but we thought if we could link the car and tire tracks to a member of a supremacist group, we might be able to solve the crime. Or at least, we might have something that could be added to the case against the suspects.

"The team found that two alleged members of local supremacist groups own RAV4s. They are Ray Parker, alleged member of the KKK, and Duke Kent, alleged member of the National Alliance. After this discovery, two members of the team were unsuccessful in reaching Mr. Parker, but they did make contact with Mr. Duke. By all accounts, the man was incensed we approached him, and he refused to answer any questions. We'll try for a search warrant, but it is doubtful it would be approved, as we don't have much to present as evidence. We'll be following up on Mr. Kent and Mr. Parker."

After responding to a few questions, Stone moved on to the murders in the campground. He reported that search warrants had been requested for the owners of the cars identified at Gopher Flats Campground, and the owners of the burned vehicles at Beggar Flats Campground. In addition, they had contacted some campers at Gopher Flats to learn more about anything that might have transpired there.

"The interviews we've had today were fruitful. The campers from Gopher Flats said similar things to the campers from the Beggar Flats Horse Campground. That is, a group from the KKK entered the camp, brought coffee and food, and tried to befriend potential new members. Like the campers at the horse camp, some thought the group was friendly, but most found this strange and off-putting. All said they had departed the Gopher Flats Campground before the melee in the horse camp, so no one saw anything new to report. We did have the campers identify photos of the visitors on-site using the photos of vehicle owners."

Stone waited a few more beats before continuing. "We strongly believe that the National Alliance was the group that took part in the melee in the campground. We had team members who went to the home of Mr. Joseph Miller, one of the deceased at the campground. The officers found photos of him with other possible National Alliance members. One person in the photos they recognized as Mr. Edgar West. He became known to law enforcement after his complaints about former President Obama, and his death threats to Mr. Obama. In these same photos we found pictures with Wilton, Speller, and a couple of others I'll discuss soon.

"For now, I'm back to the results from the warrants of KKK members. In all, the investigators retrieved six unregistered weapons, more than a kilo of marijuana, and dozens of photos that had pictures of possible KKK group members in them."

Stone told them a few arrests had been made. Mr. Ross and Mr. Brown had both refused to talk, and requested an attorney. A few other people were not in their homes when the warrants were served. Both Ross and Brown had been released. We'll work to get more information about these two men.

"While at the Rover home, our team discovered Beth Rover was recovering from a bullet wound she said was due to a 'hunting accident.' We cannot place her at the campground yet, but we suspect her 'accident' was there. She had sought medical assistance, and we have retrieved the bullet. The bullet will need

181

to be tested, but it seems unlikely another KKK member shot her. So, the weapons we have found probably were not the cause of her injury."

Carver asked for questions, and had none. He told Stone to get to the more difficult topic at hand. Stone noticed several people sit up straighter in their chairs, and a few leaned forward.

"We had some evidence from the scene of the Freeman murder that we researched. It was an AKIA coin. It turns out that the fingerprints on the coin traced to a long deceased KKK member. Yet the coin looked fairly new. It took some work, but we figured out the coin was taken from the evidence locker here."

Stone looked around. He definitely had everyone's attention now.

"I mentioned the photos with multiple National Alliance members in it. Among those were Sheriff Area Officers Blaze Edwards and Elliott Green."

Stone understood when it took a few moments for this to sink in. There were some gasps, and some shaking of heads.

"We secured warrants to search their homes, and found evidence that these officers were indeed active National Alliance members. We had hoped to locate the officers this afternoon. We found their service vehicles at their homes, but not their service weapons. Their personal vehicles were gone, and Green's safe was open and empty."

Stone again waited a beat, and then continued, "This is a lot to take in. You probably feel the same as I do. I never thought we'd tie anyone behind the blue line to supremacist groups. But now we have. There are 'be on the lookout' bulletins for them, and their personal vehicles. We're working on freezing their assets. More salient to our efforts, we have no idea how much their inside knowledge has influenced our investigations. They are the ones who discovered the AKIA coin, and it looks like they planted it.

"I understand it will be troubling to investigate our own people, but it must be done," said Stone. "Sheriff French has contacted the Federal Bureau of Investigation to take the lead in that investigation, so we don't appear biased."

Stone could see the dismay and confusion on several faces. He asked for questions, but Carver stepped in.

"We examined this thoroughly before calling in the FBI. It is likely they will want to speak with each of you to determine ways in which the two officers might have interfered in your work. Regardless of your personal opinion, and perhaps friendship with the officers, we in the oversight team expect your full cooperation." Sheriff French nodded his head in agreement.

Carver took a moment to thank each team for their work. He continued, "You've made excellent progress today. To be sure, we've had good news and bad news.

"To get back to the tasks at hand, our linkages are much like yesterday. We'll keep supremacy groups as our first category. We continue to have evidence for supremacist group memberships in the KKK, and now we are sure the second group is the National Alliance.

"Another commonality was horses. We'll retain it in the support column. We're still not sure about camping as a commonality.

"The key difference remains the different types of murder. It may take some time to unravel that difference, if we ever do.

"On another note, we've been watching media reports, and social media, related to the five murders. Several groups have called for a protest to occur tomorrow morning. While we have various reports, it seems the death of Mr. Freeman has raised the most concern. The protesters will gather at the location of the town hall meeting here in Christiansburg. We feel it is unlikely the protests would drift onto the forest, so for now all attention will be in Christiansburg. We have also heard a rumor that Antifa, who express militant opposition to fascism, is going to show up. It appears counter protesters in the form of supremacist groups will also be here."

Carver told them that most team members would be called in to protect the groups from each other, and to protect the public from the groups. They also had requested local police from several locations across four counties. He ordered everyone to wear riot gear.

This news did not surprise Stone. After Charlottesville, he figured a protest would occur. He'd seen some of the protest chatter cross his news feed that day. While he might not be surprised, he was feeling a bit disappointed. He knew most personnel would be pulled away from the investigations for the protest event. In his mind, this would delay justice.

CHAPTER TWENTY-EIGHT

Bill Harris was in his office in Forest Service headquarters. He'd had some coffee at home before coming in, but hadn't had any yet at the office. Before he could take care of that, a call came in from Carver Grayson. Bill had just hung up the phone after his early morning call. He sighed deeply. He wondered, "What next?" Then he thought, "I probably don't want to know!"

Bill headed to the coffee break room. He decided on coffee for himself, and another for Woody. He stopped at Woody's office. Woody was online and typing rapidly. It usually made Bill smile to see how fast Woody typed, as he himself was much slower. Bill was not smiling today.

"Hi, Woody."

"Hi, Bill. Oh, you brought me coffee!"

"Yes, I did."

"Thanks. I hate to say it, but you look kind of beat. What's up?"

"Virginia."

"Say no more. Oh, wait. Say more. What's happening now?" asked Woody.

"You know about all the news releases, but many on social media have been suggesting the need for protests. So today, there are protests planned in Christiansburg."

"Let me guess. The town hall?"

"Yes," said Bill.

"Another guess. Racism?"

"Good guess. You are partly correct. It looks like there will be people speaking about Mr. Freeman's lynching, and they are likely to say it is due to racism. It also looks like there will be counter-protesters, like at Charlottesville."

"You mean supremacists will be there?"

"It sure looks like it."

"What are they doing to keep it from being another Charlottesville?"

"Before I go there, Woody. It also looks like some anti-government groups will also be there."

"Wait, will the teams be pulled away from the investigations for this protest-palooza?"

"Yes. They just don't have enough people to cover everything. They were hoping for some more heavy rains, like they've had recently. They thought it might dissuade people from showing up. But Carver tells me it is actually quite a nice day there, with rains expected late in the day. 'A lovely day for protests' is what he said."

"I'm going to guess plenty of press will be there. We should turn on the television. I'll bet we can watch all that's happening," said Woody.

"That might ruin this perfectly good cup of coffee for me."

"Copy that. So what have Carver and company planned for this?"

"By 7 this morning they had cordoned off all the streets anywhere near the town hall. They're trying to prevent a car from ramming into the crowd."

"That's a good start."

"They sent out notices that no torches were allowed at the event," noted Bill.

"That's also good, and not likely to please the supremacists, I mean, counter-protesters.

"I don't know how they would enforce that."

"I agree. Even if these guys got the word, they're not likely to comply."

Bill continued, "Word was buses full of people were headed there from all over nearby local cities. They said some were on the way from Pembroke, Pearisburg, Roanoke, Blacksburg, Wytheville, and Radford. They also expected representatives from more than ten local counties, including Bland, Giles, Montgomery, Pulaski, Tazewell, and Botetourt. In Charlottesville, the counter-protesters were from all over the U.S., and there was no reason to believe today would be any different in Christiansburg."

"I'll ask again. How do you prepare for all this?"

"All the police will be in riot gear. They are going to make lines of officers to try and keep the groups from one another."

"I sure wish them luck. They don't need anything beyond the murders that have already happened. I'm going to turn on the TV. Do you want to stay and watch, Bill?"

"No, thanks. I've got a meeting I need to attend. Let me know later how it went."

Bill returned to his office to put on his suit jacket, and headed off to another budget meeting. He was sure he could tell a compelling story to convince others to increase the law enforcement budget.

CHAPTER TWENTY-NINE

By 9:30 a.m., the streets in downtown Christiansburg were full to capacity. It had the makings of a complete disaster. Stone wandered through the busy streets trying to categorize all that was happening. Stone did not like the look of this at all.

After his walk through, Stone saw Sami Foster. He said to her, "There seemed to be three groups of protesters. One's the group concerned over the lynching of Mr. Freeman. This is the largest group by far. They've staged themselves on the steps of the town hall. That's the same building where Mr. Fry had spoken.

"The second group makes less sense to me. I'd categorize these as a splintered 'anti-government' group. Some are anti-Trump, some are anti-police, and still others seem to be anti-federal government as landholders."

"Do you think they'll band together?"

"I'm not sure. They don't appear to be a cohesive group, but they are all in the same immediate area. We don't have plans in place if they conflict with each other, unless we pull people away from protecting the other groups.

"The third group, over there, is the counter-protest/supremacist supporters. There are more people in that group than I had hoped for."

"Yes, it looks larger than the anti-government groups put together. That could spell trouble for us."

Stone saw the group members were carrying torches, though those had been banned for the event. He doubted much could be done about that.

In addition, Stone pointed out to Sami that the press was making its presence known. "This has certainly caught the attention of the local press, and the national press is here too."

"After Charlottesville, I'm guessing they expect a lot of mayhem. I'm seeing what looks like people coming to enjoy a show. Do you agree, Stone?"

"Yes. It looks like a party atmosphere. They even have chairs to sit in. Look, some have ice chests with them. I doubt those are full of water. That looks like it could be trouble."

"I'll be leading the group in the middle area. The splintered protest groups. Maybe we can watch the spectators too."

"Thanks, Sami. I'm leading the officers guarding the town halls steps group. I plan to be near the top of the stairs to watch everything as best I can. I'll also keep an eye on the spectators."

Stone and the other officers had planned on doing all they could to maintain the right to protest, yet maintain the peace. Their main task was to keep the peace, to help keep the groups of protesters away from others who came to see the spectacle, and those who were in opposite protest groups.

Everyone on the three investigative teams who were not actively searching for suspects had been diverted to assist at the protest site. Like the other officers, Stone wore riot gear. All were determined that this would not be another Charlottesville. They did not want anyone there to die, including fellow officers.

Stone had left Sami and went to the top of the town halls steps. He noticed that the group protesting Mr. Freeman's lynching came prepared with signs and bullhorns. They also had a dais and a sound system running. Stone heard several speakers take turns talking about the hatred and racism evident in the country. They were incensed about the lynching of Mr. Freeman. They described an evil that must be met with prayer, and non-violent protests. They talked briefly about the death of Mr. Fry, who had recently spoken inside this very venue. They had a couple of well-known televangelists on the speaker list who fired up the crowd. In Stone's opinion this group was righteous and full of determination.

On the sidewalk closest to the town hall was where Stone could see the anti-government protesters. They were still roughly divided into three groups as they marched, chanted, and displayed their signs. They also had bullhorns so their words could be heard. It made quite a cacophony. It was definitely not music to Stone's ears. He doubted Sami was enjoying it much either.

On the sidewalk across the street from the town hall was the counter-protester group. This was the group Stone worried most about. Chris was taking the lead over there, and would call for more officers if needed. That group was also marching, and chanting, and carrying signs, as well as lifting their lit torches in the air. This group lacked bullhorns, but they had many voices joining their chants. Like in Charlottesville, they wanted it known that they thought themselves to be superior to all others. Chris had been assigned the largest contingent of officers to watch over this group.

Between the groups, on the steps and the sidewalk proximate to the town hall, was a line of police officers. These were the officers led by Stone. All had stun guns, batons, and tear gas at the ready. Stone had heard a few nearby participants comment that the shields the police had were a bit much.

The tanks that had been brought in upset some of the participants. They had not liked all the gear the police wore, and apparently thought even less of the tanks. Stone noticed the media spent a lot of time giving their versions of events from in front of those tanks.

Eleven o'clock came and went with little change in happenings; Stone thought the groups still appeared energetic, and ready to continue until noon as projected.

Around 11:45, Stone watched as the anti-government groups dissipated. The police who had been watching that group stayed in place in a continued effort to keep the protesters and counter-protesters apart.

At noon, the two larger groups began to disperse. Stone and the other police did what they could to keep the order.

Well away from the events, as people were headed back toward their cars and buses, was where mayhem began. Stone heard about it after the fact. Jeff told him, "A young interracial couple was having trouble remembering where they had parked, and had wandered into a group carrying torches. Both the young men in the couple were stabbed. They'll both survive, but I heard Anthony Stanhope will need a few surgeries to make things right again. I also heard Sergio Hernandez needs surgery, but his knife wounds appeared much less life threatening.

"It wasn't long after the stabbings that we arrived on site. We didn't catch the people who had stabbed the young men. We did find several people in the vicinity, and we tried to interview each one. Those who said they had seen the stabbings gave wildly different descriptions of the event, and of the perpetrators. It looked to me like many of the witnesses were counterprotesters themselves, and they seemed to be in no hurry to assist us. Unfortunately, the young couple was in no condition to offer their assessments."

"That's really rough. I feel sorry for those two young men."

"So do I. I hope they're both going to be fine."

Stone had not gone to that area, even when he heard a call for more officers. He and other officers assigned to him had been trying to keep the groups away from one another by the town hall steps. Stone felt they were mostly successful. Being located there meant Stone also missed the activity that would come to influence their investigations.

About two blocks from where Stone stood, some of Stone's fellow officers caught two men with their weapons drawn. Soon after Dexter Dreyfus told Stone, "The two men, Earl and Leland

Graves, were quickly arrested, and no shots were fired." He told Stone that the men were already claiming self-defense. Dexter added that the police had seen no other people with weapons nearby, so the self-defense claim was not likely to hold up. It would be later that day before the police discovered that they had two National Alliance members in custody.

Stone was told that the press had been painting the day as successful for the police, the protesters, or counter-protesters, depending on what station they represented. Chris Wray said to Stone, "From what I could hear, a few of the national news groups gave accurate reporting, and almost equal time to all points of view." He told Stone that almost all press members had been saying the tanks were out of line. Chris said they'd probably spend some time on air questioning the expense, and show of force.

"The press told us they could not wait to be able to interview Anthony and Sergio. Can you believe that a few members of the press actually left to follow the ambulance? Some press members also requested more information on the men arrested with the weapons, but we have little information to give."

Stone considered it a win. He felt really bad about the two young men, but the vast majority of protesters did not directly clash with other protestors, and no one died. If the press needed to say the police were out of line, then so be it. He felt the show of force kept the mayhem to a minimum.

CHAPTER THIRTY

Harley and Jacey had stopped overnight, and then got up at first light. They were feeling energized, having slept fairly well.

Harley thought back to the previous night. They had located a used fire pit and had settled the nearby area themselves. The pit had been cold to the touch, so if it had been used by Wilton and Speller, that had not been recently. They used it to heat water for some dehydrated beef stew, which they deemed "delicious." The water purifier had worked its magic, and the food had been wonderful.

Harley and Jacey both had small tents, and Gemma just fit with Harley inside her tent. Both had been exhausted so sleep had come easily. Gemma had moved around a few times during the night, and Harley had wondered what wild animals might be about to put Gemma on edge.

This morning Harley and Jacey talked about experiencing the A.T.

"I don't think of myself as a bird person, but I've been charmed by their wonderful songs," remarked Harley.

"I knew I could win you over. You actually saw a few birds after I pointed them out. Maybe today you'll spot some yourself."

"Well, maybe you could train Gemma to find them," joked Harley. "I can't believe there are more than a hundred bird species in the area. That's really amazing."

Jacey teased Harley about her continued confusion over identifying trees, and said she'd test her on tree knowledge as they hiked this morning. Harley commented that Jacey might as well flunk her now.

For the morning meal they tried dehydrated scrambled eggs, and coffee. Harley's assessment was that the stew was "much tastier." Jacey thought the eggs were just as tasty. She also noted she was hungry enough that most anything would taste good.

Harley checked their supplies, with particular attention to what Gemma still had in her food pack. If they were careful they could go into tomorrow before they'd need to exit the trail and re-supply. Harley and Jacey put on clean socks, stowed their tents and cooking gear, and declared themselves ready to go.

Harley said, "We'll start with trying to find a location where we can get reception. I need to get a check-in message to Violet so they don't worry about us."

"That sounds good. I need to contact Stone as well. "

It was a difficult walk through steep terrain before they found their spot. Harley was starting to worry that Violet would be concerned. Once there, Harley was quick to send a message to Violet on the data pad. Then Jacey tried calling Stone on the satellite phone. She got a voice mail message that said he was unavailable, and to contact Carver, so she did that. She learned about the protest in Christiansburg, and told Harley what she had heard about it.

"It sounds like they all have their hands full in Christiansburg. Jacey, this seems like a good spot to rest for a while. That was a steep climb, and took us a few hours. I'm famished again."

"Yes, I'd like to sit for a while. How about we split a granola bar?"

"We're okay on supplies for now, I think we can each have one. I'll bet Gemma wouldn't mind some food and water herself."

"Oh, good. Do you have the honey and oats granola bar I like?"

"Sure do. Enjoy."

After almost an hour break, they continued along the trail. At least this section was not as steep. Gemma had been out ahead of them. They spotted Gemma sniffing a bush. Then Gemma sat beside it.

Once they caught up, Harley commented, "We'll have to trust her nose. I do not see what has attracted her to this spot, but it must be important. Gemma, next."

Gemma got up and started down terrain that was off-trail.

"Jacey, do you want to wait here, and we'll do a quick check?"

"No, I'm feeling energized again. I'll come along."

Like other times though, it was simply evidence of a bio break off the trail. They retraced their steps, and continued on their way. Partway down Harley had seen hoof prints. Gemma had been correct to take them there.

Harley was feeling a bit frustrated though. They kept finding evidence that Wilton and Speller had been along the trail, but they didn't seem to be getting any closer to catching them.

"Jacey, do you think we should continue? I think it's looking more and more like the two suspects will get away. We can't seem to catch-up to them. We had hoped they'd feel like they could go slow, but it doesn't appear they're dawdling in any way."

"I'm feeling the same way. I have to say, I don't like it. I don't like giving in."

"I understand. Usually Gemma and I resolve the crimes we set out to solve. This time, I'm not so sure."

"Let's give it another hour or two. Does that seem reasonable?"

"Okay, how about this? We'll walk until we come across another trail leading off the A.T. Then we can decide what our next moves are."

"Sounds good, Harley. We can check to see if anybody has news that'll help us decide."

"Now that sounds like a plan."

Once they reached a trailhead leading off the A.T. they called in for guidance. No one had information to share. Carver thought it a good plan to exit the A.T., and reported they'd think about another tactic the trio could try.

Harley hated to give in so easily, but they could not keep chasing what could not be caught. She hated not being able to resolve the crime. For her it wasn't about her reputation, it was about getting justice.

A couple of hours after they went off the A.T., and onto local trails, they came across a pair of men hiking toward the A.T. They stopped to chat. Jacey asked the men where they had come from, and if they'd seen anyone else on the trail. The men said they'd seen a few other people just a few miles from the campground they left earlier that day. Most people, they said, were likely day hikers, and there were also two men on horseback.

That statement got Harley and Jacey's attention. They asked a bit about the people on horseback. The descriptions did not match to Wilton and Speller. That was disappointing. Jacey showed them photos of the two men, and the hikers declared it was not those guys. They knew what the men looked like because the two had requested food and water for themselves, but nothing for the horses.

Harley asked about the horses, and the descriptions matched the ones missing from the Beggar Flats Horse Campground. Harley showed them photos of the horses, and asked if these were the ones they had seen. There did seem to be a match, but the men were not completely sure. Jacey then showed them photos of the Burden brothers. Those photos were a match to the men the hikers had seen.

Once away from the hikers, both Harley and Jacey sent messages to request assistance. They might just be able to help capture the Burden brothers. It was not what they set out to do, but they'd be happy to assist.

In Washington, Violet found their current location, and noted Harley and Jacey would be coming across a fork in the trail. Each direction led eventually to a campground. They did not know which direction to take, and had not asked for more information from the hikers, since they didn't realize there were multiple options or multiple campgrounds. They decided to find that fork, and hope they went the right direction. Maybe if the rain was light, they could see the footprints of the hikers they had just met.

Jacey told Harley that she'd request teams be sent to each of the campgrounds, and if she and Jacey got lucky in picking a direction, maybe they could help with the capture. Either way, they could meet with additional police, and make plans to continue after Wilton and Speller.

CHAPTER THIRTY-ONE

Staff in the Forest Service Washington Office met to discuss joint business. The staff included people from the National Forest System and law enforcement. Bill had asked Darryl White, the Deputy Director of Law Enforcement and Investigations, to accompany him to the meeting. The meeting was held at the NFS conference room area, on the third floor of the headquarters building. To Bill, it looked much like the LEI conference room, but on a much larger scale. That made sense to him because their staff was much larger than LEI.

Bill had been feeling the pressure about all the deaths on the George Washington and Jefferson National Forests. He knew that if he was stressed, then the staff overseeing national forest management had to be feeling it as well.

Since Bill had requested the meeting, he was asked to lead it. Bill decided they should start with the current news, and then they could talk about steps they might jointly take to prevent future incidents on the forests. His first topic was Walt Newman.

As a National Forest System employee, Walt Newman was not supervised by LEI, but LEI certainly had information concerning his employment. The discussion about Newman was lengthy and passionate. Bill was told that Walt had "served the forests well in his time there." NFS had been really impressed with Walt's career, and dedication to the agency. Bill was not as sure. He told them it looked like Walt was either a friend with members of the National Alliance, or he was a member himself. Bill shared all the photos law enforcement had located.

The Deputy Chief of the National Forest System told Bill, "We understand your concerns, Bill. However, with no proof of National Alliance membership, nor proof of wrongdoing on Walt's part, we cannot discipline him. We certainly have no grounds to fire him."

This was not the outcome that Bill was looking for, but he understood it. He told them LEI would keep investigating, and if anything they found offered proof, or showed innocence, then he would share that with them.

Bill told them, "You should know that I requested Forest Supervisor Rick Givens have a discussion with Walt. I believe that Rick should ask Walt about possible National Alliance membership, and ask if Walt had shared any investigation information with the National Alliance. I'm worried that Walt may have told the National Alliance important information related to the investigation, and the National Alliance may have acted on that knowledge."

Bill did not know this as a fact, but felt the possibility could not be ignored. The Deputy Chief acknowledged the importance of the issue and would encourage Rick to have that discussion with Walt.

The Deputy Chief said her staff was quite concerned over the deaths on the forests, supremacist groups approaching visitors, and of course, Jimmy Wilson being hurt.

After that, the discussion turned to what they could do to ensure the safety of visitors and employees of the forests, and specifically the district, in the near future, and long-term. Again, on behalf of the LEI community, Bill expressed concern over the many deaths on the Eastern Divide Ranger District.

"The two campgrounds in question are now places used by both the National Alliance and the KKK. I'm pretty sure none of us think that is the best use of these places."

Bill told them he was aware that Rick Givens had to replace signs, tables, and fences. He said that Rick told him these were "expensive campgrounds to manage." Everyone there agreed that some measures needed to be taken. They needed to decide what the measures were, and if the measures were for the campgrounds, the district, or the forests.

Darryl White stepped in for Bill, as he was called away for an update from Violet about Harley related to the investigation.

Bill was happy to get the update.

"What do we know about Harley and Gemma? Where are they? Are they safe?" Bill asked.

"Yes, they are safe."

Violet relayed to Bill all she had heard today from Harley. "They've seen tracks where it looked like Wilton and Speller had gone down the trail one way, and then backtracked, and went the other way. Harley was not sure why they did that, but maybe they were lost at times.

"They also found evidence of recent campfires, possibly made by the duo. But none of the fire pits were hot to the touch.

"Harley said intermittent rains made tracking the hoof prints tricky. They were relying more often on broken branches, as well as Gemma's abilities, to keep them moving in the right direction.

"Harley did describe some 'difficult terrain,' that she said was steep in places, but they also went across some fairly flat areas.

"I should tell you that our tracking system has lost them often along the trail, so we had just general locations, and not as much precision as we'd like. I think the heavy vegetation, and the cloud cover, are the culprits."

Bill had approached Violet a few times already, asking if anyone had heard from Harley in the past few hours, where were they, and were they okay. He was concerned that they had not heard from her often enough. Then several messages had come in while he was in the meeting. Bill wished he had spoken with Harley directly.

"I didn't pull you out of the meeting just for that, Bill. I have news. The Burden brothers were spotted."

"That's great! Tell me more about that."

"Jacey, Harley and Gemma came across a couple of men hiking who had seen people on horseback. It was not Wilton and Speller they had seen, but Carl and Jay Burden, requesting food and water from the hikers. Although not confirmed, the horses were probably the ones stolen from Beggar Flats Horse Campground."

This was news Bill would be happy to go back and share.

Violet also told Bill that Harley, Gemma, and Jacey might help capture the Burden brothers.

"I certainly hope they are successful. I'm relieved the team is heading back off the A.T. I want them to have more team members with them while searching for Wilton and Speller. Those two men are dangerous."

Violet replied. "I agree, Bill."

"Thanks for the update, Violet."

When Bill returned to the meeting, the group was discussing the pros and cons of demolishing both the campgrounds. Bill relayed what he had learned of the investigations, and they caught him up on the discussion in his absence.

The group had considered a short-term closure of the two campgrounds, and agreed that about a two month closure would be reasonable to start. This would give them time to evaluate the long-term plans for each campground.

They had also talked about whether or not the entire district should be closed to use for the same time period. There was less agreement that this was appropriate. Darryl said he had told them, "If you close the campgrounds, the same people you're trying to keep out will just move elsewhere. It won't solve the problem at hand. It will merely move it. Closing the district will ensure they moved a great distance away, and they'll be some other person's problem. It's likely they would become another ranger's problem. However, we have found that when the campgrounds reopen, the same people are likely to come back.

We need to think about the campgrounds themselves, and how to discourage that use group."

That discussion had led to the thought of demolishing the campgrounds. There was concern from the National Forest System, as well as from LEI, about this. Darryl expressed concern over the precedent this would set. He'd said, "That might send the message that we cannot manage without destroying what we built." Bill concurred.

It was decided that in addition to the two campgrounds being closed for two months, funds would be added so that four additional Forest Service law enforcement officers could be transferred to the forest to help ensure safety at all other district sites. Further, they discussed that Jimmy Wilson was ready to go back to work. His job would be to oversee the Beggar Flats Horse Campground and Gopher Flats Campground as needed during the closures. He would still be armed only with knowledge and a smile, but he'd said he was up to the task.

Bill was relieved the meeting had some positive outcomes. He felt they could not go forward doing the exact same things they had in the past. This meeting showed him that everyone was taking these deaths and harm to forest employees very seriously. He knew it was important that they'd had common goals. Employee and visitor safety were paramount in his mind and theirs.

Bill was ready to head back to his office and learn more about the plans to capture the Burden brothers. He also wanted an update on plans for capturing Wilton and Speller.

It was getting late in the day, but Bill hoped law enforcement could catch the Burden brothers before dark, or at least by noon tomorrow. He'd sure like to report some good news to his boss soon.

CHAPTER THIRTY-TWO

S tone headed back to the sheriff's office mid-afternoon. There had been so much to do during the protest and after, that he could not get away any earlier. There had been a few rowdy protesters that he had followed back to their vehicles to be sure they did not cause trouble, and also to be sure they safely departed the area. There were a few more people he'd called an Uber for. They had been drinking. These were mostly bystanders. Stone was somewhat surprised they had been drinking so early in the day, but guessed they were either alcoholics, or had seen this as a party atmosphere. All these tasks were important, yet weighed on his mind because he had other things to do for the investigations.

Stone returned to his desk on the first floor. He got out his phone. He needed to check with his officers, and see if anyone had something to report on the investigations. Stone guessed though, that like him, their day had been spent elsewhere. He figured that he would not have much to report out, unless Jacey and Harley had news.

Stone dropped by the second floor to see Jeff, but Jeff was on the phone, so he'd just have to wait to see if the day brought news from Jeff's group. Stone got himself some coffee and considered his own actions. Something was contributing to his feelings of frustrations. Perhaps he'd just been too busy, but he felt he'd left some things undone. He had a nagging feeling, but didn't know why. It was not a comfortable feeling.

Stone's cell phone rang, and he hoped it was a report-in that would move the investigations forward. It was a brief call, but Stone knew he'd have information to share in the meeting.

Stone went to the conference room. The drapes were closed today and he could see that one of the overhead lights was flickering. There was only a coffee pot on the back table, so Stone walked on by. He noticed the room was pretty full today. Most people had been at the protests, and probably did not get much accomplished, so they were here, and not in the field. Stone had a bad feeling that the day had produced few results.

Carver set up the smart whiteboard, pulled up the Fry file, and requested Stone's report.

"I'll start with the investigation of Mr. Fry's murder. After leaving the Appalachian Trail, the team of Jacey and Harley came across some hikers who spotted the Burden brothers, and identified them from photos. As a plus, the Burden brothers appear to have the horses stolen from the horse camp."

Stone continued, "Jacey and Harley, along with Gemma, are hiking toward the area of the sighting. They expected to stop overnight as they covered rough terrain today, and needed some rest. Then they plan to catch up to our teams tomorrow morning. We're sending officers to two campgrounds well north of the horse campground, as the brothers could be headed toward one of a pair of campgrounds in that direction. Also, weather permitting, we expect to send some drones up tomorrow to locate the Burdens now that we know the approximate location."

"As I mentioned, Jacey and Harley will try to assist, or at the very least they will hike out, and get fresh supplies. They are requesting other teams to hike the A.T. with them after the Burden's are detained.

"That gets me to Mr. Freeman's murder. The portion of the A.T. Jacey and Harley are considering next are further north, as that is the direction that Wilton and Speller have headed. So, after we capture the Burdens, our teams will join Jacey and Harley to assist with capture of Wilton and Speller."

After fielding a few questions, Carver asked if Jeff had items to add.

"During the protests today, we arrested two men for pointing their weapons at other people. These men were identified as Earl and Leland Graves. To our surprise, these men were in photos with known National Alliance members. They have said they are National Alliance members, but will not identify any others.

"A few members of our investigation staff went through more items that were confiscated yesterday. They found photos with Joe Miller and Edgar West, which included one more person likely to be a National Alliance member, Mr. Gus Springer. They also noted it was possible that the other person in the photos, with their back to them, was Duke Kent. The person is the right size and shape, but it was a guess only. We'll seek more search warrants and check out these new leads.

"Continuing with the examination of evidence located so far, we've been looking at the weapons confiscated during the warrant searches. But none so far are a match for the bullet taken from Beth Rover's leg. You'll recall she called it a 'hunting accident.' So far, we have nothing to show it was anything beyond what she said. We'll keep investigating.

"We're sending a few of our team members, along with Stone's, to assist with the capture of the Burden brothers. They'll continue after that, with Jacey and Harley, to locate Wilton and Speller."

"Well," declared Carver, "for essentially being off the investigations today, at least most of us, that was a big report out."

Carver said that the board would change a bit from their perspective. There did appear to be ties among some of the team investigations. He said it was not clear exactly why they tied together, but they'd keep working on that. He thanked everyone for their hard work.

Stone and Jeff stopped at Stone's office to talk after the meeting.

"That really was great work you reported on today."

"Thanks, Jeff. I could try to take credit, but really, it was Jacey and Harley who carried the day for us."

"I'm glad they're coming off the A.T. There are so few tools we can use while on the A.T. that it hampers our investigation. It would be nice if we could at least use horses. I shouldn't be telling you that; I'm sure you feel the same."

"Yes, I do. It's amazing how far Jacey, Harley, and Gemma hiked, and what they learned. That is good, old-fashioned police work right there. Still, I'm all for using all the tools at our disposal when we can. Maybe Wilton and Speller have a plan we haven't figured out yet, or maybe they're running scared. I just hope they leave the A.T. They're ours if they do that."

"I agree. I just hope they hadn't planned to hide away forever along the A.T."

"Mark my words, people will see them, and be mad about the horses on the trail. Then they'll report what they saw. We'll find the men. It just may take a long time."

Jeff replied, "Let's hope we get a break on them soon. We also need to get more warrants approved, because we're likely to find more information to link all these investigations."

"I noticed that Green and Edwards did not come up in the reporting today. Did you hear anything?"

"No, Stone, but I think Rolland and Carver are feeling frustrated."

"Yeah, Green and Edwards must have a had a getaway plan in place. I'm sure they'll eventually get caught. That's going to be tough on everyone that works in this office."

"Yes that's true. But they brought this on themselves. I hope they're caught."

"Me too. Have a good night, Jeff."

After Jeff left, Stone sat at his table trying to figure out what that feeling was that he had left something undone. He pondered it some more while he filed paperwork. He would need to let it go so he could enjoy his evening with Genevieve.

CHAPTER THIRTY-THREE

Harley and Jacey had hiked a few miles when they saw what could have been the footprints of the hikers they had met. It had rained the previous evening so to call them footprints seemed a stretch to Harley. Still, Harley suggested they follow that lead. At least this area was flat, which made for easier hiking.

Harley decided to call Violet on the sat phone.

"Good morning, Violet."

"Good morning! How're you? How's Gemma?"

"We're doing just fine. Wishing for a hot meal that's not freeze-dried, but that'll happen soon enough. I'm wishing we'd captured Wilton and Speller. Have you heard if the Burden brothers have been captured yet?"

"Last we heard they'd not been. However, law enforcement sent up a drone to traverse trails near two campgrounds. They found nothing on the first trail, but spotted horses on the other trail."

"Just horses? No people?"

"That's correct. They told us the footage shows the horses, but there's nearby heavy vegetation, and some trees that may be blocking people from their view. They did see you, Jacey, and sweet Gemma headed in the right direction, toward where the horses were."

"We didn't notice the drone. It must've been high up. We're at a point where I have to make a choice about which trail to take, and I'm heading on the more north and east one. Can you tell me if that is the right choice?"

"Yes, keep going. You're not far from the horse location. Be careful, those guys, if it's them, are armed. Also, be aware that fellow officers are approaching the location of the horses headed from the campground."

"Good to know. If shots are fired, we don't want to hit fellow officers, or have them hit us."

"The drone has left the area so we don't spook whoever might be in the woods."

"Okay, I'll call you in an hour with a report."

Harley filled in Jacey about her conversation with Violet. Harley and Jacey were feeling like a break was coming their way, and stepped up the pace. It felt good to be on the hunt, and near their suspects. Harley saw the hoof prints and some boot prints. Then she saw more hoof prints, with no footprints.

Just ahead, in more open terrain, she spotted the Burden brothers on horseback. She did not want to yell or spook them. She needn't have worried. They saw her and Jacey, and headed toward them smiling, and offering a hello.

"Good morning to you two. Those are beautiful horses."

"Thanks. Your dog is a good-looking critter. What is it?"

"The breed is a Rhodesian Ridgeback."

"Never heard of it. Is it friendly?"

"Oh, yes. She'll shake your hand if you ask."

"We've been riding a long time now, and had not planned our meals well. Do you nice folks have any food to spare?"

"Sure," replied Jacey, "hop on down, and we'll get some for you. How're you on water?"

The Burden brothers got off their horses. They briefly discussed the merits of heating some freeze-dried food; instead the brothers accepted granola bars from Jacey.

Harley saw the other officers coming down the trail, and nodded to Jacey. Jacey reached into her jacket, and pulled out her service weapon.

"You're under arrest for the murder of George Fry. Put your hands behind your head. Now!"

The Burden brothers saw the other officers, and complied with Jacey's order. They did not have time to get out their weapon, or try to make a run for freedom.

Harley handed Jacey some zip ties for their wrists. Gemma watched the two men carefully. Jacey told the men their rights.

"Who's George Fry?" asked Jay.

"You've got nothing on us," sputtered Carl, "we'll sue you for false arrest."

Officer Dreyfus carefully pulled the weapon out of the saddlebag, and smiled at them.

"So what," declared Jay, "firearms aren't illegal."

Harley commented, "I'm willing to bet this is the gun that was traced to your father."

"Our father?" asked Jay, "no way! Our father didn't kill no Fry person."

"Shut up, Jay!" yelled Carl.

"No, you shut up, Carl! Why'd you take dad's gun?"

"Jay! Shut up, now!"

"You think you're so smart, Carl. You took the wrong gun! This is all your fault Carl."

"Jay, I swear I'll kill you if you don't shut up!"

Once there was a moment of silence, Jacey said, "Tell me about these horses. Where'd you get them?"

Carl responded, "We're not talking anymore. Ya hear that Jay? No talking!"

All the officers, along with Harley and Gemma, walked the men and the horses back to the campground. More officers had arrived at the campground. Two offered to take the brothers to jail. They put the men in the backseat of their service vehicle, and Harley could hear the start of a heated argument between the brothers.

"This should be good," observed Jacey, "if they keep talking, they'll turn on one another."

"Well, the case seems pretty tight to me," noted Harley, "but I'll leave it up to you officers to get whatever leverage you need for justice for George Fry's family and friends."

Dexter Dreyfus took the horses to get some water. He used his radio to request a horse trailer big enough for the two horses. He also requested feed for the horses, since he figured the horses had not been well fed.

Officers Wallace and Dreyfus would be partnering with Jacey and Harley in the search for Wilton and Speller. Wallace told them more officers were coming, so there was time to eat some food, and get some rest. Dreyfus told Jacey he'd put an ice chest in his vehicle truck. They could help themselves to sandwiches and sodas.

"Thank you, Dexter. We really appreciate that."

True to her word, Harley called Violet back.

Violet declared, "We just heard! Congratulations! You got the men responsible for killing Mr. Fry. An added bonus, you got the stolen horses back."

"Definitely feels great! I'm happy to be a small part of this."

"Oh, you! You had a big part in this."

"Sure I did. I was looking for two men, and found two different ones," laughed Harley.

"It was a great job. I'm happy to hear you laugh again."

"Thanks, Vi. Gemma sends her love to Muffin and you."

"Love sent right back to you two. Stay safe."

Harley joined Jacey at Dexter's vehicle, and selected a turkey sandwich and a diet coke. Gemma got a few treats along with her food, and a pat on her head.

CHAPTER THIRTY-FOUR

Harley and Gemma had eaten and they had napped. Harley was raring to go, but they still had four more team members on the way. Harley was rushing them along in her head. She wanted to get on the trail. It was time to try calling Violet again to see if they had any information that might help.

"Hi, Violet! We're all fine, and still in the campground. We're waiting for more team members to show up. They'll be here soon. I was wondering if you had any suggestions for us?"

"I was just about to call you. We just heard about horses being spotted on the A.T. They are about twenty miles north of your location. I'm sending you a map so you can get close to there. When you look at the map, you'll see there are some forks in the trail, and some sketchy terrain. It might be rough going."

"Do we know if these are our guys?"

"No, we don't. No one's supposed to be on horseback on the A.T., so it's likely to be Wilton and Speller."

"Yes, but it could just be some lost riders who think they're on local trails."

"True, it may not be them. Bill told me all entrances to the A.T. are well signed, so local trail riders would see those signs, and abide by them."

"Okay. Thanks, Violet. I'll talk with the others, but I think it's the best lead we have. My phone just dinged, so it must be the map you sent. You're an angel!"

"Be careful out there, Harley."

"Thanks. Tell Bill that all's well."

"Will do. Bye."

Four more team members were added to Harley and Jacey's team. These were Forest Service officers Wesley Lexington, and his newly arrived partner Greg Foster, and from the sheriff's office were investigators Chris Reynolds and Sara Levitt.

They made introductions then talked about the horse riders spotted north of their current location. No one knew who the riders were, but they thought it likely to be Wilton and Speller.

"I think we should work in teams of two," suggested Jacey, "so we can cover more ground. Oh yes, and we'll have a third with Gemma."

Harley commented, "What Jacey suggests makes sense once you look at the crisscross of trails in that area. We can have two teams start about where the suspects were spotted and head north, and the other two teams start further north, and make their way south."

"Again, we're not sure these are our suspects, but it's likely they are," added Jacey. "I'm sending their photos to your phones so we don't try to capture the wrong people."

"We have radios along for each team," noted Dexter, "so we can contact each other if we spot the people on horseback. It would be better to surround them as a group, if we can."

"Thanks, Dexter. Harley will send each team a copy of the map. Check the map and the photos I'm sending before you enter the trailhead, because you'll not have Wi-Fi later. Does everyone have water and food? How about plans and equipment for overnight on the trail? We have some supplies to share, thanks to Wesley and Greg."

They spent the next fifteen minutes getting everyone geared up, talking over the map, and memorizing faces. They all switched their radios to the same channel, and drove off to their respective trailheads.

Jacey and Harley parked at their assigned trailhead and started walking. Gray and Dexter wanted to follow them to keep the talking level down. They did not want Wilton or Speller to hear them coming.

It had now been a couple of hours of hiking. Harley and Jacey were not in an area where the data pad could pick up their whereabouts. They weren't worried, they'd been in numerous places with no coverage, and now they had additional people along the trail who could be radioed if necessary.

After being on the trail for a while, Gemma had scented something off-trail, and now they were following her. They discovered broken branches, and an occasional hoof print. It looked as if Wilton and Springer were making their own trail. It was rocky, steep, and places were fairly slick. It was not where Harley would prefer to make a trail.

Jacey commented, "This is a really steep area. Do you think it is merely a pit-stop off the trail for Wilton and Speller?"

"I don't know. You could be right. I think, though, we should keep going now that we see prints to follow."

"My concern is that Gray and Dexter will not know where we went off-trail. I don't think our radio will work down this hillside."

"I hear that. How about I wait here, and you go back, and carefully mark our position so they know where to turn? You can radio them while you're there."

"Okay, but wait here. Okay?"

"Okay."

Harley waited about four minutes, thought she heard something, and decided to go just a bit further.

Harley saw the horses. She stopped, and waited for Jacey, and perhaps for the others, to join her. Harley signaled to Gemma to sit and wait. Soon the hair on Gemma's neck was on end, and too late Harley saw movement from the corner of her eye. A quick glance told her it was Wendell Wilton.

Harley got knocked on her shoulder, stumbled over some

rocks, and lost her balance. She slid down the hillside. She did not tumble far. It was steep, but she was able to stop her slide.

Harley shouted, "Attack!"

Harley could hear Gemma attack Wilton. She heard what was likely Gene Speller running away.

Wilton hollered, "Call off your dog, or I will shoot!"

Harley yelled at Gemma, "Cease!" She called Gemma her to her side.

Unfortunately, Jacey had the radio, and Harley did not.

If felt like hours before Jacey got to her. By then, Harley was sitting up, and assessing the damage done. She'd checked Gemma before she dared look at herself.

CHAPTER THIRTY-FIVE

Stone had just heard the news about the Burden brothers being transported to the sheriff's office. This was feeling like real progress. He walked upstairs to Jeff's office, and knocked on his doorframe. He noticed the desktop was mostly clean, and the trash had been taken away.

"Come on in! Great job, Stone!"

"Thanks, Jeff. Jacey, Harley, and Gemma were the ones who did the work. I heard they tricked the guys into getting off the horses, and then arrested them."

"So I heard. Apparently these two guys were not the sharpest tools in the shed."

"Maybe not. Though I did hear they were starving. I know I think better on a full stomach. Did they confess?" asked Stone.

"Not yet, we'll talk with them more soon. They should arrive here most anytime now. Have you called the Butler and Duvall families about their horses?"

Stone answered, "I'm waiting for the horses to arrive here. They're probably an hour away still. It took a bit longer to get the horse trailer to them. I want to be sure they're safely here before contacting the families."

"That's probably a good idea. I'm sure those families will be thrilled to have their horses back."

"Yes. All in all, it was a good day. Now, if we could catch Wilton and Speller, I'd be having a really great day."

"Here's to hoping you have a really great day, Stone. Hey, did you hear we brought in Edgar West and Gus Springer?"

"No. What did the gentlemen have to say?"

"They said they 'wanted their lawyers,'" recounted Jeff.

"Well, that's too bad, but it is their right."

"It is. We found lots of evidence at their homes that we're going through right now."

"What did you find?"

Jeff replied, "In Springer's house we found a small cache of unregistered weapons. We'll be checking those to see if anything is in the system. With luck, we can have a really good reason to arrest him. Like some of the others, we found photo evidence, but here they were hidden behind a wall. Springer kept glancing in that direction, or we would not have thought to open the wall."

"It's amazing how much people give away when they're under pressure."

"We're glad he did. Now, we have some items of value to us."

Stone asked, "What about Edgar West's home?"

"Not much there. Some photos, so we'll go through those. His weapons were all registered, and nothing popped from the system. We didn't have enough to hold them, so both were released a while ago. Do you remember that from the earlier warrants we missed a few guys who were not at home?"

"Yes. Junior Kendall and Gerald Brown, right?"

"Yes. We have officers going to try for an interview with them again," said Jeff.

"Good. With enough pressure some of these guys are going to talk."

Jeff added, "We're also bringing in two more men whose cars were identified. These are Herb Smith and Ben Rover. I look forward to chatting with Rover more about that gunshot wound to his wife. I think he knows more than they're saying about that. I think there are pieces of this puzzle we're not aware of yet."

"Yes, it does seem like we have a lot of pieces of investigations open at the same time."

"Yes, but it sure beats having no idea where to look next," laughed Jeff.

"Your office is looking better."

"And I'm feeling better," responded Jeff.

Stone returned downstairs to his office. His desk was cleared of detritus. He wished his mind were cleared too. He had moments where he felt they had so much to do yet. There were other moments when he realized how much they had accomplished already.

Stone had not been sleeping well, he had been worrying over this feeling he was missing something. Perhaps it was just the puzzle pieces not fitting together yet, or how he'd left most of the wedding planning to Genevieve, or was it something else?

Stone had been trying to balance his personal life and his work life. His work life had been easier before Genevieve had come along, but in many ways, his personal life had been harder before her. Stone was sitting in his temporary office considering all the wedding tasks they had discussed the previous night, while he was also considering all the tasks yet to accomplish before this task force would be considered done. He had done the same thing last night, thinking about work, while he and Genevieve were talking about wedding plans. He startled, and thought, "Genevieve would kill me if she thought I was comparing murder investigation tasks to our wedding tasks!"

Stone went back to compartmentalizing and considering only the next step in the workday. After that, he worked on updating several of the murder files. He was busy when Jeff came to see him.

"Hey, Stone. Got a minute? I just talked with Smith and Rover. Do you have time to hear what we learned?"

"Yes, indeed. I was wondering if you'd had them in yet."

"Unlike some of the other KKK members we've brought in, these two could not keep quiet."

"Well, that sounds promising. Anything in that dialog that matches to what we know about Mr. Fry's murder?"

"Yes. They discussed the Klavern meeting they'd had soon after Mr. Fry spoke at the town hall meeting. They told us that Mr. Fry's talk was discussed in detail. They said in the end, several members thought that nothing should be done about it, and for the Klavern to let it go. But Smith and Rover both said the 'inner circle' must have decided otherwise, and taken action. They claimed not to have any idea about what would happen to Mr. Fry. Both men said had they known, they would have tried to stop it, or they would have called the police."

"Yeah, right. I doubt they would have called us," observed Stone.

"Yes, but other parts of what they said rang true. Actually, I wonder if they just might have called. They seemed remorseful for Mr. Fry's family and friends, and they did tell us all they knew. So, maybe they would have."

"Okay, maybe they would have," said Stone.

"They were scared that Mr. Fry's death would be blamed on them. It worries them because they might go to jail, they'd had no say in the decision, and didn't kill him themselves."

"Well, I guess the courts are going to decide that. But their speaking out might help them in the long run."

"They said that at the same meeting, the Klavern discussed recruitment at the campgrounds. We know how that turned out. Both of them had been at Gopher Flats, and then moved to the horse campground. So now we know several members went from one place to another."

"That's true. We only knew for sure about one person and vehicle making that move. What else did they say?"

"They said they didn't know the people who had come to the horse camp behind them. They said they'd been shouted at, and then shot at. They claimed they didn't enter either campground with weapons, and were unprepared for that kind of confrontation. They said the other men yelled at them that the camps 'belonged to them,' and not the KKK. They were shocked by the deaths of the Wright brothers, and regretted leaving the bodies behind."

"It sounds like the National Alliance was responsible for the deaths of the Wright brothers. It's interesting that the National Alliance really did consider the campground as home turf," observed Stone.

"Apparently so. We have some photo evidence that shows National Alliance members in both campgrounds."

Stone said, "These guys were really helpful. Did you learn anything else?"

"Yes, and this solves another question we had. Rover told us that his wife was not hurt in a hunting accident. She had been shot at the horse camp during the melee. Neither man saw who did the shooting."

"Maybe if they see a photo array of possible suspects they'd remember?"

"No," replied Jeff, "we tried that, and they didn't identify anyone. They said it was chaos in the campground. Also, Herb Smith claims that he was grazed in the leg by a bullet at the campground. He revealed that he'd told people he'd been hurt on a plumbing job. He thought he recognized one of the men in the photo array, but he was not sure enough to make identification.

"All that, and we got some lab results back. The bullet that hit Beth Rover came from a weapon confiscated at the Springer residence."

"That's big news. Has Springer been arrested?"

"I believe it is imminent, if it hasn't happened already. I presume he'll continue to 'lawyer up.'

"We also found photos of Duke Kent at Springer's house. As you know, Kent's known to law enforcement, and has a long history of bad behavior. We have a 'be on the lookout' for him, and his RAV4. Adding to the news, we also found photos of Wilton and Speller at Springer's house."

Stone was starting to piece together the puzzle. "So now it appears we have evidence that the persons responsible for the killing of Mr. Freeman were associated with people at the campground melee. This is some crazy puzzle."

"Yes," observed Jeff, "and the day is relatively young."

After Jeff left, Stone thought about all the connections. He knew the oversight team had been considering each linkage as news flowed in, but it did not stop him from trying to work it out himself. Stone was encouraged, and hoped the remainder of the day went as well. If it did, maybe he'd sleep better tonight.

CHAPTER THIRTY-SIX

Bill was in his office, on the phone with the Deputy Chief of Research, when another call came in. He put the first call on hold.

"Hi, Bill. This is Rick Givens."

"Hello, Rick. I hope you're doing well. I have to apologize. I'm on another call. Can I can you back in about five minutes?"

"Sure. Talk with you soon."

Bill was thinking about Rick right after he finished the first call. Bill had visited the forest supervisor office previously, so he could envision what it looked like there. He remembered being surprised that the building was so small, given the people there managed two forests, which meant a very large land base.

There were only six offices in all; one was the forest supervisor's, which also served as the conference room, when one was needed. It had Rick's desk, some file cabinets, and also a conference table and chairs for twelve people. Bill thought he would have picked another office if he was the forest supervisor, and made the conference room part of the break room. Since he had not been there for a few years, maybe that change had already been made.

Bill thought about the rest of the spaces. There was a small office for the deputy forest supervisor; a position that Bill knew was currently vacant. With all that was happening right now, it might be hard to focus on filling that position. Three other offices were for storage, the break room, and the reception area.

The reception area was where the photocopier and employee mail slots were located. The last office was larger than all the others, but held several desks meant for people juggling all the other forest duties, including recreation, lands, and engineering. It was a crowded space. When Bill had been visiting, it was also a rather noisy space. There had been people in the room, and some were speaking to each other, while others were on the phone. It wouldn't have been Bill's favorite choice for office space, but they seemed to be making the most of it.

Bill had noticed on the visit that the exterior and interior of the building had shown signs of wear and tear. He'd guessed then that diminishing budgets meant lots of maintenance went into a backlog. Bill doubted much had changed since; budgets had not been increasing. Still, he recalled the beautiful wood of the conference table, and all the desks. He'd been told the wood had all been harvested from the forests. All in all, Bill thought it was probably a great place to work.

Bill could imagine Rick pacing his office waiting for him, so he called Rick back.

"Hi, Rick. Glad you called. How're you doing?"

"I'm better now. I had a discussion with Walt Newman in my office. I had been dreading it."

"If you feel better, it must have gone well. Tell me about it, if you can."

"I have to say I wanted to be sympathetic, but mostly I was feeling disappointed in Walt. I said, 'Walt, I have to ask. Are you a member of the National Alliance?' Walt declared that he was not, but he was a friend of people who likely were members of the National Alliance.

"Walt told me 'I never asked them straight out about it, and they never said they were.'

"So I asked why he didn't tell us earlier about this. He said, 'I didn't know for sure. These are people I thought were my friends. I couldn't do that to them.'

"That ruffled my feathers a bit. He could hold out on us, but worried about them. I told him I was disappointed that he waited until we could prove he had a relationship with them.

"Walt told me that he only recently figured it out for sure. Then he said, 'Now I think they only were friends with me because I'm a Forest Service employee, and they could get information from me. I feel like I was used by the National Alliance. And now I feel like my own agency doesn't understand me.'

"Bill, I was not fond of the idea that Walt was acting like a victim. I told him as much. Then I asked him, 'Have you provided any information from the investigations to members of the National Alliance?'

"Walt didn't hesitate at all. He answered, 'No, I have not. The only time I see them is in the campground, and they've not been back there since the melee. I don't have their addresses, or their phone numbers. But, I do know their names and faces if you need verification of who's who.' I told him we might need him to do exactly that.

"Walt told me he loved our agency, and wanted to do what he could to keep his job, and get back in good standing."

"That's good to hear."

"I think Walt was pretty scared when he came in the office, and I think he was humbled by the questions I asked. He seemed to understand the importance of being the topic of discussion in the headquarters office.

"Finally, I told Walt that I expected him to do everything in his power to get back to his job, and concentrate on doing it well."

"Thank you, Rick, for taking on that difficult conversation. I'm pleased that Walt had no contact with National Alliance members after the melee. I think we can take him at his word. Frankly, I'm relieved he didn't interact with them."

"I am, too. As hard as that conversation was, I'm grateful you nudged me into it. Now I know where Walt stands, and I think he and I can continue to work together."

"Call again if anything else comes up, Rick."

After hanging up, Bill considered the conversation. He found he was relieved that Walt didn't interfere with the investigations, yet Bill was still feeling uneasy. He could not figure out what that was about. As Bill considered the feeling, Harley had popped into his head. He hoped she was okay.

CHAPTER THIRTY-SEVEN

Harley was mad. She had let the rodeo man get the best of her. To make matters worse, she almost got Gemma shot in the process. Then it occurred to Harley that Wilton had not shot at her. He'd had a chance, and he didn't take it. She was grateful for that. She was not as grateful about the precarious slope she was currently on. At least there was some tree cover here. Harley was feeling hot and sticky. She considered it might not just be the humidity. She might be embarrassed about her predicament.

Harley felt the knot on her head. It hurt. She examined the scrapes on the pads of her hands. They hurt, too, but not as much as her head. Her ribs were feeling the impact from all the items she had stuffed in her vest, and her back was telling her she'd regret that slide.

"Damn it," she thought, "I should have known he was there." Harley wondered how Wilton had not been seen, or smelled by Gemma. Harley knew she'd been focused on the horses. Maybe Gemma had been as well. Harley decided she'd think more about that later. Right now all that mattered was Gemma was fine, and Harley would be fine. Now she needed to get back up the slope, go find that bully, and arrest him.

"Harley! Harley! Where are you? Gemma?"

Gemma barked.

"Down here, Jacey, I'm down here!"

"Oh my god! What happened?"

"Wendell Wilton is an ass. That's what happened."

"Wait there. I'm coming down to help you."

"Okay, but be careful, it's slick and steep. Better yet, does any-one on the team have a rope? It might be better to get pulled up, than chance you falling down. I do not recommend the landing."

"Hey, there's a rope on the horse over there. Great idea! I'll be right back."

It took a bit of effort, but Jacey got the rope close enough that Harley could grab it. She scooted uphill a bit and tied it around herself. Jacey pulled her up, and Harley climbed. Gemma was sitting by Jacey, just watching the proceedings. Harley arrived at the top just before Dexter and Gray arrived. Everyone made a fuss over Harley until she got mad at them.

"You'd think I was an old woman the way you're acting. I'm fine. Never better."

"Sorry, Harley," said Jacey, "let's go find those guys."

Dexter added, "Let's do that, but first, how about we tie down those horses before we go? We'll know where to come back for them later."

"Well, it's definitely off the beaten track so I doubt anyone will come take them, or disturb any evidence that might be in the saddlebags," observed Jacey.

"I like that these fools are on foot now. Makes our tracking job much easier. Let's go, Gemma." Harley did her best to not show her aches and pains to the others.

CHAPTER THIRTY-EIGHT

Bill Harris had just returned from another meeting between Forest Service LEI and the National Forest System staffs in their headquarters office in Washington, D.C. Woody Brooks had attended the meeting with him.

Woody commented, "I'm happy with the revised regulations, Bill. I think they really listened to the law enforcement input about the issues on the Eastern Divide Ranger District."

"I agree, Woody. I know that when we make requests they don't have to take our advice. I'm glad they did this time. How much gets done, and how quickly is still a question in my mind."

"Mine as well. I'm headed to Vi's office. I told her I'd update her after the meeting. Did you want to join me?"

"Sure," replied Bill, "I want to get the latest news about Harley."

They approached Violet's office. Woody knocked and said, "Hi, Vi."

Bill noticed most of the wedding decorations were still in place. He'd have to check and see if any of the food or cake remained.

"Hello, Woody. Bill, I'm glad you are here. I have news. Let me start by saying Harley is fine."

"Oh. That doesn't sound good. Guess you'd better tell me

what happened."

"Harley, Jacey, and Gemma went off-trail following Wilton and Speller. Jacey left Harley to go mark the turn they took, so the follow-up team would know where to turn. While Jacey was gone, Harley ran across the two men. They were off their horses. One surprised her, and knocked Harley down an embankment. She had Gemma attack the man, but he threatened to shoot Gemma, so Harley called her off."

"Is Harley really fine? How about Gemma?" asked Bill.

"Yes, they appear to be fine. Harley thinks she may have hit her head, she's going to have bruises and bumps. Harley thought it took Jacey a long time to return, and she is not sure if that is because she blacked out, or she just lost track of time. Jacey said she was away from her at most ten to fifteen minutes. Gemma had no cuts. She had some blood around her mouth, so she apparently got a bite or two in."

"Good dog," remarked Bill. Then he asked, "Do they need medical assistance to their location?"

"It might be a good idea to get medical as close to this area as possible," suggested Woody.

"Okay," Violet responded, "but Harley said she was fine for now. They're back on the trail. This time the men are not on horseback."

Woody said, "Well, that's an upside to Harley taking a fall. I wonder why they left their horses? I'm glad they did. They'll be easier to catch on foot."

Bill asked, "Is Harley still off-trail? Can you locate her on the app?"

"I couldn't see where she was off-trail, due to her location. She showed up again, and called in. I can't find her right now, probably because of the vegetation cover. When she shows on the app again I will let you know. We do have the general vicinity, and we can see where it is likely they'll head next on the trail."

"Okay, I'll call the sheriff about getting medical to that general area, or at least the nearest location they can drive to, after we're done here."

"Thanks, Bill."

Woody added, "We have news as well. The forest supervisor will institute several rules for the district. For starters, groups of more than six can only camp after registering in advance at the district office. One member of the group will have their driver's license copied, and it will be shredded later, after crews have determined no damage has been done to the campground."

"That sounds reasonable. They're not banning group camping, just adjusting it."

"Vi, your data helped us state a strong case."

"Thanks, Bill. I appreciate knowing that."

Woody continued, "There'll be no hunting, no shooting, and no gathering of forest products for six months. Plus, they'll not allow any solicitation in the campgrounds."

Bill added, "The district is going to temporarily fence off access to the two campgrounds. That would free Jimmy Wilson to return to his home district. They also decided to do more upgrades to both campgrounds, and make them less primitive. The thinking is that more families would want to camp in the area if the sites are not so primitive. They'll focus most changes on Gopher Flats, where the National Alliance had been frequenting most often, and make it different than what might have attracted them before."

"It sounds to me like they listened to several of the concerns we had. Did they talk about increasing law enforcement?"

"They're still working on that. They'll have lots of costs associated with the physical site changes in the short-term. My guess is they'll examine budgets, and at least make a temporary change to enforcement. That probably won't happen until they reopen one or both campgrounds. Thanks, Vi, for the update on Harley. Let me know when she's back where you can track her."

"Will do, Bill."

Bill returned to his office to think about Harley getting hurt. He'd had a bad feeling about this investigation before she left. He didn't want to make it seem like she was incapable in any way, but he should've listened to his gut. Bill laughed and thought "Yeah, like that would stop her." She was a bit bull-headed, but he really did trust her to know her limits. Bill would try not to spend his time worrying.

"'First things first," thought Bill. He'd make that call to get some medical assistance. Bill made a mental note to himself that when he and Harley next talked that he would not over-react about her injuries. He'd let her know he was concerned, but supportive.

CHAPTER THIRTY-NINE

Harley and the others walked the trail a bit. She could easily follow the boot prints that remained as Wilton and Speller ran away. Harley could see no evidence that the two had backtracked. Had it been her, she might have wanted to get back on those horses.

Jacey asked, "Did you identify yourself to them in any way?"

"No, I really didn't have time. All I could do was shout for Gemma to attack. She had some blood on her muzzle, so she got in some bites before I called her back."

"It's going to be hard to see the blood drops, if there are any, so we'll keep following Gemma and the prints," advised Jacey.

Gray added, "I doubt then that they know police are on their trail."

"Well, not by anything I said. It might occur to them that there was a reason I was off-trail in the same place they were."

"Good point," Gray replied.

As they walked it occurred to Harley that the rope Jacey used was for her safety, unlike the rope used on Mr. Freeman. That thought made her shudder. These were bad men they were chasing. It'd be best to keep that in mind. She'd been caught up in the tracking process before, without really thinking about why. She considered that she might not have taken a tumble had she been more aware of how dangerous these guys were.

"Did I tell you that Wilton said to call off my dog, or he would shoot her? So we know they're armed, or at least Wilton is."

"Yes, you told us that Harley. You sure you're okay?" asked Jacey.

"I was just thinking about how dangerous these guys are, and want everyone to be aware. Guess you guys generally presume that to be the case."

"Not always, but we do often think about our safety in unknown situations," said Gray. "We do know some members of the National Alliance have weapons, and we know for sure these guys do. We'll approach with caution. Dexter, can you radio the other teams and alert them?"

"Roger that."

They walked for another fifteen minutes before Harley commented, "Look at these prints, and compare them to the ones back there. This is where they started walking, rather than running. They ran pretty far for wearing cowboy boots."

"Looks to me like they're staying together. Am I reading that right?" asked Gray.

"You're correct. Look over here," Harley said as she pointed to some prints. "This looks like they wandered here a bit. A lot of boot prints overlap. Probably stopped to talk about their next options. They may not have much food or water without their horses. I wonder what their plan is."

Dexter noted, "If it were me, I'd be thinking about finding a place where I can watch who is coming along the trail, or I'd find a place where I was protected, and people could only come at me in one direction. Of course, that presumes they think people are coming. If I were on the run, I'd presume police are on their way."

Harley added, "I think they'll do what they can to protect themselves. They had a run-in with me, so now they'll be wary. What do you think, Jacey?"

"I agree, Harley. Even if they thought you were harmless, there's a chance you might tell other people, and then the chase would be on. It's safe to say they know someone is coming. They don't know when, or how many."

They walked another ten minutes in silence.

"Listen," whispered Gray, "do you hear talking?"

Gemma had her ears up and was looking up the trail. Jacey signaled the others to wait while she approached the sounds. Using multiple trees for cover Jacey moved very slowly. Gemma growled quietly, and Harley restrained her, then signaled Gemma for quiet.

It was a very long half hour before Jacey returned.

Quietly she said, "Both men are about a half mile up the trail. Looks like they selected a place to protect themselves. It looks like they plan to make a stand. They are armed. It is best to contact the other team, and let them know where we are, so it's a group approach. With enough people, maybe they'll give up. Harley, do you have a connection to Violet right here?"

Harley checked, "Yes, I will text her, and have her text Wesley."

They waited for another five minutes before a return text came in saying Wesley and the others were about ten minutes away from Wilton and Speller.

Jacey said, "Let's get closer ourselves. Harley, you're not armed, so you and Gemma stay to the back. Okay?"

"We're good with that."

"Do you want my second weapon?" asked Jacey.

"No, you know I don't like guns."

Harley watched as they covered the ground slowly, and quietly. Jacey had the lead, and signaled everyone to stop. A few moments of quiet passed.

The unmistakable sound of gunfire was shocking in the quiet of the forest.

Harley stayed where she was as Jacey, Gray, and Dexter rushed forward.

"Police! Drop your weapons. We have you surrounded!"

More shots rang out.

"I'm hit!" yelled Chris.

Sara called, "Stay down, Chris. I'm coming for you."

"I'm hit!" yelled Sara.

"Sara, back up this way" declared Wesley, "I'm going to get Chris to safety."

"Damn it! Lucky bastard got my leg," said Chris.

Harley saw Sara back up while continuing to shoot. Her left arm was bleeding, and she was trying her best to land shots with her right hand, though she was left-handed.

Greg laid down several shots, while Wesley pulled Chris behind a tree. Harley learned later that Chris would not be assisting any further. His leg was badly damaged. Meanwhile, Wesley was doing his best to assist Chris, and stop the bleeding.

Jacey, Gray, and Dexter took up positions behind trees and shot at Wilton and Speller.

More shots rang out.

This was not going the way Harley had wanted. She couldn't understand why Wilton and Speller would want to fight it out when they were so outnumbered. Even after hurting a few team members, Wilton and Speller were outnumbered. Couldn't they see it was futile? At this rate, someone was going to die out here. Harley prayed it was not any of her friends.

Harley was trying to keep herself and Gemma safe. Harley had some gun safety and shooting training, but guns still unnerved her. She hoped the injuries to the others were not bad. She hoped the shooting would stop soon. She hoped no one else got shot. She hoped she'd stop shaking like a leaf.

CHAPTER FORTY

Harley wished she had a hot cup of tea to help settle her nerves. She decided to focus on Gemma, and try to calm herself. She was petting Gemma, and whispering words of encouragement, though they were more for herself than her dog. She was wishing for this madness to end. At least she had stopped shaking.

Though she had not heard anyone approach, she saw Gemma react. It startled Harley.

"Harley, take my other gun," whispered Jacey. "If these guys decide to move, they could easily come your way, and being unarmed won't make any difference to them."

"Of course, you're right, Jacey. Sorry to be so obstinate."

"Keep the gun out. Point and shoot. You've got this. Stay behind these trees so you have good protection."

"Okay, I've got this. You need to get back, and help the others."

Harley watched Jacey move from tree to tree and make her way closer to the action. Harley peeked from behind her tree and watched Jacey take aim at Wilton or Speller. She could not discern which one from this distance and the trees obstructing her view. Jacey got a couple of shots off, but Harley could not tell if she'd hit anyone.

"I'm hit!" yelled Jacey.

Harley did not hesitate; she and Gemma ran fast to Jacey's side. She had a head wound that was bleeding a lot. Harley pulled a bandana from her pack, along with some gauze and water.

"Okay, relax Jacey. It doesn't look bad, only bloody."

"Likely a graze. Clean me up so I can continue with the team."

"Maybe you should just rest."

It took a few minutes, which seemed to pass slowly, but Harley finished the cleanup. Jacey had winced a few times as Harley worked.

"Jacey, you should probably sit for a bit. This could bleed again if you move too much. How do you feel?"

"Exposed. I think we're both a bit exposed here."

Harley said, "I've got us covered. Plus, we have Gemma watching out for us."

Then Harley looked around. She had been really focused on Jacey, and had not been paying much attention to everything else going on around her. She was back now, and would not let her partner get hurt any more than she had been. Jacey was right, though, they did seem exposed. She helped Jacey move further behind some trees. She checked to make sure Jacey was not bleeding more after the move.

"They're splitting up," yelled Gray, "Dexter and I have Speller. Wilton headed your way, Jacey!"

"That means we have Wilton, Harley."

Greg called out, "I hit Speller! Damn, he's still running!"

Harley peeked from behind a tree, and then aimed Jacey's weapon toward the last area she'd seen Wilton. He wasn't running though. His pace slowed, and then Wilton stopped. He was looking toward where Speller was.

Harley heard Wesley yell at Speller to drop his weapon. She looked the same direction as Wilton and saw Speller get shot again after he fired toward Wesley. Speller fell to the ground.

Harley felt bits of tree bite into her arm as she steadied herself to shoot. Wilton started to head her way.

Harley was not scared. She had Gemma, and she had a gun. Wilton was not going to get past her.

When Wilton got close, she called out, "Stop. Police. Drop your weapon! Surrender or you will be shot!"

Wilton kept walking toward Harley. It was strange. He seemed to be in a bit of a trance. He wasn't running, but he wasn't stopping either. She released Gemma.

"Attack!"

Gemma knocked down Wilton. Harley and Jacey grabbed to get his gun away from him. It was not much of a struggle. Jacey got the gun away.

Wilton shouted that he surrendered.

"Cease! Good girl, Gemma!"

Gemma sat very close to Wilton, and focused solely on him. She was not going to let him move a muscle.

"I should've shot that damn dog!"

Harley wanted to kick him for saying that. "Very good girl, Gemma! Extra treats tonight!"

"Speller is deceased," called out Wesley.

Jacey cuffed Wilton, as Wilton started crying.

"My friend! What have you done to my friend? He's my rodeo partner, my best friend. What will I do without him?" wailed Wilton.

Harley was finding it difficult to work up any sympathy for the man. This was the man who had a part in killing Mr. Freeman. He was involved in the shooting of three officers in the last hour. Nope, she just could not work up any sympathy.

Harley looked at Jacey. "Jacey, you're bleeding again. Let me work on that," said Harley.

After being taped again, Jacey called out, "Greg, what's your status?"

"Chris has a badly injured leg. We've stopped the bleeding, but he needs help."

"Sara? How about you?"

Sara called out, "I'm fine! Gonna need some help myself, but I'll be fine."

Dexter reported, "All good here. That was a good shooting, Wesley. Harley, if you still have a connection, can you send for the paramedics and the crime lab. Do you think they can make it out here?"

Jacey replied, "Not much choice. The lab techs are likely going to be working in the dark."

Harley confirmed she had reached Violet. Violet told her medical assistance was on the way, but because of the difficult terrain near the trailhead they would not be able to bring a gurney. The crime lab techs were also coming. They were all several miles down the trail.

Harley gave water to Jacey, made her eat another granola bar, and generally fussed over her.

"Harley, you weren't happy when we fussed over you. Kindly stop fussing over me."

"Okay, you're right. However, I got bruised, and my ego was hurt. You got shot."

"Just a graze, and I don't know if I was grazed by a bullet or tree bark," laughed Jacey.

"See, you've lost your mind. I'm staying right here until the paramedics examine that thick head of yours."

"How about checking on the others to be sure they've had water and something to eat? I'm fine, really. Just being silly, and somewhat relieved. What time is it?"

"Just past 5:30 p.m. Why?"

"We just missed the last check-in. They should know our status."

"Don't worry. Violet said she'd be sure to have Bill get a message to Carver. So they'll know we'll all be fine, that Wilton has been arrested, and Speller is dead."

"Good work, partner. Now, will you go check on everyone else?"

"Sure thing. Don't go anywhere."

"Funny."

Harley had Gemma stay with Jacey while she went to check on the others. Harley admitted to herself that she had been scared to death. When Jacey got hit, she flew into what she considered "savior mode," she rushed in to help, but in doing so she'd exposed herself to danger, and probably Gemma too. That was not her best moment.

Harley could still feel the adrenalin in her system. That was probably why she felt sickened and elated at the same time. It was probably what was responsible for her shaking earlier.

Time was starting to feel normal again to Harley. She thought it was funny how time went from passing so rapidly, to hardly passing at all.

Harley had checked on everyone else, and returned to Jacey's side.

"How're you doing, Jacey?"

"I've got a bit of a headache that I didn't feel before. Stop looking so worried, Harley. It's just a graze, and nothing big."

"We'll let the paramedics decide that. Here they come."

"I see that, and the crime lab folks, too."

Jacey had needed her wound cleaned and redressed, but it looked like she would be fine. It was suggested she see a medical doctor before she headed home, just to be sure all was well.

"See," giggled Harley, "I knew your hard head would be fine!"

"Oh boy," said Jacey, "I'll never live this down."

Sara was going to need to have the bullet removed from her arm. It would be a while before she would be back to fighting speed. Still, she joked and laughed it off as another day's work.

Chris was looking quite pale, and seemed to be in a lot of pain. The paramedics splinted his leg while Wesley and Greg found sticks, and whatever they could to devise a gurney to carry him out. Harley and Jacey offered their sleeping bags for the make-shift gurney to keep Chris comfortable. Chris had been offered a horse to ride on, but he didn't want to get on it. He said it would be too difficult to get on and off, and besides, he had said, they were on the A.T., and no horse use was allowed.

While the crime scene techs worked the scene, took photos, and interviewed everyone, Dexter had gone for the horses. They used one to carry out Speller after the crime scene crew had everything they needed. Everyone else, including Wilton and excluding Chris, would be walking out. Gemma led the way.

CHAPTER FORTY-ONE

Stone sat in his temporary office and thought back to his day. He had assisted with several interviews, met with Jeff a couple of times, and talked with some of his team members. Every once in a while his thoughts would return to Edwards and Green. Each time Stone considered what they had been part of, he got angry. In his opinion, no police officer should be engaged in supremacist activities.

This had opened Stone's eyes. He was starting to understand how people got so very angry with police harming black men. Stone didn't know if the officers were part of the lynching, but they were part of a cover-up. He thought if word got out about these two officers, and their allegiance to the National Alliance, this might confirm the worst fears held by a lot of people. Stone would consider this a great day if those two former officers were arrested.

Stone wondered, "Who knew how much damage they had done to these investigations, or across their careers?" Stone imagined a lot of time would be spent examining all their police and non-police activities.

Stone had a message from Carver, saying he had good news. So Stone wandered upstairs to Carver's office.

"Have you heard?" asked Carver.

"Depends. Heard what?"

"The good news," replied Carver.

"The suspense is killing me. What's happening?"

"Our former sheriff colleagues, Blaze Edwards and Elliott Green, have been located."

"Wow! That's great news. Have they been detained?"

"Yes. They're in FBI custody as we speak."

Stone asked, "How'd they find them? Do you have details?"

"I have some. What I've heard so far is that facial recognition software located the pair at an airport in Columbus, Ohio. They had fake identification on them, and credit cards to match those fake names."

"Sounds like these guys had been planning an escape in case they were found out."

"I agree, Stone. But now they've been caught. These two have a world of trouble headed their way."

"Although I hope they do, maybe they'll turn in evidence against others, and work some kind of deal."

"They could try that, but their details would help us locally, and the FBI may not be so willing to cut them slack."

"You could be right. I guess it'll depend on what kind of information they can supply, and just how valuable it's deemed to be. Will they be brought back to Virginia? What about their service weapons?"

"We don't know any of that yet. We have asked they get returned here so they can face charges from us."

Jeff came into the room. "Who? What charges?" Carver caught him up on the latest regarding Edwards and Green.

"That's big news," noted Jeff, "I wonder how people here in the office are going to feel about that? Some were angry with those two, especially their membership in the National Alliance. However, there were some who more concerned for Edwards and Green's well being than anything else. That might be something to talk with Rolland about."

Stone returned to his office, and thought the upcoming close-out session might be really interesting. He presumed most everyone had heard about the capture of the two sheriff area officers, at least those here in the same building likely had.

Stone also thought the puzzle had been becoming clearer.

What had begun as seemingly unrelated events was starting to be clearly linked. It was not crystal clear yet, but they weren't finished with all the investigations.

Stone hoped the teams on the A.T. were closing in on the last people still running free, Wilton and Speller. If that happened, maybe law enforcement could figure it all out.

After another hour, Stone made his way to the large conference room. The drapes were open and Stone could see clouds outside. He figured it was warm and muggy outside. At the back of the room the coffeepot seemed to be calling his name. He fixed a cup, and selected a seat. He could sense a current of energy in the room. He guessed discussion of the day's progress had made its way throughout the building.

As usual, Carver had the smart whiteboard up and running. Instead of starting with Mr. Fry's death as he'd done before, he had the words "Edwards and Green" on the screen.

Carver said, "The really good news today is that Edwards and Green were captured. I won't go into specifics, because everyone here has heard about it by now. What you may not have heard yet is that they are being extradited from Ohio back to Virginia.

"As with most good news, there is also more challenging news. A firestorm of media coverage has begun. As you can imagine, a story about police who have 'gone bad' makes for a juicy story. I know this will be especially difficult for those who work here in the Sheriff's office. All calls and all questions from media need to go directly to the public affairs office.

"We do not want any speculation about what any of you may have known, or not known, about those two officers. So don't share information with anyone outside the building, including your families. Everyone who works in this office will be interviewed tomorrow or possibly this weekend. We expect you to cooperate fully.

"Those of us who have reported here for the investigations, but don't normally work here, will also be interviewed. Again, your full cooperation is expected. These interviews will take place tomorrow or over the weekend.

"Let me take your questions about this before we move on."

There were few questions so after answering, Carver commented, "Moving on. Congratulations to Stone's team on the capture of the Burden brothers! Is there anything to add from the interviews, Stone or Jeff? I know you two have been combining efforts."

Jeff answered, "Yes, the Burdens have confessed. They were worried their father would be held responsible for the death of Mr. Fry. Both said they had borrowed the weapon, and it had nothing to do with Toby Burden. They said only the 'inner circle' made the decision about Mr. Fry and took action."

"Excellent," said Carver. "You'll note on the board it indicates this case was 'resolved.' Still, we've been learning more about the case as more KKK members are interviewed. We're sure we have the actual killers, but we may have many more people who could be held responsible. The District Attorney will have to decide who gets charged beyond the Burden brothers."

Carver continued, "We're also learning there are quite a few overlaps in people involved. People found to be involved in Mr. Fry's murder are some of the same people involved in the campground melee. Some other people likely involved in Mr. Freeman's murder were involved in the melee. We're hoping to figure how out how it all is pieced together. We're not there yet. Let's move on to additional reporting."

Jeff resumed speaking. He spent time relaying what he had learned from the investigations, including the evidence found at Gus Springer's home. "We do know that Mr. Springer shot Ms. Beth Rover, and we do know that the bullets from his weapon didn't match the bullets in either Wright brother. We interviewed Springer once, and he requested his lawyer. Then we later arrested him for the shooting. He's not talking, except through his lawyer."

Jeff mentioned he'd been working with Stone on interviews and going over test results. He explained, "As Carver mentioned, it just seemed more expedient to work together."

Then Jeff told them about the photo evidence, and the "be

on the lookout" for Duke Kent. He added, "That gets me to the latest interviews with Junior Kendall and Gerald Brown. These were exceedingly brief interviews, with both requesting their lawyers. We tried telling them we knew about Mr. Fry, we knew about the recruitment, and still neither had anything to say."

Stone added, "During our investigations today we found matches to two sets of fingerprints on the plastic ware found at the horse campground. One set belongs to Melba Ross, and the other to Ella Parker. We brought both women in for questioning. Ms. Ross continued to claim she had not been at the campground, but had merely made some food for others to take. However, two campground visitors have identified Ms. Ross's photo as someone who had been at Beggar Flats. They also identified Ms. Parker as having been at the same campground. Ms. Parker admitted to being there, and being a member of the KKK. She also remarked that she'd never leave the KKK, and would continue to recruit members as soon as she could."

Stone added, "Related to campground updates, I'd like to pass along kudos from the Butler and Duvall families. They were very happy to get their horses back, and thank everyone here for making that happen."

Carver noted that additional news was just reaching him. "We just got word that Duke Kent, and his RAV4, were spotted across state lines in Bristol, Tennessee. Kent has been arrested, and will be brought back here. He was seen tossing things out his window as he tried to outrun the police. The police in Tennessee have recovered four weapons that had been tossed. Those will be sent to the lab for processing. They said that Kent was uncooperative. He tried his best to hit some officers, and he kicked at the patrol car door as they tried to load him into the car. My guess is they'll add charges of resisting arrest to other complaints."

Stone added, "I've previously mentioned the skin found under Mr. Freeman's fingernails. The skin found under Mr. Freeman's fingernails is a match to Kent. "

Carver then said, "Kent will likely be held without bond. This is due to the severity of the crimes, and his propensity to flee. I look forward to the testing of Kent's weapons. Maybe they'll match to the shootings at the campground.

"Stone, did you have more?"

"Yes. On another topic, as most of you know, we have four teams still in the field trying to locate Wilton and Speller. One team member had a brief run-in with Wilton, and now the suspects are on foot. We're hoping that makes catching them much easier."

Carver had checked his text messages, and said, "I'm just getting a few messages in about that exact thing. This news comes to us from Bill Harris with the Forest Service. Bill has learned that we have three injured officers in the forest. One of those injuries, the one to Chris Reynolds, appears life threatening. He's lost quite a lot of blood. The team out there is doing all they can for Chris. We'll get his blood type, and after the session if you match, please go to the hospital in case they need your donation.

"Paramedics haven't yet been cleared to approach the area where a shoot-out has happened between our teams and Wilton and Speller. Also injured is Sara Levitt, who kept shooting with her right hand after her left arm was hit. Another injury was to Jacey Jenner. A bullet grazed her head. Both Sara and Jacey are said to be fine, though both will need medical attention.

"Okay, another new message coming in. Good news, the gunfight is over. One suspect, Dave Speller, is deceased. The other suspect, Wendell Wilton, has been arrested. There are no additional injuries to team members, and the paramedics are on the way to assist the injured officers."

Stone spoke up, "I'd like to assist in interviewing Mr. Wilton, if you'll let me join you in the interview, Jeff."

"Yes, of course Stone."

After the meeting broke up, Stone wondered how long it would take to get Wilton back to the office. If they had a long walk out of the forest it could be hours. He told Jeff he'd take a dinner break, and head back to the office later.

Stone went to a nearby diner. He'd been there a few times already this week, and knew where he preferred to sit. He asked for a seat near the back, where he could watch the door. The server smiled at him. She noted he must be law enforcement because they never sit with their backs to the door, and often request the table that Stone had. She had it right on all counts.

Stone was enjoying his meal, thinking about how much had been accomplished in a week. But then he also thought about all the things they still didn't know. He mused that it was a good thing he liked to work on puzzles. Stone decided to head back to the office. He hoped they had Wilton there, or at least nearby. It had already been a long day. He dodged several reporters and answered no questions as he entered the office building.

CHAPTER FORTY-TWO

Once Harley was awake she thought back to the previous evening. The group of officers had walked from the trail to the campground. Harley recalled being worried for Chris. His coloring had looked poor, and she was sure the trek out of the forest had caused him even more pain. Most of the way was fairly flat, but the last mile or two had been very rocky and steep. By the time they got to the trailhead, it looked like Sara was really uncomfortable too. Jacey had told Harley she was fine, but still had that headache.

Harley remembered how tired she'd been. She had elected to go back to her motor home with Gemma, and get some rest. She'd already made the decision that in the morning she'd visit Sara and Chris at the hospital.

Harley recalled saying her goodbyes to Jacey. She had thanked her for being her partner, and gave her a hug. Jacey had said she had loved working with her, and Gemma, and hoped to partner again someday. Then Jacey had said she'd be going to the morning meeting at the sheriff's office, but Harley told her she would not.

After their goodbyes, one of the officers had given Harley a ride to her motor home. It was still parked at the sheriff's office. She had been happy she hadn't needed to move it. She had been too tired to consider driving anywhere.

Harley giggled at recalling just how bedraggled she and Gemma had looked, and felt the previous night. They had both had some food, and then Harley showered before bed. She had put on the shorts and t-shirt that served as her pajamas, then brushed Gemma, and had checked her for ticks. Gemma had wanted a piece of late-night cheese, but she'd had no interest in more walking. Harley hadn't either. They had been exhausted.

This morning Gemma had woken Harley around 7. Seemed like Gemma needed a walk now. That was fine with Harley. They'd go to a local park, walk a mile or so, have some breakfast, and drive to the hospital. First though she'd leave a voice mail message telling Stone of her plans. He could call her if she needed to stay around. Since she and Jacey had worked together, Harley figured Stone could get any information he might need from Jacey.

After finishing her tasks, Harley drove to the hospital. She had to find street parking because the hospital parking lot wasn't built for motor homes. Harley left Gemma to rest, and headed into the hospital. Once there she found that Sara had already been treated and released. Chris had required surgery, and was in his room, recovering. He was sleeping when Harley entered, so she pulled up a chair to wait for him to wake. A few more people, friends and family, had looked in on him as well while Harley was there.

"Hey, Harley."

"Hey, Chris. Should I ask how you're feeling?"

"I've been better. I'm thirsty. Can you get me some water?"

"Here, just sip a bit. You sure scared me yesterday."

"Yep, I kind of got scared myself. Wesley and Greg really helped me a lot. Where's Sara?"

"I was told she was treated and released. My guess is she'll hit the morning meeting, and come by here. I imagine most everyone will head this way after the morning session."

"I was told a dozen officers came by here last night. All donated blood, in case I needed it, even if our types didn't match."

"That is so amazing."

"I have to ask. Have you heard anything?"

"You mean about Wilton? No, nothing yet. I think he was

really torn up about Speller. While I admit to little sympathy for him, maybe he'll tell all he knows now that he lost his friend."

"I sure hope so."

"How long will you be staying here?"

"I don't know yet. My mom and dad probably grilled the doctor, so I expect to know more soon. Before the surgery, they made it sound like a bit of time here, followed by rehab."

"Can I get you anything?"

"Nah, I'm good. How long are you staying in our neck of the woods, Harley?"

"I'm out. I'm headed to Nevada to see my sister. I think Gemma and I need a change of scenery."

"Safe travels, Harley. We owe you and Gemma a debt of gratitude."

"Well, I was going to say the same to you. You take care, Chris."

CHAPTER FORTY-THREE

Shrimp had been struggling since he watched Orville and Wilbur die in front of him. He'd seen it over and over again in his dreams. He'd wake up in a sweat, often screaming. His parents were trying to deal with the deaths themselves, and didn't have much left in them to help Shrimp.

Big Lou had not seen most of what happened in the campground, and told Shrimp he was being a sissy. She said she ought to knock some sense into him. He didn't doubt that she would do exactly that next time he found himself alone with her.

There was added pressure on Shrimp since the police had shown up at their home twice looking for Junior. The first time they came Junior was not home, but the next time Junior had been taken to the sheriff station, and questioned. Shrimp had been very worried that his dad would be arrested.

Shrimp had sought Red's advice.

Red had told him, "My dad was taken in for questioning. He refused to talk, and requested an attorney. Your dad was already advised to do the same. If they don't talk to the police, they'll likely be let go. At worst, they'll get questioned again at some point. There's no way they'll get hit with any charges, or jail time."

"Are you sure? I don't know what our family would do without Dad around."

"I think you need to relax a bit, Shrimp. You're worrying over things that probably aren't going to happen. I'll take you to the Klavern meeting tomorrow night. We're going to talk about what's happening with everyone. You'll feel better if you hear what everyone has to say."

The evening after that the Klan members returned to the Klavern meeting place, and everyone took their usual spots, with Shrimp sitting next to Red.

Shrimp asked, "Where are Ma and Pa Wright?"

"You didn't hear? They're too upset to attend the meeting. But they told everyone to stay strong, and stay together."

"Well, then why aren't they 'together' with us tonight?"

"Really, Shrimp? They're in mourning. Give them a break."

"I'm in mourning, too. Give me a break."

The big news at the Klavern meeting that night had been about the Burden brothers getting caught, and having the weapon used on Mr. Fry with them. They had simply taken the wrong weapon. Their dad said he felt awful, that it was his fault. He told everyone to learn from his mistakes. The brothers would likely be going to jail for a long time.

Shrimp had said, "I thought the Klan was supposed to get the brothers to safety, Red."

"They were, but I heard no one could figure out where they were."

Shrimp asked, "Will Carl and Jay ever get out of jail? Their parents are really shaken up. This is ruining their family."

"They'll be fine. I heard a few of the men considering how to break them out of jail. Their dad said not to do that. He told them that the Klan could grow during this time, or it could fall apart. If we broke out his sons, it might destroy the Klan."

"Red, for fuck sake, who cares about the Klan? Shouldn't we care about Carl and Jay?"

"You watch yourself, Shrimp Kendall, " growled Red, "the Klan is what makes us all family. No one goes against the Klan."

After returning home and crawling into bed, Shrimp had

thought about the meeting. He knew better than to say things like that, but he'd been considering all his options, and right now, the Klan did not rank high on his list. All the trouble they'd had recently was because of the Klan. Other members of the Klan thought everything was the fault of the National Alliance, but Shrimp could not see how Mr. Fry's murder had anything to do with that. He had tried to discuss that with Red, but that had made Red very angry. Shrimp felt like he had no one he could talk to anymore. It seemed like Red would not even listen to him, he'd just get angry at Shrimp.

For the third time that week the Klavern met, Shrimp went to his usual spot by Red.

"Hey."

"Hey, yourself."

"Are you still mad at me, Red?"

"Nah. Just quit saying stupid things, and we'll be fine."

They listened as news of more police interviews was shared. Some people had not heard about Melba Ross and Ella Parker getting questioned. So far, though, most every person questioned had been released.

Red whispered, "Did you notice Herb Smith and Ben Rover aren't here today? It's because they talked about the Klan to the police. They've been thrown out of the Klan. My brother, Buster, has been telling the family today that we need to do more recruiting to make-up for losing people lately. He said the time's right to find new members. All the news coverage has renewed interest in the Klan. Buster says now is the time to gather more people into the fold."

"Losing people? How about we call it what it really is. Two Klansmen are dead, two are arrested, and more are identified to the police."

"See, Shrimp, talk like that makes me think you don't support the Klan."

Shrimp decided to walk away before he said something to permanently damage his relationship with Red. He waited outside until the meeting broke up, and rode home with his family. Shrimp hadn't even stopped to see what sweets Ella Parker might have made for him.

That night at home Shrimp asked what else had happened at the meeting, and what would become of the Klavern. His dad said he had been selected to be the new Klavern leader, and along with a few others would be selecting a new inner circle. His mom said several people noted it was time for a more active role for the women of the Klavern. She said she could support that, and wanted an active role herself. Both his parents looked quite happy. They noted that Buster would stay on in his capacity as Kleagle. They wondered what role Shrimp, and his friend, Red, might want to have. Shrimp replied he'd have to give it more thought.

Shrimp, though, had already made up his mind. He went to his bedroom to consider his next steps. He needed to break from the KKK. It seemed like a matter of life and death to him.

Shrimp was less than a year away from his birthday, but it seemed like forever at this point. When he was eighteen he could move away, no one could stop him. It meant he'd break his friendships, and it'd cause a huge break with his family.

Shrimp wondered whom could he talk to. He knew he couldn't talk with Red about this. He knew Big Lou and his parents would be very mad, so he could not talk with them. There was no one. Shrimp had to figure it out himself.

Shrimp thought about it for a while. He decided to reduce his time with the KKK. He would find reasons to stop attending Klavern meetings. Shrimp would need to curtail his time playing Fortnite with Red, and slow down their interactions. He'd think of things to keep busy, and away from the house. Shrimp would find clubs to join for his senior year, maybe join some sports teams. He would start considering colleges far away from home. Shrimp knew he could no longer be associated with the Ku Klux Klan or people who did.

CHAPTER FORTY-FOUR

Stone was in his office once again. He looked around and was pleased that all his paperwork was under control. It had taken time and effort, but it had paid off. He could lay his hands on everything he needed, when he needed it.

Stone was feeling some relief, and not just about the paperwork. He felt that many pieces of the investigation, that he'd come to think of as a puzzle, were falling into place. A completed puzzle seemed to be within sight for four of the five murders, with the death of Joe Miller left as the biggest unknown. Whoever set the car fire was directly responsible. So far, no one had confessed to doing that, and the police had no leads on it.

Stone thought it would be nice to move out his temporary office here after he was interviewed, and move back to his home office in Wytheville. There were not many miles that separated the offices, but it felt a long way away. Stone thought it'd feel great to have his own filing system, desk, and chair again. Not that Stone really spent much time sitting around. Still it was something to look forward to. Plus, Stone would be that much closer to Genevieve. He had stayed in Christiansburg a couple of nights this week. Stone had really missed not being able to talk as much with her. There was little he could share from his job, but he hung on her every word when she talked about her day.

Stone could just envision them cuddling on the couch, and talking about their upcoming wedding. Today might be the day he could make that move.

Stone had conducted the Wilton interview the evening before, which had continued into the early morning. Like most of the interviews, there had been valuable information that came from it, as well as parts that were not believable. He thought, "How was it that people could lie to you, and think you would believe them?"

When Stone and Jeff spoke with Wilton, they could tell he'd not had a good day. Wilton had not yet had a shower, so had been wearing the same filthy clothes that he'd had on for a few days. He had not shaven either, and his beard was past the scruffy stage. His eyes darted back and forth from Stone to Jeff, and back again.

At first Wilton had little to say. Once he started talking, his story changed. He'd said he was innocent, that he and a buddy were merely riding the trail so they'd have stories to tell their kids someday. Later, Wilton cried over the loss of his friend. He'd told them that he and Speller had been responsible for Freeman's death. He claimed they'd been driving along in his truck, and spotted a broken down car. The black man had flagged them to stop. So they did. Wilton said he was not sure why they decided to hang him, but that was what they did. Yes, just the two of them. They had the rope in the truck because they always carried rope.

The story Wilton described was partly credible, but parts stretched the imagination. As Stone and Jeff walked Wilton through the actual events, it became clear to them that Wilton was having trouble explaining how just the two of them were able to accomplish the lynching. Wilton though would not budge. He said it was just he and Speller involved. When told there was evidence that another person was involved, Wilton refused to admit it, or say who the other person was. When asked about a RAV4, Wilton said he'd never been in one before. He had claimed not to know anyone named Duke Kent.

Stone knew there was more to the story, but he and Jeff had to settle for the confession that identified Wilton and Speller as the murderers of Mr. Freeman. Plus, they had DNA evidence for Duke Kent. Three people might have pulled off the murder. It was possible they now had everyone responsible.

When the oversight team met with the two investigators they learned all that had transpired in the Wilton interview. Stone suggested getting more information from Edwards and Green if possible. Plus, they might be able to get Kent to talk, though it didn't seem likely to them.

Stone thought about the former officers, Edwards and Green. Maybe they had full information on the Freeman murder. Maybe some deal could be struck so they'd tell all they knew. Then they'd finally learn all that happened to Mr. Freeman. Then it occurred to Stone what had been bothering him. He'd seen both officers on their phones after the first meeting there in Christiansburg. Maybe what he saw was them providing inside information to National Alliance members. He realized that the order had been to keep things quiet, and it was odd they were on their phones. At the time he guessed they just had business to conduct, or were calling family members. He bet that if the team traced the phone calls they'd find those officers had been calling the very people they were not supposed to contact. Stone was sure it would all be investigated anyway, but decided he'd talk with Carver to be sure phone records were checked. It might result in the identification of more National Alliance members.

This time as Stone went into the conference room, he considered it could be the final meeting for this group. There was quite a bit of talking, and the room held more people than it had since the initial meeting. On the back table, in addition to the usual coffee pot and pastries, there was fresh fruit, cheese and crackers, cut-up beef stick and salami, and what looked like freshly baked bread. He gratefully helped himself to some of everything.

Carver had set up the smart whiteboard a bit differently this time. On the board was listed "KKK" followed by several names.

Carver said, "Before we start, welcome back to many of our intrepid trail hikers! We're so glad to have you back. Sara and Jacey, we're really happy you both are well enough to join us today. Chris came out of surgery well. He will have a long recovery. He appreciates all the visitors and blood donors. He is open to visitors after our meeting today.

"We've made inroads in identifying local members of the KKK throughout these investigations. Deceased are Orville Wright and his brother, Wilbur Wright. Arrested are Carl Burden and his brother, Jay Burden for the murder of Mr. Fry. By all accounts these four men were the inner circle of the local KKK.

"We also have Toby Burden's gun, and are listing him as a KKK member. From the campground investigations we found Klan members including Hank Ross, Melba Ross, Ella Parker, Herb Smith, Ben Rover, Beth Rover, and Gerald Brown.

"Within a week we now have identified twelve Klan members. We will be taking a closer look at their families and friend connections to see who got by us. That's a job well done.

"Let's move on to the National Alliance. We'll start with Duke Kent. We have tied him to the murder of Mr. Freeman. Plus, our ballistics tests now tie him to the murders of the Wright brothers from the Ku Klux Klan.

"Also tied to Mr. Freeman's death were Wendell Wilton and Dave Speller. Mr. Wilton has confessed, and Mr. Speller is deceased.

"We have also identified as National Alliance members the deceased Joseph Miller, plus Edgar West, and Gus Springer, who was responsible for shooting Beth Rover at the campground. We also arrested Earl Graves and Leland Graves for their actions at the protest.

"That brings us to eight National Alliance members which is precisely eight more than we were aware of earlier this week. Just like the KKK, we will be examining family relationships and friends to locate any remaining National Alliance members. That's also a job well done.

"Before we get too carried away, I need to note that some work is incomplete. It appears we have finished with Mr. Fry's death, but we still have questions on Mr. Freeman's death. For example, we need to know if only the three men were responsible, or if others were involved. Also, we don't know who started the car fire outside the campground causing the death of Joseph Miller. Nor do we know who shot Herb Smith in the campground. We feel confident these issues will be resolved in time.

"I have to say that it was a pleasure to have each of you on the team. Your ability to work with other agencies is something others should emulate. Though she is not here today, special thanks go to Harley Fremont, and her dog, Gemma. They provided valuable assistance in capturing the Burden brothers, and in ending Wilton and Speller's escape from justice. We had heard about Harley's reputation as a resolver, and she did nothing but bolster that reputation in her work here.

"During these investigations we changed things up a bit. We started with separate teams, but we found over time that tasks and perpetrators were intertwined. As you well know, we have not yet figured out everything to our satisfaction, but we did figure out that it was better to let go of our seemingly arbitrary 'teams' and work as one. I thank you all for your efforts, and your willingness to be flexible.

"Earlier in the week, I was thinking our investigations might take a very long time. However, we are close to calling these investigations closed. The items remaining to reach closure are left to the Sheriff, Rolland French, and his team to complete. All others are officially released, once your interviews and paperwork are completed.

"Now it's time to enjoy the treats brought in for this special occasion."

Most everyone had full plates already and stayed seated to eat. As he ate, Stone considered his next items to do. He knew he had enough paperwork to keep him here at least through the end of the day, but he'd head home soon enough. He'd been scheduled for his interview in early afternoon.

Stone finished his food and then talked with every person before heading back to his temporary office. Jeff told him he was scheduled for interviews on Saturday. He jokingly told Stone he'd miss all the pastries Stone brought in every day. Stone laughingly told him to buy his own pastries.

Stone was proud of the effort everyone put in, and looked forward to working with each person again in the future. When he saw Jacey, he reminded her that they would all be going out to dinner soon. He knew Genevieve would love to see her.

"Good thing you have a hard head, my friend."

CHAPTER FORTY-FIVE

Bill Harris was in his office at headquarters. He had been kept apprised of the ongoing investigations. He was most anxious to hear from Harley. It had sounded like a very close call with Wilton. Bill had a feeling early on that this outing might be dangerous for her. He sighed as he thought about that. He knew he always worried about her. But this time he truly felt it might be unsafe. Was he just thinking like that because he adored Harley? Yes, he thought, that was probably it. Still, his premonition turned out to be true. One of the killers had walked toward her, and likely meant to kill her in his attempt to get away. He had shuddered when Violet shared that news with him.

Bill had been very happy that he and Harley had been to a target range a few times. He was sure that if pressed, she would have shot the man, if only to protect Gemma, if not herself. Bill guessed that her partner, Jacey, had probably provided the weapon. Bill was relieved that Jacey had only a minor wound. He'd have to call Jacey, and congratulate her on a job well done.

Bill had heard about Chris Reynolds and his injuries. Bill knew just where he'd find Harley when he called her. She'd be at the hospital checking on Chris. That was just who she was.

Bill had decided not to call Harley the previous night. He had an idea of how long the walk was from the forest, but didn't know how long it would take her to get back to her motor home. Bill was pretty sure it would be late, and Harley would be exhausted. He had decided to wait this morning for a call from her, and if she did not call by 10, he'd call her. Bill was about to call Harley when a call came in from Rick Givens.

"Hi, Rick. I'll bet you are feeling relieved."

"Yes, I am. I wanted to call and thank you for all the advice you have provided throughout these investigations. I appreciate that your work has helped move along some changes in thinking, and some changes coming to the forest."

"Thanks, Rick. I appreciate hearing that. I think you were wise to agree to four additional law enforcement officers on the district. That kind of coverage will really help you turn things around."

"That was one of the things I wanted to thank you for. I know it took a lot of effort to pull those officers from other places. You and your staff have been great about suggesting, and then supporting us, with enforcement and investigation staff."

"I will pass that along to my staff here. You can always call me as the officers' details progress, either with suggestions or kudos."

Rick added, "Your officers will be working every weekend at all the open campgrounds on the district to be sure no recreation visitor is bothered by other people. Over the next month or two they'll be getting a lot of hours.

"Soon enough the Beggar Flats Horse Campground will open again, and we'll add that to their rounds."

"I'd heard Beggar Flats was opening in a month or two. I know the Gopher Flats Campground is going to get an upgrade, so it'll be slower in opening."

"Yes, the opening will likely not occur for another year or two. We'll keep it blocked off from use until we can make those changes. We have a landscape architect doing some planning, and then we need an environmental review, followed by public comments."

"Yes, I know those changes can be complicated, and time consuming. Did you hear we renewed the contract with the Sheriff French? It includes more hours and more coverage than you previously had."

"I had heard. I can't thank you enough for doing that. I know forest visitors are going to feel much more safe."

"What else is being done to assure the public, Rick?"

Rick replied, "I listened to your advice. I've started engaging more with some of the local communities. So far I have arranged for community meetings in Pembroke and Bland next week. Then I'll have more meetings coming up in Pearisburg, Roanoke, Blacksburg, Wytheville, and Radford. We might expand out to more cities after that."

"That sounds encouraging, Rick."

"Thanks. At each meeting, I'll be telling the story of the clash of the KKK and the National Alliance on the forests. I don't expect the meetings to be easy, and I do expect many hard questions to be asked. I will talk about how my own staff may have been complicit, though it appears to be an inadvertent complicity."

"How does Walt feel about that?"

"Walt was surprised I planned to bring it up, but then he realized the value of sharing it. We expect people will respond well to the honesty of it. We hope they'll hear the truthfulness of it. Walt has decided to join me at almost all the future meetings, and tell his own story."

"That's great news. I'm happy he's making amends."

"So far the community people helping me plan the sessions are open to hearing me out. They still have concerns about how other community members will react. They expect some will be supportive, and others may be angry. They tell me to be sure to talk about our plans for additional coverage by officers. I will also talk about future changes to the campground.

"Some of the community members helping me plan have voiced concerns about making the campgrounds too urban park-like. They said they prefer them to stay primitive. They guess that others in the community will embrace the changes we have planned, and would not mind additional changes, like Wi-Fi being added, and flush toilets."

"The planning process will help you decide what is best for the land. Your decisions, of course, will be to have the best fit of land base, and human desires. Never an easy decision."

"It's complicated, but we'll get there. Also, I'm hoping Rolland French or Carver Grayson can join me for a few of the future meetings. I wasn't engaged in the investigations, but they were. They'd be better able to tell that part of the story. The public will definitely be interested."

"Yes, I imagine there's a lot of curiosity about it. However, there are still aspects of the investigations that are not complete, plus there might be some jury trials. I imagine Rolland and Carver would be careful about their involvement."

"Yes, I had considered that. Maybe they'll let one of their officers tell what they can."

"We could have one of our officers take that role, but it would need to be carefully considered by Rolland and Carver before we did that."

"Sounds reasonable. Again, thanks, Bill. Your leadership is very much appreciated."

"I'll talk with Rolland, and get back to you about officer involvement. Take care, Rick."

Bill had not expected this level of engagement by the forest supervisor. It appeared some good things were resulting from the bad experiences. Maybe someday Rick would go on to a higher leadership post in the Forest Service. Bill hoped that would be the case.

While he'd been talking with Rick, a text had arrived from Harley. She would be calling him in another hour or so, after she finished her visit with Chris at the hospital.

CHAPTER FORTY-SIX

Harley returned to Gemma and the motor home. She had texted Bill earlier, and thought she'd call before hitting the road. She wanted to think through the past week before calling.

After every case, Harley liked to spend a bit of time reviewing her actions. She also analyzed the agency, and how they responded to different parts of events. This time, she would be thinking about several agencies, and how they worked together.

Harley started with Gemma. Harley was really impressed with Gemma, and how well she tracked the fugitives, and their horses. For being only two and a half years old, Gemma had shown stamina, strength, and courage. Harley was less sure how Wilton had been able to get so close to her without Gemma reacting faster. She decided the wind direction must have played a part in it. It was also possible he'd been behind a nearby tree, but then why did Gemma not sense him? Maybe the horse smell was too strong? She knew that if she could not resolve the dilemma, then certainly she could not train Gemma to do anything differently.

Harley thought about the fall she had taken, and was pleased that she remembered her training on how to fall the right way. She imagined it could have been much worse. She thought about her vest with so many things in it. Had it cushioned her, or contributed to her aches and pains? It was probably a bit of each. She'd have to think about what she carried, and where it was in the vest.

Harley was less pleased with the way she handled the rope and knots issue. She had it in her mind that it was rodeo related, and ran with that, without considering all the other types of jobs that might use the same rope or knots. It was a hunch that paid off, but for her the lesson was not to move so quickly without considering multiple angles. Normally she'd asked herself, "What haven't we considered? What are we not seeing?" She hadn't used that exercise this time. It was something she vowed to be better at next time. The lynching had rattled her; there was no denying that.

Harley rarely partnered with others in addition to her dog, but had partnered the entire time with Jacey. It was really good to have a competent human partner on the trail with her. She'd have to consider partnering again, if the situation warranted. Harley was happy Jacey was not hurt too badly. She was sure Jacey would have a great career ahead of her.

Harley also considered how long she and Jacey were on the trail without reinforced supplies. Clearly, they were at a disadvantage to be on foot while the fugitives were on horseback, and they should have known to carry more with them. She felt it was kind of a screwy rule to not allow horses on the trail, but she knew special places often came with their own quirks and challenges. Next time she might study the place in more detail before heading out, as it might result in more solid decision-making. In the end, though, it was good other people had joined them, and they were able to make the arrests.

As Harley considered the agencies she had to smile. They had looked somewhat shocked that she and her dog were going to do pretty much as they pleased, and yet, they gave her the space to do so. No one knew Gemma's skills as well as Harley, so no one else was in a position to redirect their activities. She thought perhaps it was the addition of Jacey to the team that made acceptance easy.

Harley was impressed there was not much jockeying for leadership, and that each team looked for the strong points that each member could bring to the partnership. Sometimes different agencies had different agendas, and it could get ugly. This time the agencies had acted like a well-oiled machine.

Harley felt that progress came only when people worked with each other. She preferred people didn't keep things secret from each other. Nor did she like when people pretended things were other than they appeared to be. Harley felt this team had met her usual standards. They had worked well together, they told the truth even when it was difficult, and they didn't pretend things were different than what the data showed.

Harley had been shocked to learn about the disappearance of the two area officers. Despite that set back, each team had been focused, yet freely shared information so that others might benefit from what they knew. Plus, the oversight team showed true leadership, and it made everyone want to do a great job. Harley was glad this was over, yet was proud of her contributions toward resolving the investigations. She hoped the families of the fallen had taken some solace from their work.

Harley called Bill. She told him all the thoughts she'd been having about things that went well and things to improve. Bill shared that Violet and Emmylynne had put in many hours tracking her, and other employees, and provided detailed information when needed. Harley told him she would be sure to call and thank Vi and Em for their efforts.

"That was a job well done, Harley. How about coming back to Washington to celebrate, and you can thank Vi and Em in person."

"I'll likely come back in a month or so. I already called Hazel, and made plans to visit with her. As soon as we finish the call I'm off to Nevada."

"I'm disappointed. I wanted to spend more time with you."

"We will, but later. Let me work on my relationship with Hazel, before I take on a new one with you. Okay?"

"Yes, okay. I know you want to improve your relationship with your sister. Speaking of relationships, I wanted to tell you about Emmylynne and Scott. Scott has been scrambling to get their honeymoon plans revamped. He asked when were the best dates for them to leave, and we told him after this weekend. Scott had hoped their hotel would be flexible with them after they postponed before. Their hotel in Bora Bora was very accommodating. Scott said they would leave Monday for paradise, with their overwater bungalow and their underwater adventures."

"That sounds wonderful. Please give them my best wishes!"

"Will do, Harley. You have a safe trip to Hazel's."

Harley was thinking about goodbyes. Many years ago, Harley had worked with a very gracious young woman named Marla. It was a summer job, and Harley was sad to see Marla leave for school. She had never worked with such a polite and sweet person. Harley decided to take Marla, and her other employees, to a local restaurant where they celebrated birthdays, and other events. On previous visits there, Harley had heard them sing *Happy Trails to You* as their going away song. It would be a nice send-off for Marla. Their crowd enjoyed their lunch, and the restaurant employees gathered to sing to Marla. Harley was a bit shocked when they sang, "*Hit the road Marla, and don't you come back no more, no more, no more, no more. Hit the road Marla and don't you come back no more...*" It took a while, but it eventually became humorous to Harley.

It was that time once again. "Hit the road, Jack," is what she typed, and hummed, as this adventure ended, and a road trip began. She sent Jack the message before heading out to put diesel in the motor home. It was time to crank up Patsy Cline and the music.

"We're off to another adventure, Gemma. Are you ready?"

In response, Gemma barked once. Then Gemma lay down with her toy tucked under her. She was always ready for a new adventure, especially if she could nap first.

ACKNOWLEDGMENTS

For reading a very early draft, and correcting rookie mistakes, I thank my son Alejandro. He offered ideas and expertise that were hard to hear, but necessary. I appreciate his honesty and his insights.

Sue VanKley offered many editorial comments on an earlier version of this book. She was surprised when I accepted many of her ideas. Of course I did, she's fabulous.

Reader review thanks go to Deborah S. Carr-Taylor, Cindy Justice Perser, Ann K. Putney, and Joanne F. Tynon, Ph.D. They all had remarkably similar comments, showing me how to make this a better novel for the readers. I truly appreciate the time and thoughtfulness this task required.

ABOUT THE AUTHOR

Deborah J. Chavez, Ph.D. retired from the USDA Forest Service in 2015, after 25 years of service. She resides in southern California with her husband, son, three dogs, a dozen koi, and a few dozen tropical fish. The humans are outnumbered. This is her first effort at novel writing. She plans several more Harley Fremont and Gemma books. The second book is called California Juncture and takes place in southern California.

Made in United States
Troutdale, OR
08/24/2023